In Our Memories

Three trucks, engines screaming, roared into Gamursh and stopped with squealing brakes. Nine Turkish soldiers in sandy-coloured uniforms jumped down, while an officer climbed out of the cabin of the lead truck and stood in front of the church. Holding a sheet of paper which he didn't read, he announced that all men between the ages of 18 and 48 were to be conscripted, while soldier-drivers sat behind steering wheels and stared vacantly into the distance. Meanwhile other soldiers, rifles at the ready, searched the village from end to end. The bakery, the butchery, the grocery shop, the blacksmith's forge, each house, and even the church. One by one, the men of Gamursh between the ages of 18 and 48 were assembled in front of the church.

They were roughly prodded to climb into those three trucks. Soldiers got in behind, tailgates were slammed shut, and after awkward turns, three trucks roared out of the village, while women, some with babes in arms or young children at their legs, watched the caravan disappear out of sight, leaving nothing more than the putrid smell of fumes. Anoush stood shocked, even though it was as Zeki predicted six months before. Tuesday July 20 and it was too late.

In Our Memories

by

Mark Morey

Mark Morey

http://markmorey.blogspot.com

Copyright ©

978-0-6480647-5-6

Published In Australia

November 2017

Other Works by Mark Morey

The Red Sun will Come - June 2012

Souls in Darkness - August 2012

The Governess and the Stalker - July 2014

Maidens in the Night - September 2014

One Hundred Days - September 2015

The Last Great Race – April 2016

The Adulterous Bride – October 2016

No Darkness – March 2017

Prologue

The cart rolled eastward on a fine autumn day, further into the Anatolian countryside. Anoush heard the music faintly in the distance, but louder and louder as the crowd closed. Beautiful Armenian music; bright and happy with an infectious beat. Women in bright clothes dipped and twirled with hands in the air; men in their best outfits danced and clapped while they surrounded the two carts as an escort into the small village. Many eyes were on Anoush; newly married at the side of her husband Emni. The driver, Berj Hagopian, uncle and godfather to Emni, turned the cart into the village, and they rolled between whitewashed mud brick houses lining the smooth, gravel street. All well-sized, two-storey homes, with the tall pointed roof and tower of the Apostolic church part-way along. Maybe 40 or 50 houses, a few shops, and home for less than 300 souls. Anoush saw the blacksmith shop and the house of her in-laws beside, with a welcoming fire outside. When the cart stopped Emni jumped down, and offered his hand for Anoush to climb down. The musicians: quamancha, duduk, oud and dhot played while the wedding guests: Anoush's family, Emni's family, and friends from both sides, danced exuberantly; clapping the beat and whistling to the tune. As much as Anoush wanted to dance with them, she couldn't. She was expected to remain quiet, even sombre, because she was leaving her family in the city of Ourfa to

move to her husband's family in the village of Gamursh. A wedding was a time of celebration, but for a bride a wedding was also a time to mourn the end of her old life.

"You're not allowed to dance," Lori, her sister, said with a big smile.

"Your turn will come," Anoush said quietly without wiping the serious look from her face. "And when it does I'll dance until I'm exhausted, and then I'll dance some more!"

"You would too."

Indeed she will.

At the house a plate was shoved at Anoush. She grabbed it; went inside and broke it on the floor of the courtyard for good luck, as Emni broke his plate. Through the courtyard and into the barn, where a large table was set for the feast to come. Emni escorted Anoush to that table while the dancers trailed, and there he left her. "Dance with Emni," Anoush said to Lori still at her side. "He's your family now."

The dance was formal, with men and women holding hands in two long lines; dancing steps that hadn't changed for thousands of years, to music that hadn't changed for thousands of years. Many thousands of years and before the time of Christ. Lori disappeared into the crowd and soon she was dancing with her new brother-in-law. Anoush took the bride's place at the table and drank some wine. Her mother-in-law sat beside her.

"That's a lovely dress," her mother-in-law, Mayr Gayane Hagopian, said.

"Thank you," Anoush replied. She wore a simple, white cotton dress with coarse, gold-coloured embroidery at the waist and at the hem. Over that she had a short, dark red jacket; heavily embroidered in gold and fastened by a broad, gold-coloured belt at her waist. A simple, black hat trimmed in gold-coloured fabric, and that was covered by a fine, white scarf looped over her head and around her neck.

After a time the food was brought out, and the women of the village had cooked long and hard to produce such a lavish feast, especially the large pot of harissa made from meat and roasted wheat; cooked and stirred for hours. Shaslik: grilled meat on skewers, stews, salads and freshly-baked lavash bread, accompanied by bottles of wine and bottles of cognac. It was a boisterous feast as Armenian weddings always are boisterous, followed by more dancing which Anoush could only watch. It was quite late when Emni returned to his bride. He was a handsome man, with dark eyes and a slightly hooked nose. Average height for a man, slightly taller than she, but broad and strong from his work.

"We must go outside to the fire," he said quietly; too shy or perhaps too embarrassed to look her in the eyes. The fire was to give the newly married couple fertility for their next duty to come.

Anoush took his hand and they went to the fire raked low. There they jumped that fire to the claps and cheers of their guests, and jumped it again, and again for a third time. Once more holding hands they returned to the courtyard, but went upstairs to his room lit by a flickering lamp, and closed the door. Below, the music and dancing would continue, with the door doing little to muffle the noisy festivities beyond the courtyard.

"This is a modest room but I hope you're pleased," Emni said.

There was little space given the double bed, a bedside table, and a chest for clothes. Hard floor with a rug, white walls, and shutters open. Their home, until she gave birth and they could move into their own house. "It's a lovely room," Anoush said.

Emni closed the shutters and there they had privacy.

"You know what to do," Anoush said.

Emni unwrapped and removed her veil and then he removed her hat. She unpinned and unbraided her black hair which fell to her waist. Emni held Anoush around her waist and kissed her gently; the first time they'd ever kissed. His moustache tickled! He kissed her for a time and then backed away, and as much as she tried to fight it Anoush couldn't stifle a yawn. It had been a long day after many days of preparation.

"You're tired," Emni said quietly. "We can sleep if you want, and make love tomorrow morning."

Anoush hugged his waist and kissed him lightly. "No my sweet; we will make love now," she said. Although they'd only met twice before, Anoush sensed that Emni was a good and gentle man; and she really wanted to make love with him. She was sure that he would be good for her. Anoush held Emni's hands and looked deep into his eyes, and she was sure that he would be good for her.

* * *

Mehmit Talaat paced his room in the Hotel Nea Metropolitis while silently reading his speech. On the bed Hayriye watched him. This conference and his speech was the most important in Taalat's career. He'd risen from postal clerk to minister of interior affairs; a senior minister and therefore a Pasha, and now he had the opportunity to create a better and more secure future for Turks. It was absolutely essential for Turks to strike first, before they became victims.

"You seem anxious," Hayriye said quietly.

Talaat stoped pacing and turned to face his wife of eight months. November 1910; and much had changed for Hayriye Bafrali in recent times. "We must bring an end to the Armenian problem," he said.

"How do you propose to do that?"

"By ridding Anatolia of them."

"How?"

"First I must get my strategy accepted at this conference, and the how will come in good time."

"Is this the speech you're working on?"

"Yes it is," Talaat said.

"Can you read your speech to me, and I can tell you what I think?"

Talaat thought that might help. "In the year ten seventy-one, our ancestors conquered Anatolia, and since then we have built the greatest Muslim empire the world has ever seen. But when I look around me now, I see that our people have been put at risk in their own land. For many centuries we've allowed the previous inhabitants of Anatolia: Armenians, Greeks, Assyrians and Kurds, to live amongst us as equals in the Ottoman Empire. But Armenians, Greeks and Assyrians can never be our equals, as the Balkans war showed.

"In that war, the prime aim of Bulgarians and Greeks was to drive Ottomans out of those countries. They did just that, and many thousands of Ottomans died when they were forcibly expelled after that war. As long as millions of Armenians share our land, we will never be safe from them. We have seen Armenians agitating for independence for many decades now. These Armenians will fight us sooner or later, and in the process they will spill much Ottoman blood. What worked for centuries will not work in the future. There can be no question of equality, until we have succeeded in our task of Ottomanising the Empire.

"I call on the Committee of Union and Progress to make Ottomanisation of our Empire our official policy."

Talaat looked at Hayriye. "Do you think this is sufficient?" he asked.

"That's a good speech," Hayriye said. "It's clear and concise in explaining the problem facing Ottomans, meaning us Turks, and implying the solution to that problem is to make Anatolia the home for Turks only. I don't think your speech can be improved."

Talaat nodded his head. "Good," he said. "Tomorrow I will present my speech, and I expect my plan to be passed."

"Then what?"

"Soon, war will be coming to Europe. When that war comes, we will deport Armenians from Anatolia to the desert of Syria. Under the cover of war other countries won't intervene, because they'll be too busy with their own problems. By the time this war is over, we will have solved our Armenian problem."

Hayriye smiled. "You have it all planned, my love."

Talaat smiled too. "Tomorrow we will agree to the what, and the how will come in good time."

Hayriye smiled even brighter. "You need a clear head for tomorrow," she said.

"Meaning?"

Hayriye began unbuttoning her dress. "Meaning I can help you to solve the Armenian problem." Hayriye peeled her dress from her shoulders. "Are you interested, my love?"

Talaat laughed big and boisterous, while Hayriye stood to remove the rest of her clothes.

Chapter One

Anoush carried the urn across the courtyard and hung it above the fire in the kitchen. After lunch, she always relaxed with a cup of tea before deciding what to do for the afternoon. The front door opened on creaking hinges, and Anoush recognised the voices of her sisters-in-law Maral and Sona while they crossed the courtyard, before they opened the door to the kitchen.

"Parev Maral ist Sona," Anoush offered as a greeting.

"Parev Anoush," they both replied.

"Would you like some tea?" Anoush asked.

Maral nodded, and Anoush placed two cups on the rough-hewn table, and two extra scoops in the teapot. She grabbed the woollen mitten and poured the now hot water into the pot to let it brew.

"Have you heard the news?" Maral asked.

Indeed Anoush had, from her children when they came home from school. "The Ottomans have entered the war on the side of Germany," she said.

Maral nodded. "Why did this happen?" she asked.

Anoush kept as straight a face as she could manage. The women of the village, including her family, thought of her as a sage or something like that. "Russia has threatened the Ottomans in recent times, and their only option was to side with Germany against Russia."

"Can they beat Russia?"

The Ottoman Empire was once strong, but was rotting from the inside. Just a few years ago they even lost the Balkans War. Anoush poured three cups and slid two across the table. "They're weak and they should have stayed neutral," she said.

"Could they do that?" Maral asked.

"They could."

"Stupid...," Sona muttered. "As long as they don't conscript our men."

"They don't let Armenian men fight," Maral said. "They only support the troops."

"Armenian radicals could side with Russia against the Ottomans," Anoush said.

"Surely they wouldn't do that?" Maral gasped.

"You know how it's been."

For many years there had been tension between Ottomans and the Armenians, although not between everyday Turks and Armenians. But the tensions were quite destructive at times. Indeed in Ourfa just 20 years ago, 10,000 Armenians were killed by the Ottoman Army; including 3,000 massacred in the Cathedral of the Holy Mother of God, which was then desecrated. The original causes of those tensions were innocent and well-meaning, but once started the momentum was impossible to stop.

"On Sunday I will pray for peace," Maral said.

"I will pray for common-sense on both sides," Sona said bluntly.

Anoush thought that might be too much to ask for. She finished her tea, and noticed that Maral and Sona had finished as well.

"Thank you both for visiting me," Anoush said.

Maral laughed brightly. "Thank you for painting a vision of a war within a war!"

Anoush didn't know what to say. "Maybe it won't come to that," she eventually said.

"It's good to know what could happen," Sona said before standing. "Muhnak parov Anoush," she said.

"Muhnak parov," Anoush replied, as did Maral, and they left Anoush to contemplate her afternoon. She went upstairs to get the dress she was embroidering, and then she sat by the fire in the kitchen where it was cosy and warm. Her house was similar to most houses in Gamursh: two-storey built of mud brick with a flat roof, and larger than houses in Ourfa. The front door opened onto the courtyard, which like the rest of the house had a flattened, earth floor and whitewashed mud brick walls. The courtyard contained the well and the bathing basin, where the family bathed and Anoush and the girls washed clothes, and timber stairs to the porch upstairs. The courtyard led to the kitchen which had a fireplace and an oven, a table for food preparation with four, simple, timber chairs, and many cooking utensils on wooden racks or hanging from hooks. On a separate rack were glasses, cups and dishes. A door led to the provision room, which had racks, barrels, bins and much more besides. Up the stairs was the porch, open on one side and with no ceiling, and the family slept in the porch on hot nights. There were three bedrooms off the porch, one larger and two smaller, and a dining room with a fireplace.

As the shadows outside lengthened, Anoush began preparing a dzhash of mutton and pumpkin, to be accompanied by bulgur wheat. By that time the children had returned from the American missionary school in Ourfa, about an hour's walk away. As always they were hungry but chores came first. Karine split some wood, Taniel carried this wood to the kitchen and to the fireplace upstairs, while Lilit lit the oil lamps and then carried the cups and plates to the table.

Karine came into the kitchen; frowning deeply. Anoush didn't want to pry, but clearly something troubled Karine.

"Would you like a cup of tea?" Anoush asked.

Karine nodded silently.

Anoush put two scoops in the teapot and poured water from the hot urn. Karine fetched the cups and soon they were drinking lovely, refreshing tea.

"How's school?" Anoush asked; while guessing that was Karine's problem.

"School's good," Karine said. "Today we wrote poems in English."

"I wish I could write poems!" Anoush said, and laughed.

"You can't write poems?" Karine asked; surprised.

"I like reading poems, but I can't write poems to save myself."

"They asked us to write a poem about our mothers," Karine said quietly. She reached into her dress, pulled out a neatly folded sheet of paper and handed it across. Anoush unfolded the poem on the table.

> *My angel is a woman who walks upon the earth,*
> *she shows me my potential and all that I am worth.*
> *When I am sick she heals me and makes me feel*
> *better,*
> *and makes sure that in times of need that we are all*
> *together.*
> *When we get into all trouble in our life,*
> *my angel comes out strong as a mother and a wife.*
> *My angel has raised me to be good and kind,*
> *and makes sure that I have a strong and intelligent*
> *mind,*
> *my angel is my guardian.*
> *my teacher and my friend,*
> *but most of all my mother until the very end.*

That was a lovely poem and Anoush was touched. "Thank you very much," Anoush said. "I will keep this poem for always."

"I hope I'm as good a mother as you," Karine said quietly.

Anoush saw part of herself in her oldest daughter, who liked to live some of her life in her head. Karine liked reading books and poetry, and when she was younger she often played pretend games with Lilit. But there was a touch of ruthlessness in Karine; a burning drive to win; something Anoush didn't recognise in herself or in Emni. Anoush hoped that trait wouldn't get in the way of a happy marriage. "Open your heart to the love that your husband will bring to you, and that love will come," Anoush said. "Open your heart to the love that your children bring in those early days when they most rely upon you, and that love will come too."

"Is it that easy?"

Anoush got up and hugged Karine's shoulders. "Love will come to you, even at the very first, if you open your heart to your husband and to your children."

"It's not long for me."

"We will find someone good in Ourfa."

Karine turned her head to look at Anoush. "I don't want to leave you, Mama," she said.

Anoush hugged her again. "There are good men in Ourfa, and a special man for you." There were few young men in Gamursh, and none of those men were good enough for Karine.

"I understand."

"What is it, Mama?" Lilit asked.

"Karine wrote a nice poem for me," Anoush said.

"Karine's good at English."

"Yes she is."

"Can you help me with my English?" Lilit asked Karine.

Karine sighed deeply like that was a big burden.

"Alright," she eventually said, before they went upstairs together.

Anoush stirred the dzhash which smelled quite lovely, while outside was getting quite dark. Soon Emni would be home from his work at the blacksmith's forge with his father; a business which will be his one day. There was much work for blacksmiths beyond horse shoes, including repairing farm equipment and even making hinges and fastenings for new houses. For the past six years since the overthrow of brutal Sultan Abdul Hamid by the Young Turks and the restoration of democracy, Armenians had felt safe. Safe enough to put the effort into building new and bigger houses. Anoush hoped her concerns about the war would come to nothing.

Emni always came to the kitchen when he got home, and always he kissed Anoush on her cheek. "How was your afternoon?" he asked, as always.

18

"Fine," she said. "Maral and Sona came for a cup of tea. How was your afternoon?"

"Busy, as always. What's for dinner?"

"Mutton and pumpkin."

Emni smiled brightly. "You know how to spoil a husband."

Anoush laughed. "It's just a dzhash."

"The best prepared dzhash in the world! It's been a hard day and I must bathe."

He headed to the courtyard and the bathing basin, while Anoush took a cask of wine from the provision room to the dining room upstairs. Shortly after, the family was gathered around the dining table and sharing a hot meal on a cool evening.

"Jivan came to see us at the forge," Emni said.

Maral's husband. "Did he talk about Armenians and Russians?" Anoush asked.

"He did."

"I'm sorry about that."

"How do you come up with such ideas?" Emni asked, incredulously.

Anoush drew a big breath and wondered how far she could go. "As you know I visit friends in Ourfa, and when I go there we discuss world events."

"Can you tell me how we've come to this?"

19

Anoush could. "American missionaries run the school in Ourfa where I was educated, and where our children now go. When these missionaries first came to Anatolia, as Christians they felt an empathy with Armenians, the world's first Christians. They set up schools and churches, and they preached that Christians are superior to Muslims. Through this superiority they encouraged Armenians to take charge of their destinies, rather than being subservient to Muslim Turks. In Constantinople and other cities, for the first time Armenians began to agitate for independence. This led to the massacre at Hamidan, and other tensions since then."

"We were here first and Turks invaded us."

"American missionaries would say the same thing, but that doesn't help us when we're outnumbered, and when they hold social and military power. We should be realistic about our situation, as we were for hundreds of years."

"Is this true, Mama?" Karine asked.

"I don't want you to have bad feelings about your school and your teachers," Anoush said. "This happened a long time ago."

"They say things at school about Muslims."

"You know many Muslims, Karine. Almost always they're good people, is that not so?"

Karine paused. "Yes," she eventually said.

"The difference is they worship God, the same God as we worship, in a different way to us."

"Is that all?" Karine asked, clearly perplexed.

Anoush looked her oldest daughter in the eyes. "Do your lessons, pass your exams, master English because that could be useful one day, but keep an open mind about religion."

"Is this what you did?"

"I discovered these things later, in discussions with my friends."

"Will these problems go away, Mama?" Taniel asked with the simplicity of a twelve-year-old boy.

"I truly don't know." Anoush sighed. The genie had been let out of the bottle and there was no putting it back.

* * *

Emni came into the room, eyes blazing, and closed the door behind him. Anoush knew that look. She sat up in their bed to toss blankets and sheet aside, and to remove her nightdress too. Emni couldn't wait and he grabbed Anoush and kissed her hard, before unbuttoning his shirt and tossing it aside, and unbuttoning the waist of his trousers. Soon those trousers were gone and he was kissing Anoush again, before climbing on the bed to straddle and kiss her, while fondling her breasts. He bent down to kiss her breasts and tease her nipples momentarily, before resuming his kiss.

Anoush murmured with the delight of their kiss, and murmured more with the delight of his big, powerful hands kneading her. Nothing delicate; just pure desire. Pure lust.

His hard member pressing against her while he kissed her, and she wrapped his muscular body with her arms. Firm and muscular, and all for her.

Again Emni kissed her breasts, and this time he stayed there. Anoush shuddered when he filled her, and they made love mouth to mouth. Strong, manly, masculine. She; the vessel of his desire. Again she wrapped his muscular body with her arms; almost light-headed at his power channelled through her and into her. Still they kissed; right to the end when he pulled out and slid his member along her stomach, and she felt his warm juices on her. Momentarily Emni nibbled her ear before kissing once more. Then he looked down with his dark eyes sparkling.

"I love you," Anoush said quietly; but those trite words didn't describe how she really felt.

"I love you," Emni whispered in a hoarse voice. "We'll be together forever."

"We will be together forever," Anoush echoed, and she hoped they would be together forever. She loved him; she truly did.

* * *

As always at lunchtime the staff dining room was busy, and echoing with a hundred conversations, or more. Paul got to the start of the queue and grabbed a plate and cutlery. In turn, the plate was stacked with grilled veal, watery gravy, pumpkin, carrots and peas. At the end he paid 12 francs and took his meal to an empty table. He was about to start when someone took the seat opposite. Without looking up he knew who it was.

"Guten tag Maria," he said.

"Guten tag Paul," she replied. "How's your lunch?"

"The usual."

He ate some and it was better than it looked.

"How are you today?" Maria asked.

"Fine," Paul replied. "And you?"

"Busy."

"How's your father dealing with retirement?"

"He kept a few patients who he sees at home."

"That's good for him," Maria said.

"He will consult to the end."

Paul ate more of his lunch.

"We're having a friend for dinner on Saturday night," Maria said. "You're welcome to join us."

Paul tried to stifle his smile. "Are you match-making your cousin again?"

"No, no, no," she professed. "But Gretel is nice."

Paul knew nice. His mother was nice and devoted her life to begging and scraping after his father, and Paul didn't want that. He wanted someone who knew herself, like Maria. Someone who would have her own life in marriage, beyond looking after a husband.

"I told Gretel about my tall and handsome cousin, with wavy black hair and penetrating green eyes," Maria said. "And she knows you're a doctor."

Maria told him that so he couldn't refuse. "I will be pleased to come for dinner on Saturday night," Paul said.

"Come at eight," she said.

He put his knife and fork down and was about to say 'I'm only twenty-four and there's plenty of time', but Maria knew that already. "I will," he said. Besides, he thought, Gretel might even be the one.

"This war is terrible," Maria said. "I'm glad Switzerland has the good sense not to get involved in such things. But to think of such terrible suffering so close to us."

Bern, Switzerland, was quite close to some of the worst battlefields, but in the staff dining room of the Bern University Hospital, you would never know. "I know what you mean," Paul said. "Over there, you and I might be behind the lines tending the wounded."

"That's very true. Sometimes I would like to ease their suffering."

"They have their own doctors and nurses."

"The Red Cross in Geneva have volunteers looking after prisoners."

Paul was surprised. "I didn't know that. Are you thinking of volunteering?"

"I would if I could but something else has happened. "We're going to have a family."

Paul was so pleased to hear that. "Congratulations," he said.

"It wasn't that hard," Maria said with a smirk.

"My time will come, and not when I'm almost fifty!"

"I know, and you will make a good father too, because you know what not to do!"

Paul looked into her sparkling, brown eyes. Mischievous sparkling brown eyes. "Are you returning to work after?" he asked.

"I would like to work part-time."

She was a good nurse and they would do that for her.

"A governess for our child, and me working part-time," Maria said.

"That sounds ideal." Paul looked at the clock and time was slipping away. He finished his meal before folding his knife and fork together. "I must go," he said before standing. "Bis spatter Maria."

"Bis Samstag Paul," Maria said.

He looked forward to Saturday, although not so much for Gretel.

* * *

It was late, well into evening and dark, when Paul eventually arrived home. It was a large house about 30 years old, in a street of large houses in the Kirchenfeld district. Three storeys with attic rooms for the maid and gardener; it really was too big for a family of three. Frida the maid worked particularly hard, and the house was always spotless. Father was fastidious, and Paul had to be particularly careful not to make greasy marks on polished woodwork, or track dirt inside. He climbed the stairs to his room, large but not cosy, and there he changed for dinner. He heard the clock in the entry hall chime six, and he'd made it home just in time. He went downstairs.

The dining room of that large house was particularly austere. Dark mahogany timber skirting boards and a mahogany mantel above the fireplace, the fire bright and crackling on a November evening, dark green walls with dark brown trim, and a long, mahogany table with six mahogany chairs. Father always sat at one end of the table, Mother at the other end a distance away, and Paul sat half-way; away from the fire.

"You were home late today?" Father said.

"Work was busy," Paul said.

"When are you going to get a real job?"

"I have a real job Father. I'm a good doctor, and I prefer to work at the hospital where I can help the good people of this city."

"I mean a job which earns decent money."

Father was a specialist neurologist and patients needed a fat wallet to afford his fees. "I earn a good income," Paul said.

Father crossed his arms and glared into the distance.

"I met Maria today at work," Paul said to his mother. "She has good news. She's pregnant."

"Oh that's wonderful!" Mother exclaimed.

Paul glanced at Father who now glared at Mother; still with his arms crossed. Paul always suspected that Father wanted a wife to care for him and for other things, but children were not part of his plan, and being a doctor he could arrange that. But somehow, something went wrong, although maybe not accidentally. Paul's theory was that he wasn't planned and Mother had never been forgiven for that. "I'm visiting Maria and Hans on Saturday night," Paul said.

"Give them my best wishes," Mother said.

"I will."

Father said nothing, as to be expected.

Frida brought out their traditionally German dinner of bread with cheese, cold meat, and sausage. She then poured three glasses from the crystal wine decanter, before slipping from the room. Paul ate in silence as they always ate in silence, while sipping his wine from time to time. Paul finished and waited for his parents to finish. He then made an excuse, bid them both 'tschüs', and went upstairs to his room, now warm with a fire set by Otto the gardener.

Paul sat on his bed with the only sound being the crackling of the fire, and then the clock chimed seven. He really needed to get out of that house, although it wasn't conventional to leave home until married. He didn't want to marry just anyone to get out of that house though. He wanted to find a woman like Maria: warm, caring, intelligent and independent. And then he remembered Maria's conversation about the Red Cross. That would get him out of that house, and broaden his horizons beyond Bern too. Nursing was a bigger part of medicine than doctors, and that might be an opportunity for him. That might be a wonderful opportunity for him in many, different ways. Paul sat at his desk, pulled out a pad and his fountain pen, and pondered what to write to the Red Cross in Geneva.

Chapter Two

The road to Ourfa crossed farms on the fertile and treeless plain, with many fields fallow in late January. Anoush accompanied her children early on a cold, mid-winter morning, while they walked to school. Anoush was absorbed by many thoughts and mesmerised by the vapour from her breath. They closed on Ourfa and entered through the Assyrian Quarter, and after crossing farms and fields, and after the broad, spaciousness of Gamursh, Ourfa felt tight and claustrophobic, squashed between farmland to the east and hills to the west; those hills topped by the ruined castle. The street was tightly hemmed by tall, stone houses, while narrow, cobbled lanes zigzagged in all directions, with buildings all but blocking the sun. As always the city bustled. Arab men in long, white robes and white ghutrahs; some dwarfing small donkeys and some with a camel train recently arrived from the south, accompanied by the pungent smell of animal and dung. Turkish men in their squat, Fez hats, going about their business or talking in small groups. Women always rushing, unlike men who had time to socialise. Further on the street widened at the Samsat Gate, just a simple, stone arch from ages past, before they headed right into the Armenian Quarter and along Mousali Meydan, passing Armenian shops: butchers, bakers, wine merchants, fruit shops, clock maker, lawyer, insurance agent, accountant and more. Again stone buildings mostly blocked the sun, and they kept clear of the centre drain perpetually wet from rains of days and weeks past. A little further on they reached the large and impressive Armenian Protestant Church, flanked by the American Girl's and Boy's schools; all fine structures built from brick.

Anoush hugged Karine, Taniel and Lilit in turn, and bid them 'muhnak parov' before heading past the Apostolic Cathedral of the Holy Mother of God, the grandest and largest building in Ourfa by far. Beyond the cathedral was a large courtyard containing countless tombs. She then went past a mosque and along a narrow lane past a bathhouse to the Turkish Quarter, and to the market and shops, noisy and bustling with merchants calling customers for their wares. Fruit, vegetables, meat, kebab vendors, rolls of fine material, carpets, jewellery: every essential and luxury one could possibly want. Sights, sounds and the scents of fresh produce. Most had stands in front of their shops, with merchants calling each customer who passed to inspect, for surely they had the best quality and cheapest prices. Each merchant had the best quality and the cheapest prices, and that was a fact! Anoush avoided eye contact while she marched through the chaos to her destination. She opened the door and went inside, where it was quiet and musty. Peaceful and relaxing, with shelves of books lining each wall, and standing free along the centre too, with a counter, unattended, near the door. Creaking on the timber stairs, and Anoush turned to face her friend who hadn't aged a day but was truly showing his years.

"Selam Zeki," Anoush said. "Nasilsin?" she asked.

"Selam Anoush," Zeki said. "Lyiyim."

He was fine, as always. Maybe around 50, greying on his hair and his trimmed beard, and with lovely smile lines around his eyes.

"I thought I would be seeing you," he said in Turkish. "Come upstairs and I'll make some coffee."

Anoush followed him up the stairs to the small apartment where there was a table with five simple, timber chairs, and a spirit stove for the inevitable cups of coffee. She had been there many times: alone with Zeki or with his friends, discussing philosophy, religion, Turkish events, world events and much more.

"That's a lovely dress," Zeki said.

"Thank you," Anoush replied. "I finished it the other week."

"Armenian women have the nicest clothes. Often in red which is quite attractive."

"This one is warm for a cold morning."

"Please sit," Zeki said as he poured a small cup.

Anoush sat and Zeki sat too. She sipped the coffee and it was superb, and better than she was ever able to make.

"How's your husband?" Zeki asked

"He's fine and his work is busy at the moment. My sister-in-law will be making him lunch."

"And your children?"

"Fine too."

"How old are they now?"

"Karine is fifteen, Taniel is twelve and Lilit is ten."

"How they must be growing. Soon it will be time for...."

Anoush laughed. "Don't remind me! It seems like yesterday that we were married, and soon we will be looking for a husband for Karine."

"It seems like yesterday when you first came here."

Anoush remembered; she was maybe a little older than Karine now. "I wanted to look at your books and dream about reading some of them, only you had a copy of James Ferrier on the counter and I read the introduction to myself."

"That's when I realised that you speak English."

"That's right. With my English and your self-taught German, and books in Turkish...."

"And Armenian."

"Yes. But you have to have an interest in learning about the broader beyond."

"You do."

Anoush nodded her head slowly. "People would never understand us."

"One day women will have freedom. I think Armenian women are more independent than Turkish women."

"How so?" Anoush asked, surprised.

"It seems that you have province over the domestic sphere, and men the external sphere."

"Compared to Islam?"

He nodded.

"I told the family about American missionaries preaching the superiority of Christians over Muslims," Anoush said.

"That's good," Zeki replied.

"I know my children get a good education from the Americans, as long as they understand that we're more the same than we're different." Anoush thought about why she came to Ourfa. "Is it true that Russia defeated the Ottomans at Sarikamish, and Enver Pasha blamed Armenians for siding with the enemy?" she asked.

"It was as we forecast."

"What would you do?"

"Armenians are now the enemy within. Perhaps the Ottoman Government will arrest and detain Armenian men of fighting age."

"Could they do that?"

"They have the resources to do that."

"We should leave."

"To where?"

"Away from war. Bulgaria maybe."

"To start over?'

"If they arrest Emni and put him in a prison for years; that would be worse than starting over."

"This is a big decision, Anoush."

"I'm only a woman and this is not my decision. I will try to persuade Emni, because I see no good coming out of this war."

"Good luck."

"I will need good luck to persuade my husband to leave family, friends and a prosperous business." Anoush realised that she forgot something. "How's your wife, Zeki?"

"A happy grandmother many times over."

"That's good for her. One day I'll be a grandmother many times over, but I need more than that, in my head at least."

Zeki stood. "I have a present for you."

He went down the stairs and returned with a second-hand copy of Handan by Halide Edib.

"Oh Zeki, this is so wonderful!" Anoush gasped. "She's my favourite author."

"Look after it as always, and bring it back when you're finished."

Anoush carefully turned the pages of Turkish script. Edib had divorced her husband some years past, and her stories inevitably pointed towards women's equality. "I can't wait to read this." She stood and hugged him, and he held her lightly. "You're my best friend," she said quietly. "People would never understand us."

"You're a good friend Anoush, and people would never understand us."

* * *

Emni paced their bedroom while Anoush sat on the bed and watched him.

"You say they might arrest us and lock us away?" he asked.

Anoush nodded. "They have an army large enough to do this," she said.

"But to start over in a new country, on the basis of what might happen?"

"Until now, things have happened as I suggested they would."

"You're not a prophet Anoush. I know the women here think you're the sage of Gamursh, but you're not infallible."

"My friends in Ourfa think about issues and suggest the most likely outcome."

Emni put his head down and frowned. "To start over with nothing...." He looked up at her. "I would have to tell my family and they would leave too, but if nothing happened...."

Anoush understood that made for another dimension.

"You don't want your brothers to be arrested," she said.

"I don't want to turn their lives upside-down, if nothing comes of this. The whole village will know and they will leave, and we will be responsible for them too."

Anoush sighed. Emni was right; it would be the whole village. However, Zeki was seldom wrong. "I believe that something bad will happen."

"This is just a few radicals siding with the enemy. Until now, we've been safe in Ourfa. I can't imagine the authorities arresting every Armenian man of fighting age, just for the actions of a few radicals." He crossed his arms. "We won't be going."

Anoush knew that look, one Emni didn't show often, but when he did that was the end of the matter. She thought it was a mistake but a marriage was two people, and both had to agree on major decisions. "I understand," she said, even though she felt it was wrong.

* * *

Monsieur Gabriel Martin came from behind his desk and shook Paul's hand.

"Good morning Dr Lang," he said in English. "Thank you for visiting us here in Geneva."

"Good morning Monsieur Martin," Paul replied. "Thank you for finding the time to meet with me."

"Please sit."

Paul sat, and Monsieur Martin sat behind his imposing desk.

"You're interested in volunteering to care for prisoners of war?" Monsieur Martin asked.

"I believe I'm old enough to have the experience to help," Paul said. "And I'm young enough not to have family commitments. Also, I speak German which might help."

"Actually, we've had a good response from German-speaking Swiss Doctors," Monsieur Martin said. "So what we're looking for are doctors for the Eastern Front."

Paul was surprised. "Russia?" he asked.

"There are fair numbers of prisoners from the campaign at Gallipoli, under the care of the British in Cairo, Egypt. Soldiers from the Ottoman Empire; mostly Turks."

That pricked Paul's interest. Cairo, Egypt. Pyramids, the Sphinx, the Nile River, Cleopatra and more besides. That would be interesting.

"Are you interested, Dr Lang?" Monsieur Martin asked.

"Are there other doctors there?"

"We have one doctor but he will be leaving shortly, so you would be the only doctor for us in Cairo."

"Tell me how this would work."

"We arrange your travel, accommodation and pay for your meals, and arrange an interpreter. We will also pay you a doctor's honorarium."

"I don't want to be treated specially just because I'm a doctor."

"Your honorarium is meant to cover expenses invariably incurred when away from home, so you won't be out of pocket. This is only fair."

Paul thought that was reasonable. "I'm interested in your proposal, Monsieur Martin," he said.

"Good. I have your details from your letter, so we can book your travel and accommodation now, and arrange a visa too. My secretary will compile an itinerary and the contact details for your interpreter. I expect you will be sailing from Marseilles within the next two weeks. Would that give you enough time to arrange your affairs?"

Paul thought. He had to apply for leave from the hospital, and then he would be free. "Two weeks will be fine."

Monsieur Martin stood. "If you leave your passport with my secretary, she will be in touch by telegram with your itinerary."

They shook hands and said goodbyes, and soon Paul was on his way to the station to catch a train home. He wondered what to tell his parents. That he was volunteering for expenses and an honorarium? No. That he was working for the Red Cross, which would save him a lot of drama, although his mother would be quite shocked. But still, months or even longer in Egypt? That sounded truly fascinating.

Chapter Three

Three trucks, engines screaming, roared into Gamursh and stopped with squealing brakes. Nine Turkish soldiers in sandy-coloured uniforms jumped down, while an officer climbed out of the cabin of the lead truck and stood in front of the church. Holding a sheet of paper which he didn't read, he announced that all men between the ages of 18 and 48 were to be conscripted, while soldier-drivers sat behind steering wheels and stared vacantly into the distance. Meanwhile other soldiers, rifles at the ready, searched the village from end to end. The bakery, the butchery, the grocery shop, the blacksmith's forge, each house, and even the church. One by one, the men of Gamursh between the ages of 18 and 48 were assembled in front of the church.

They were roughly prodded to climb into those three trucks. Soldiers got in behind, tailgates were slammed shut, and after awkward turns, three trucks roared out of the village, while women, some with babes in arms or young children at their legs, watched the caravan disappear out of sight, leaving nothing more than the putrid smell of fumes. Anoush stood shocked, even though it was as Zeki predicted six months before. Tuesday July 20 and it was too late.

* * *

Anoush sensed something was happening. Nobody had visited and she hadn't been outside, but something was happening out there. The hinge creaked, just as Anoush went to the courtyard to meet Sona looking quite peculiar.

"What is it?" Anoush asked in panic. Despite the cool she felt flushed and sweaty, and her heart beat painfully fast.

"You must come," Sona said.

"Where?"

"To the forest to the west. Bodies have been found."

Anoush gasped and put her hand to her mouth. "Men's bodies?"

"I don't know."

Anoush followed Sona outside on a cloudy day, and joined the women heading away from the village; some with their children. In silence they trudged along little-used dirt trails towards the green smudge a few kilometres away. Into the forest of tall fir trees, almost dark despite it being near midday; the trees blocking much of the light. On and on until a clearing, but strangely still dark from heavy, grey clouds. Anoush felt something; an eerie, other force. Haunted? She wondered. She felt restless spirits in that place.

A woman cried out while other women ran to a long ditch with dirt piled to the far side. They wailed; a pitiful, mournful sound of anguish. Anoush went to the freshly-dug ditch and looked down at naked bodies of men lying in the grave they'd dug. She felt strangely unmoved despite the tragedy at her feet. She dodged around women crying,

41

wailing, and even pounding the ground in grief. She walked slowly while checking each man, and then stopped with a quiet gasp. Never again would Emni come home, kiss her cheek, and cheerfully ask how her afternoon had been. Anoush knelt beside the open grave; while realising Emni had gone from this world to a better place. There were many things Anoush would miss about Emni, but mostly she would miss his love for her, and his love for their children. Emni's love was all-encompassing and all-enveloping. Anoush cried with near-silent sobs at the terrible tragedy that befell her husband, and the terrible tragedies that befell the good men of their village.

Alongside lay Emni's brothers Mayis and Jivan, and only then was Anoush aware of Sona beside her; kneeling at the grave for her husband Mayis, and also crying to herself. To her other side was Mayr Gayane Hagopian and Anoush briefly touched her hand. A wife had lost a husband but a mother had lost three sons. Beside Sona; Maral was inconsolable.

"I will miss him," Anoush said between sobs.

"I will miss him," Sona said between her sobs.

Anoush grabbed Sona and hugged her tight. Tears flowed between the two sisters-in-law. "Emni will live in my heart for eternity," Anoush said.

Chapter Four

It was hot, stiflingly hot, and too hot for a suit, shirt, tie and cap. Cairo was noisy chaos. Trams rumbled by, bells ringing continuously in an attempt to forge a path through the crush of cars, busses, donkeys, camels and pedestrians swarming over the road. The crush of pedestrians on footpaths was even more unbelievable, with most men dressed in long, white robes; and most women hidden in black. Vendors at stalls and barrows shouted for business, while there was a mournful cry from a nearby mosque with a tall tower and a dome-shaped roof, echoed by hundreds more cries from all over the city. Cairo smelled smoky from fires, mixed with pungent scents drifting from cafes or wafting from street vendors.

The foyer of Shepheard's Hotel was somewhat calmer but still busy. That foyer was quite huge, with ornate columns, marble floors, stained glass windows, leather sofas and more marble forming the reception counter. Swiss-owned and Swiss-managed; Paul was booked into a room on the second floor. His room, his home for the next while, was surprisingly opulent with ornately-carved timber trim in cream and gold, contrasting with maroon coloured walls, and thick, maroon rugs. Furniture: bed heads, wardrobe, desk and chair, were also elegantly carved and finished in cream and gold; the seat having a red velvet cushion. Unfortunately because of the heat, Paul had to keep the window open, which let in the cacophony of noise from the street outside. Because of the heat, he removed his jacket, tie and cap.

Paul left that behind to wait in the foyer, but in the swarm of customers coming and going, he wondered how he would ever identify his translator.

"Excuse me," the man in a casual white jacket without lapels, and a squat, black hat asked. "Are you Dr Paul Lang?"

Paul turned to face this middle-aged man with a haggard face, and a mouth of twisted teeth. "I'm Paul Lang. Are you Asil Toral-oglu?"

"Yes I am," he said in quite accented English, but easy enough to understand. "You have just arrived?'

"Yes I have," Paul said. "Tomorrow we will start at the prisoner of war hospital, and then we will go to the camps."

He nodded, and smiled in a way which seemed more like he knew everything and was merely tolerating the Swiss doctor. Paul would have preferred to work as a partnership of equals, where one had the medical knowledge and the other had the local knowledge.

"Can you meet me in this foyer; tomorrow morning at eight?" Paul asked.

"Yes Dr Lang," Asil said.

"I will see you then."

He left, and Paul headed to the dining room. It was quite massive, with maybe a hundred tables beneath towering ceilings, and had many windows overlooking magnificent gardens beyond. It seemed as if there was one waiter per table, which was astounding. Paul waited to be served.

* * *

Anoush held the door while her children went inside Zeki's shop, and then she followed. Zeki was at the counter serving a young, bearded man; a Turk by his Fez. The young man thanked Zeki for his carefully wrapped purchase and headed to the chaos outside. Zeki came to Anoush who put her suitcase down. He held her shoulders and looked into her eyes.

"You have my deepest sympathies for what happened," he said in Turkish.

"Thank you Zeki," Anoush said. "Zeki, these are my children Karine, Taniel and Lilit. Children, this is my friend Zeki."

"Merhaba Karine, Taniel ve Lilit," Zeki said.

"Merhaba Bayim Zeki," they said in near unison.

He looked at the bags carried by each. "You're moving to Urfa?" he asked.

Anoush nodded. "I will stay with my parents for now. I'm worried that soldiers may come to Gamursh for the rest of us."

"Yes, of course. Come upstairs and I will make coffee."

They went upstairs to the apartment, where Anoush told her children to leave their bags to one side. They sat at the table while Zeki worked at the stove. Anoush sipped her coffee while he joined them, but the taste didn't register.

"When I heard about what happened at your village; I never thought they would do that," Zeki said. "Then I head about deportations of Armenians from Erzinjan, and I realised this is more than the threat of Armenian independence."

Anoush was terribly confused. "Do you know what this is about?" she asked.

"I don't know if this is for the ears of children."

"Their father was killed for no good reason, and I'm worried that whatever's happening will involve us sooner or later."

Zeki nodded thoughtfully. "Like your husband, all men of fighting age are being separated and dealt with. Women, children and old men are then marched to a camp at Der-el-Zor. There's little food and water and many die on the way, while the camp in just a paddock in the desert and it has little food or water."

"Where's Der-el-Zor?"

"In the desert of Syria, hundreds of kilometres south-east from here."

"So many hundreds of kilometres for those from Erzinjan, with little food or water on the way?"

"Yes."

Anoush was quite shocked. "They mean to drive us out of Anatolia, and if we die that's of no consequence." But there was more, because the camp was a death sentence too. "They mean to kill us for being Armenian."

"I believe it's for being Christian, and this is too organised not to have been planned in some detail."

"You said that being Muslim was just worshipping God differently to us," Karine said.

"That's true," Anoush said. "But too many fixate on the differences between us."

"But they're killing Christians just for being Christians!" she exclaimed.

"This is actions of the government and not of the Turkish people."

"Turkish soldiers shot my father."

"They were following orders," Zeki said. "Like all soldiers if they don't follow orders they will be in serious trouble. Other Turks fixate on the differences between us, like the government."

"Some Turks are good and some are bad?" Karine asked.

"Some are good, some are bad and many are ignorant."

Karine looked at Zeki with her mouth open. "I understand," she eventually said. "They're ignorant of how similar we are, and how we can live together peacefully."

"That's right."

"Do you have any ideas?" Anoush asked Zeki.

He drew a deep breath and blew out his cheeks. "Gather every rifle and every bullet, because you have nothing to lose. If you can tell other cities and towns to fight to the last person standing; this is your only chance. You will be opening a third front to the war: Russia to the east, Britain to the south and Armenians within. The Ottomans don't have the resources to fight a war like this, and their priority must be Russia and Britain or else their borders will be overrun."

"We're city workers, not soldiers!" Anoush said in exasperation.

Zeki put his hand on her hand. "I wish I didn't have to say this, but you have no other choice."

Anoush realised her heart was beating fast, yet again. She sipped her coffee, drank some water and contemplated what Zeki said. Persuading every Armenian city, town and village? Even persuading the Armenians of Ourfa would be close to impossible! She looked at her children, young and innocent, and realised she had no choice.

* * *

After the heat, noise and chaos of the streets of Cairo, the prisoner of war hospital was cool, calm, quiet and well-ordered. Paul waited for the commanding officer, and shortly after he heard boots stomping on hard, timber floors.

Captain Morris, maybe in his thirties in a crisply pressed khaki uniform, strode to Paul and clearly was about to salute before he thought better of it. Instead he extended his hand.

"I'm told you're Doctor Lang," Captain Morris said in a sharp, crisp tone of voice.

"Yes I am, Captain," Paul replied in English.

"We're more than happy to have the Red Cross participate, but I'm afraid you won't find much to concern you."

Paul nodded while he thought. "What was this place before the war?" he asked.

"It was a private clinic. We had to fit more beds so it's a bit crowded, but it has good facilities."

"I understand. This is my interpreter, Asil Toral-oglu."

Captain Morris shook hands. "Pleased to meet you Mr Toral."

"Thank you Captain," Asil said in his accented English.

"There's nothing much more that I can offer. You're free to check on the prisoners, and if you have any questions please speak to the nurses but not the doctors."

"Thank you Captain Morris."

Captain Morris left.

"We should go," Paul said to Asil, before he pushed heavy, solid wood double doors to a ward. It was crowded indeed, with perhaps double the number of beds he would normally have expected. A modest-sized room in a building maybe 50 years old, with tall windows allowing light to flood in. Immaculate with ornate timberwork, which was to be expected in a ward of a formerly expensive private clinic. Ceiling fans lazily stirred the air and were surprisingly effective. The ward was hushed and quiet, while nurses in black and white uniforms glided from patient to patient. The first bed had the name Private Dado Mustafa-oglu written in chalk on a small blackboard, and amputated finger. Paul opened his notebook, took a fountain pen from his pocket, and wrote down those details before he inspected the dressing. All good as Captain Morris promised, and he went to the next soldier, Private Pavo with no surname, suffering from a bullet wound to his left leg.

"Excuse me Asil," Paul asked. "This soldier has no surname."

"Turks have no surnames," Asil said.

That was odd and must be rather confusing. "What did the Mustafa-Oglu for the other private signify?"

"Oglu means son of."

"So his children will be known as Dado-oglu?"

"That's right Doctor, but to use a second name is entirely optional."

"I understand and thank you."

Asil smiled in a smarmy sort of way. Like he wanted to help Paul, but at the same time he was too superior to help. Paul took notes, inspected the wound dressing where all was satisfactory, and then he moved to the next soldier. He checked every soldier in the ward, all were satisfactory, and he wondered why he was there. Had he volunteered and been sent to Cairo for no good reason? He wondered indeed. There was another ward, and just through the double doors was quite a scene. A soldier was shouting and thrashing about, but nobody was in the least bit interested. Paul went to that soldier, Jabir Rafa-oglu, who'd had a leg amputation.

"Ask him what his problem is?" Paul told Asil.

"Senin sorunun ne?" Asil asked.

"Cinayet Ermeniler," the soldier said.

Asil frowned, and then turned to face Paul. "He said he doesn't have a problem."

Paul looked at the soldier who repeated "Cinayet Ermeniler Doctor."

"What does cinayet Ermeniler mean?"

"It means nothing," Asil said, while looking down and fidgeting with the button on the cuff of his jacket.

Paul knew that wasn't right. He put his bag on the bed, opened it and pulled out a thermometer. He shook it, slipped it under the soldier's tongue while holding the soldier's wrist and counting his pulse. Pulse was 130 which was high but not extreme, and temperature 39, which was again a bit high but not extreme.

"English?" the soldier asked.

"No, Swiss," Paul said, and then he realised. "Yes, English."

"Murder Armenians."

"What does that mean?" Paul asked the soldier.

"Many, many," the soldier said.

"Asil?"

"I don't know, Doctor," Asil said.

"What is it, Doctor?" a nurse asked.

"This soldier seems upset and I thought he may be delirious, perhaps with gangrene after his amputation. But his signs are reasonable: pulse one-thirty and temperature thirty-nine."

"Both a bit high."

"Remove his dressings and check for infections."

"I will do that now."

Paul checked soldiers in the remaining two wards, and finished by four. He went to reception where he was intercepted by Captain Morris, who clearly was kept up to date with the activities of the Red Cross doctor.

"I hope everything was to your satisfaction, Doctor Lang?" Captain Morris asked.

"Your hospital is excellent, Captain Morris," Paul said.

"We have more coming from Gallipoli in the next few days."

"I will be back on Monday next week, and I will be at the prisoner of war camp over the next days."

"Good."

"There is only one thing," Paul said. "A soldier in ward two told me 'murder Armenians; many, many'. Do you know what that might mean?"

"Not at all."

"Oh well," Paul said. "Thank you very much for making your hospital available to me."

They shook hands and departed with farewells. On the way down the stairs, Paul had to raise his voice to be heard above the commotion. "Asil," he said. "Meet me in the foyer of the hotel; tomorrow morning at eight."

"Yes Doctor," Asil replied.

"Goodbye and thank you."

"Yes Doctor."

Paul walked around the corner to the hotel, grabbed his key from reception and climbed the stairs to his room. There he removed his jacket, tie and cap; washed, changed his shirt, and wondered what to do until the dining room opened at six-thirty. Loneliness was the biggest problem of being away from home, family and friends. Hopefully he could make a difference at the prisoner of war camps, but in the process his existence was transient and gypsy-like. He went outside without a jacket and tie; crossed the Nile and walked through nearby gardens on an oppressively hot day. Despite the heat and general chaos of Cairo, it was quite fascinating to be strolling past the Nile River which had seen so much history over the millennia. Paul headed back to the hotel and to the large but almost empty dining room, where a waiter showed him to a table. Eating alone in dining rooms was another awful thing about being away from home, family and friends.

At the next table were three men talking quite loudly in a nasally type of English. Paul ignored them while he ordered a glass of wine, and checked the menu which hadn't changed. Despite being a Swiss-owned hotel, the food was rather stodgy. He ordered a steak, and sipped his wine.

The three men at the other table, dressed in open-necked shirts like he, were maybe in their forties, and were drinking beer while they waited for their meals. Beer made more sense on a hot day. One of them said 'what're we goin' do 'bout the Armenians?' and that pricked Paul's interest. The second time he'd heard that word that day. Another replied 'pressure needs to be applied before it's too late', with the answer being 'it's almost too late now'. The answer to that was 'there's thousands in those camps and we gotta do somethin'.' Paul became even more curious, and he wondered if he should. But if he didn't ask then he wouldn't know.

He got up and went to their table. "Excuse me," he said. "I overheard you talking about Armenians, and I heard that word today at work and I wondered what might be going on."

"Sure," one of the men said, smiling brightly before he stood to shake hands. "My name's Jack Bennet, and with me are Mike Sallis and Bill Lohman."

"My name's Paul Lang."

"You wanna join us?"

"That would be too much to ask."

"Armenia's a long story, so you ought to."

"If you don't mind."

Mr Bennet nodded so Paul took his drink to their table.

"I'm working for the Red Cross," Paul said. "Today I came across a Turkish prisoner who was quite distraught. He said 'murder Armenians' and 'many, many'. I don't know what that means."

"I'll explain," Mr Bennet said. "Armenians are a group of Christians living in Turkey, and they're being, and I don't know the right word but I reckon eliminated describes it."

"Pardon?" Paul asked; surprised by that.

"Turks are killing Armenian men, and then marching women, children and the elderly across country where many die on the way, to camps in the desert of Syria to die."

"To die?"

"No food or water."

Paul got the most dreadful shock. He mouth felt dry and sipped some more wine. "Why is this?"

"There's been friction between the two groups for a while now, but none of that justifies this."

"The soldier I saw today might have been involved with this in some way, and it might have affected him."

"For a soldier following orders, I reckon it would."

Paul thought that quite by chance he'd discovered something big, although only fragments of it and unproven. But it could be big and even tragic. "I should let the Red Cross in Geneva know about this, if you don't mind me quoting you."

"Sure, no problem."

"How do you know this?"

"We're missionaries, and we've just returned from Damascus where there are camps nearby. Some of the camp inmates told us through an interpreter."

"If I was to telegraph the Red Cross that a Turkish soldier told me that many Armenians are being murdered, and American missionaries confirmed that Armenian men are being killed, and Armenian women, children and older people are being marched to camps in the desert to die because there's no food or water; that would be an accurate summation?"

"If you add that most women, children and old people die from exhaustion and starvation on those marches; that would be accurate."

"I will do that." Paul sipped his drink. "This is really quite dreadful. Do you know how many are involved?"

"It seems to be a lot."

"I will telegraph Geneva tomorrow."

"We're tryin' to do our bit with the 'States."

"We're both doing the same thing then?"

"Yeah."

Their meals arrived and it was steaks each.

"Tell me Paul," Mr Bennet said, and Paul was surprised by his familiarity. "What're you doin' here for the Red Cross."

"I'm a doctor volunteering."

"You're lookin' after their bodies, and we're lookin' after their souls."

"That's right."

It was a good meal: the steak was cooked just right and pink in the middle, with a lovely Diane sauce.

"You from Geneva, Paul?" Mr Lohman asked.

"I'm from Bern, which is the German part of Switzerland. I was concerned about the terrible slaughter of this war and hoped I could help."

"Like us?"

"Yes; like you but in a different way. I never expected to be sent to Cairo, but war is war and here I am."

They ate their meals in a relaxed and friendly atmosphere far removed from the stuffy formality of Switzerland. After they finished their steaks, the three Americans ordered desserts of treacle sponge pudding while Paul made do with a glass of port. After, he bid them farewell and headed to his hot room; noisy with the window open. He sat at the desk, straightened the pad with the Hotel logo on top, and contemplated what to write. Telegrams had to be brief, but also had to be clear.

'Come to my attention Ottoman government or Ottoman army massacring Armenian men, and marching Armenian women, children and old people to desert camps in Syria with many dying from exhaustion and starvation on the way. No food or water at camps and many more expected to die. Seems very serious situation.'

Paul was pleased with that. He pulled on a pair of short pyjama trousers and slid into the big bed, and hoped he would sleep in the heat.

Chapter Five

Anoush joined maybe two hundred women carrying food and water, as they headed past Samsat Gate to the open ground beyond the German Orphanage. There were many tents in that space, patrolled by gendarmes with rifles slung over shoulders. But it was known that local inhabitants could assist caravans camping in Ourfa, so Anoush ignored those fierce-looking men while she walked to the township of tents.

Slowly bedraggled women and children emerged. Anoush had baked six loaves of lavash bread, which was simple but filling, while other women had cold meat, cheese, fruit, and wine casks of water. They were soon surrounded while Anoush tore her loaves into pieces and handed them to greedy hands. The poor wretches were in a terrible state: with dirty, worn clothing, collapsing shoes and boots, and were gaunt and haggard so clearly had lost a lot of weight.

One woman maybe the same age as Anoush had two boys and two girls, and Anoush guided that woman and her family away.

"Parev," Anoush said. "My name's Anoush Hagopian."

"Parev Tikin Anoush," the woman said. "My name's Talar Sargsyan with my children Yeter, Ara, Penik and Emma."

"Parev to you all," Anoush said. "Where are you from?"

"A village near Sivas. We've been walking for about three weeks now."

"How has it been?"

Talar sighed deeply. "Unbearable. We were told we were being deported, but we didn't realise what we were in for. All of our men were taken away and killed, while the rest of us were sent onto the road. Many have died from disease and exhaustion, while the gendarmes take joy from brutality. Maybe one in ten have made it this far."

Anoush was shocked. Zeki said that many died on the way, but she never realised that most died on the way. She wondered how they died. Perhaps gendarmes shot them.

"I don't know where we're going or how long that will take," Tikin Talar said.

Zeki knew. "You're going to Aleppo, which is about three-hundred kilometres from here," Anoush said.

"So far! There won't be many left." Talar ate some of her bread. "Thank you for this. We've had little food and water so far."

"Our turn will come," Anoush said quietly.

"I'm sorry for that, Tikin Anoush."

"Is there anything I can do?"

"They mostly keep off main roads and away from towns and cities, so you only pass through villages except for here. If you had money maybe you could buy food and water at those villages, but they search thoroughly, even inside mouths and inside women." Tikin Talar shrugged her shoulders. "Keep positive and maybe you will be lucky."

Anoush wanted more than luck. "I will do that," she said. "Good luck for you and your family, Tikin Talar."

"God bless you for this food, and good luck for when your turn comes."

Anoush left them while she pondered her options. The more she heard the more obvious it was that they had to fight for survival, because they were going to die regardless. If not on the march then when they get to Aleppo. There was no other option. If they fought to the last Armenian alive, then that would be worthwhile. If they could fight to the last Armenian across Anatolia, that might even mean survival. Fighting for survival was their only option. Anoush handed out the last of her bread with a resolve to bring Armenians to war.

* * *

Anoush stomped into the house, across the courtyard and slumped into a chair in the kitchen. Her head pounded and she hadn't slept much either.

"You look like you need a cup of tea," Mama said.

Anoush looked up. "Yes please Mama,"

"Just wait there."

Soon the urn was boiling and Anoush had a warm cup of tea in her hand.

"How did your morning go?" Mama asked.

Anoush sighed. "I spent two hours with Apraham Attarian and got nowhere! You know what I told you about the deportations, and surely it's obvious that we just can't just wait for near-certain death. But when it comes to fighting Turks here and in other cities, they're our friends and they will protect us!"

"You know that there is friendship between Turks and us, and I'm sure they will protect us."

"When the army comes with rifles and orders; friendship between Armenians and the Turks of Ourfa won't count for anything."

"I don't understand where you came up with these ideas."

"Caravans of deportees have passed through here these past weeks, and they've told us. We've helped them with food and water and they've told us. If we don't fight, the army will kill all the men like they killed Emni, and then they will take women and children to die by the road or in the desert." Anoush sighed; she was so frustrated. "I don't know what to do, Mama."

Mama sat on the other chair. "I know you want to help us all...."

"I must help us all to help my children, and to help this family."

"When the army moves on us, men like Apraham Attarian will realise they're looking at a disaster, and then they will listen to your ideas."

Anoush sipped her tea and thought that Mama was right. When it's nearly too late then she may be able to make a difference. But sadly, she had no chance to incite an uprising across all Armenian communities. To do that she needed the support of men like Apraham Attarian now, but that would only come at the last minute, if it came at all.

Anoush didn't have to wait long. The next day, August 15, Turkish soldiers came to the Armenian quarter, and soon it became clear who they were after. Specific homes and business were searched, and Armenian community elders were taken away. Two days later soldiers posted notices demanding Armenians to take their guns to the police station, which they didn't course! Soldiers returned a day later to enforce that order and there were scuffles and shots. Some were killed and there was much tension in the air. It was clear that the Armenians of Ourfa knew they were on their own and fighting for survival.

Word went around that a meeting was to be held in the Boy's School the next evening, and Anoush couldn't wait. Surely they would resolve to fight, although that was probably too late. There were more than 30,000 Armenians in Ourfa, but she doubted if there were many rifles. The Armenians of

Ourfa couldn't defeat the Ottoman army without the help of Armenians in other cities.

The classroom was full with every seat taken and more standing around the perimeter of the room, and even lined out the door. Anoush sat with her Papa, her brother Misak, who like her late husband worked with his father but as a cobbler, her sister Lori, and Lori's husband the moody Garnik. The remainder of the family, including children, remained at the family home. The room buzzed with hundreds of conversations.

Suddenly, two young men and a young woman strode the length of the room and turned to face those waiting.

"My name's Mgrdich Yotneghparian," the taller of the men said. "With me are Harutiun Rastgelenian and Khanum Ketenjian. The time for action has come."

The conversations rose to a near roar and Mgrdich put up his hands for quiet. The noise died down. "We have two choices: we can go meekly to our deaths or we can fight our oppressors. I know that some in this room have been making the same case, with no effect, but the men who ignored reality are now dead. Now it's time for us to make a decision, and I say we fight...."

One man stood and pointed at them. "We can't defeat the Ottoman Army!" he shouted.

"We've been planning this," Mgrdich said. "We have rifles, we have more than enough people, and we have the high ground to the west. Those who wish to fight for freedom are welcome to join the Resistance Movement of Ourfa, and those who don't wish to fight, I do implore you to hand over your rifles and ammunition so they can be put to good use."

Again the conversations rose to a roar until the woman, Khanum Ketenjian, stepped forward. "I'm looking for women volunteers who want to play a part in the defence of our lives and our families," she said. "I know that some women have been pushing for this, and now is the time."

Anoush knew who Khanum Ketenjian meant, and immediately she stood. "That was me and I will join your cause," she said while her Papa pulled at her hand. Anoush snatched her hand away and looked to the threesome at the far end of the room. Soon, many men and more women stood to pledge their allegiance, and other men shouted they had rifles for the cause. Maybe there were a few thousand in the room and maybe half of those volunteered, including 20 or 30 women, but not her brother Misak or her brother-in-law Garnik.

"You have your children!" Papa exclaimed above the noise.

Anoush bent down. "We will die regardless, but in the meantime I hope you and Mama can care for their grandchildren while I do what must be done."

Papa's mouth fell open and his eyes were wide with shock.

"They mean to kill us all," Anoush said. "Soon."

"The men who will fight for our freedom come to me," Mgrdich Yotneghparian said. "The women please go to Khanum."

Anoush joined the women, and they were all so nervous! Khanum led them to a house near the Cathedral of the Holy Mother of God where all was chaos, but there was method in that chaos. Men's trousers, jackets and caps were heaped on a table, while several maps of Ourfa were on a chair. Introductions were made by the 27 volunteers: names, ages, and all were single except for Anoush.

"You're not from here?" Khanum asked.

"I was born and raised in Ourfa," Anoush said. "For the past seventeen years I've lived in my husband's village of Gamursh...."

"Where the men were executed?"

Anoush nodded.

"I'm sorry for your loss," Khanum said.

Anoush nodded again.

"Now ladies, we must get organised," Khanum said. "We've gathered men's jackets, trousers and caps, although you will have to shorten arms and legs, except you Anoush. You're tall enough, I think. Tuck your hair under your caps

66

so Turks can't see that we're women. Over there we have 25 rifles; have any of you used a rifle?"

Four had.

"We will train starting tomorrow, although ammunition is limited so training will be limited. There are twelve entrances into the Armenian Quarter, and we will build barricades, starting tomorrow. The Quarter has been divided into six sections and thirty-two positions. We've been assigned the far end of Mousali Meydan, just past the spring. This women's brigade needs four messengers, so I'm looking for volunteers. Those of you who know how to use a rifle will be on the front line in shifts of eight hours. Because you're tall Anoush, you'll be on the front line as well. You have better line of sight. We have two-thousand volunteers to man other positions, and if we need we can retreat to the high ground to the west and fight from there. The Ottoman Empire's best troops are on the front line, which means we're up against reluctant and inexperienced conscripts, so we do have a chance."

"If other cities fight like this, we have a better chance," Anoush said.

"By forcing the Ottoman Army to fight a war within its borders?"

"Yes."

"I wish I could incite an uprising from one end of this country to the other, and I've prayed for one every night.

We've been in contact with colleagues in Sivas and Angora, but after the arrest and murder of our leadership in Constantinople in April, there's nobody left to pull a resistance together."

Anoush was glad they tried, but was disappointed that nothing came of it. At first those deported wouldn't have known what was in store, and in Ourfa they knew from speaking to deportees that Armenians still didn't know what was in store for them, until it was too late.

"There's one other thing," Khanum said. She went to a cupboard and returned with small packets wrapped in paper. She gave one to each woman. "These are strychnine tablets. If we're ever captured by Turks, you know what would happen to us."

"So we take one of these?" Elsapet asked.

Khanum nodded while Anoush contemplated the tablet wrapped in paper. Despite their dire situation, that seemed wrong. Where there was life there was hope, regardless of what happened. Maybe she felt differently because she was a mother. Regardless, she doubted that she would ever use that tablet. She put it aside and sorted through the clothes piled on the table to find a jacket and trousers that came close to fitting. Khanum was right; she wouldn't have to shorten and hem her clothes to fit.

* * *

Karine, Taniel and Lilit shared the room Anoush once shared with Lori, while Anoush had the room once used by Misak. Anoush climbed the stairs to her old room, where Karine and Taniel were playing a game of Tama. Anoush sighed deeply while wondering what to tell them. She waited until their game was over, and Karine won as she usually did.

"There's something I must tell you all," Anoush said. "Please sit on the bed."

They sat on one bed while Anoush sat opposite.

"You will remember what happened to Papa," Anoush said. "That will happen here, if we don't stop them."

"Like what Zeki said?" Karine asked.

"Yes, exactly. So starting tomorrow we're going to fight a battle to stop the same thing happening here, and I'm part of this battle. Over the next weeks I'm going to be away from home for hours at a time, and while I'm away you must do whatever Grandpa and Grandma asks you to do."

"Why you?" Karine asked.

"Because I want to protect my children who I love, and I want to protect my parents who I love."

Karine nodded silently, and clearly she understood.

"If anything happens to me, Anoush said. "Your grandparents will look after you."

"I don't understand," Lilit snapped with frustration.

"Come to me, Lilit," Anoush said, and she sat Lilit on her knee. "The men who killed your Papa now want to kill all

69

of us, and I will do all I can to stop that from happening to the most important girl in the world. Does that make sense?"

Lilit nodded.

"I can help," Karine said, and Anoush was touched.

"Come here Karine," Anoush said.

Lilit climbed down and Karine stood close. Anoush hugged Karine who'd had to cope with a lot over the past weeks. "I wish this wasn't happening, my darling," Anoush said.

"I know Mama, but it is. You will do what you have to do, and I will do what I can do."

Anoush hugged Karine tighter. Karine was smart and strong, she'd shown that over the past weeks. "I love you my darling," she said, and like when she said those words to Emni, they could never convey the emotion she truly felt. "Mere words can't describe how much I love you all."

"You're going to fight a battle to protect us," Karine said. "That means much more than words."

That was the truth of it.

Chapter Six

Anoush sat with her back against the stone wall, and with her rifle in her lap. To one side was a barricade of bricks, stones, tables, chairs and cabinets, topped by barbed wire. On the other side of that was a Turkish guardhouse, just a few metres away. A few shots cracked and echoed from the far side of the Armenian Quarter on an otherwise quiet day, made quieter by war. A shot cracked above her head and Anoush ducked before looking up, and realised Turkish soldiers were using the roof of the Halil-Ur-Rahman Mosque to target resistance fighters. Indeed, her own position was perilous. She looked around and nobody moved, but that was stupid! Anoush stood close to the wall for protection and ducked low to creep along Mousali Meydan where Khanum was with Mgrdich.

"Excuse me," Anoush said. "Soldiers from the guardhouse are on the roof of the mosque to shoot at us."

They both turned around and looked up. Anoush followed their eyes and the view from that roof was substantial.

Khanum unfolded a map from her pocket and frowned. "We will take the guardhouse," she eventually said.

"Are you sure?" Mgrdich asked.

"Look at this," and Anoush looked over her shoulder. "If we cross from the Pond of Abraham here we can take the guardhouse from behind, and then build a barricade using that guardhouse. Tonight, when it's dark."

"Alright and good luck."

"Are you ready for battle tonight?" Khanum asked Anoush.

"Yes," she replied quietly.

"All soldiers are frightened," Mgrdich said. "Even the soldiers up there. In war, it's not possible not to be frightened."

Anoush looked up once more and thought he was probably right, but surely they were not as frightened as she.

As rostered, Anoush was relieved at two in the afternoon and free to sleep for a few hours. She lay on her bed tossing and turning and wishing she could sleep, for her head had to be clear for what was to come. But sadly, sleep wouldn't come. When the church bell chimed ten she left her parent's home and returned to the barricade where all was quiet, and Khanum was with the evening women: Knar, Elsapet, Lala, Kadara, Tatush, Yeva and Maro.

"Paree eereegoon Anoush," they greeted.

"Paree eereegoon," Anoush replied.

"You know the plan?" Khanum asked.

"We use the boardwalk past the Pond of Abraham to get to the path beside the Halil Ur Rahman Mosque, and then to the guardhouse."

"They won't be expecting a night attack."

72

That was probably true, given how quiet the evening was.

"Let's go," Khanum said, with their way lit by a sliver of moon. Onto the timber boardwalk with creaking boards sounding so loud, if anyone was around to hear. Past the mosque to where it was much darker, but Anoush's eyes were used to darkness by then. The guardhouse was light and bright, and Anoush realised that like a house with shutters open at night: it was possible to see in but impossible to see out. The guardhouse was noisy too, with the men playing games perhaps. Their game of cards were about to be interrupted.

Khanum gestured for the women to spread along the wall of the Halil-Ur-Rahman Mosque, and also along the wall of the bathhouse opposite. Anoush pressed herself against cool stone; rifle in hand and heart beating fast. Khanum blew her whistle, and just as she'd practiced, Anoush sighted her rifle to one of the bright windows and squeezed the trigger, and just as she'd practiced the rifle kicked hard against her shoulder. She ejected the cartridge, grabbed a bullet from the pocket of her jacket, slipped it into the breech, and aimed at a Turkish soldier now at that window. Again she squeezed the trigger and saw, in intense detail, that soldier fall backwards. Another soldier took his place, this one with a rifle in his hand, and Anoush shot at him with no effect. A shot came from Yeva to her left, and this soldier also fell away from the window. The men came to all windows to point rifles at the women, but clearly they couldn't see into the darkness.

Khanum shouted in Turkish for them to surrender, but the soldiers bellowed insults accompanied by a random volley of shots, while Anoush carefully aimed and fired again, and again a soldier crumpled. Soldiers fired and women fired back until there were only shots coming from the mosque and the bathhouse. Khanum blew her whistle and the women stopped firing.

Anoush held her hot rifle tight while Khanum kept low and crept close to the guardhouse. Slowly she put her head up and looked through a smashed window, and then she gestured for the women to come. Anoush looked inside and was horrified! Seven, no eight soldiers sprawled on the floor, and so much blood! The floor was red with a river of blood running out the open door. Khanum went around the guardhouse and through that doorway. Anoush watched her look around.

"There are no officers," Khanum said in Armenian. She smiled brightly. "The officer ran away! He ran through that open door!"

Khanum came out to count her brigade. "Eight," she said. "Eight dead in there, and eight unharmed out here. Well done."

Anoush felt sick to her stomach at the sight of those men, the bodies of those men, all tangled and twisted on the floor of the guardhouse. One or maybe two were dead from her. Husbands, fathers, sons; never to return home. But the Resistance Movement of Ourfa had captured the guardhouse, protected the Armenian Quarter, and not one was injured. You shall not take a life, the commandments said. Anoush wondered if that applied to war.

"This guardhouse is our new barricade," Khanum said. "From here we protect the southern approach to the Quarter."

"What will we do with the bodies?" Elsapet asked.

"Remove their ammunition belts so we can use their rifles. Then take them to the courtyard of the mosque. Four of you for each body: Lala, Kadara, Anoush and you. The rest of us will clean inside."

Anoush went inside and propped her rifle against a wall. It took many hours to move the bodies and to mop the blood to a point, while Khanum and Maro kept watch for a counter-attack; especially likely given the Ottoman Army was defeated by women. But all remained peaceful, and at the end of her roster Anoush trudged home, slipped the Ottoman Army rifle off her shoulder, unhooked the Ottoman Army ammunition belt from her waist; stripped off her boots, jacket, shirt and trousers, and fell into bed.

Chapter Seven

Anoush woke with a start. She slept so soundly. She got up, dressed, and then went to the courtyard to wash at the bathing basin. Feeling clean and fresher, she went to the kitchen.

"Anoush!" Mama exclaimed. "Was that you last night?"

Anoush knew what she meant. "Yes Mama," she said quietly.

"Do you want something to drink? It's almost time for lunch and Papa will be home soon."

"I will have some coffee. I can make it."

"Nonsense!"

"It's alright Mama. The children went to school?"

"Yes."

"Good."

Anoush made coffee, and it was never as good as the coffee Zeki made. She sat at the table and sipped, when Papa burst through the door. "I heard the women's brigade took the guardhouse at the Halil-Ur-Rahman Mosque!" he exclaimed. "Congratulations."

"It was all of us," Anoush said.

"Congratulations to your colleagues."

Anoush felt empty and drained, and she knew what it was. Mgrdich said that all soldiers felt frightened, but she wondered if he would say that all soldiers felt sick at the thought of the men they killed. She also thought about Emni. The solder who shot him in the back of the head was following orders, just as she shot Turkish soldiers silhouetted in a window. Who was to blame? Not the soldier who pulled the trigger. No, the men in Constantinople who give those orders. The Three Pashas were responsible for everything that happened.

"How many did you kill?" Papa asked with morbid curiosity.

"One or two," Anoush said flatly.

"How do you really feel?" Mama asked with more sympathy.

Anoush looked her in the eyes. "At the time it was automatic, but later it was tough. I wish we didn't have to do this and I'm sure the men on the other side feel the same."

"But they're trying to kill us," Papa said.

"They're conscripts following orders."

"Do we have a chance?" Mama asked.

Anoush thought about that. "Last night was easy because we were in the dark and they were in the light. If they put their lights out they would have stood a chance. But even if we take a guardhouse and kill eight, they will send eight more. The only chance we have is if other cities do the same."

"Will that happen?"

Anoush thought not. Ourfa was a major city on the road to Aleppo, with deportees passing by. But those deported said they didn't know they were heading to near-certain death, until it was too late. For sure Armenians in villages and small towns wouldn't know until the army, following orders, rounded them up and sent them on their way. "In some cities maybe," Anoush said.

"When do you return?" Mama asked.

"Four this afternoon."

"I will serve lunch."

Eight hours on and eight hours off, and spending as much time with her children as she could. Days blurred into weeks of skirmishing and sniping, but nothing of any consequence. September passed with the weather cooling, especially at night, and no rain as was typical for that time of year. October started with an assault by the Ottoman Army. On the first of October, the army stormed barricades and sniped from the rooves of buildings, losing many men and retreating by the evening. The next day the attacks started once more and this time they didn't retreat. Day and night the Ottoman Army fought to breach Armenian positions, with many Turkish casualties and many captured Ottoman Army rifles too. But it seemed that for every soldier killed, another soldier took his place. Mgrdich, Harutiun and Khanum met with brigade commanders, and the next morning Anoush was given new orders. They were to move

78

away from their barricades, and conceal themselves to shoot at soldiers attempting to breach positions now abandoned.

Anoush pressed herself into the doorway of a house in a street about 100 metres from the guardhouse, waiting. Clear and distinct was the buzz of Turkish voices, unable to believe that they'd been given free reign into the Armenian Quarter. She heard creaking and crashing as most likely the barricade around the guardhouse was dismantled, and she gripped her rifle tighter. All 25 surviving women of the brigade were called to duty, in this street and in a lane further along. Turkish voices closed and Anoush took a deep breath. Some distance away there was much shooting from another defensive post, but tall buildings caused noises to echo and swirl about, making it impossible to determine where that battle was being fought. The first shot caught Anoush by surprise, because it came from the direction of Mousali Meydan! Turks were advancing from the Pond of Abraham, and clearly they'd breached the defences of another brigade. In reflex, Anoush aimed her rifle and squeezed the trigger at the sight of a sandy-coloured uniform. Automatically she ejected the steaming cartridge, just in time to snipe at another soldier. More and more soldiers entered the street and she was terribly exposed and under fire too. Dalita fell, and keeping close to the wall, Anoush eased towards her fallen comrade. Still the soldiers came, and from her new position Anoush continued to shoot at them, forcing them back for a moment. Women from the lane joined the battle, and the Turks retreated. Khanum looked up and down and then came to Anoush while she reloaded her magazine.

"We've lost three," she said bluntly.

"They've overrun the Pond of Abraham," Anoush said.

Suddenly shots came from the other direction, from the abandoned guardhouse barricade, and the women were surrounded! Turks from the Pond of Abraham on one side, and Turks from the abandoned guardhouse on the other. Anoush knelt and aimed, and hoped her shots were hitting their targets. A bullet whizzed past so close she seemingly felt it. Anoush aimed and shot again, and a bullet hit the wall just above her head with dust falling into her eyes. Anoush brushed that dust away, and while she reloaded she noticed there were more dead and injured women than alive. She kept firing as the army moved into the street. Anoush backed away before firing, and backed away further, along with Khanum and four others. They were hopelessly trapped, hopelessly outnumbered and only a miracle could save them.

Anoush reloaded, and suddenly heard a shot and felt an excruciating pain in her arm. She dropped her rifle in shock, reached for her right arm and felt warm wetness. Blood. She picked up her rifle and tried to aim but the pain! Her arm was useless and she had no way of defending herself. She looked to Khanum for help just as Ottoman soldiers closed to within a few metres, but Khanum and the others were too busy for a fallen comrade. Anoush tried to aim but the pain was too much. She eased away from the battle and slipped around the lane. There she hid in a doorway; waiting to be found and killed. Her heart beat faster and faster while the battle raged so close, and where she knew death was only a matter of time. Anoush quietly prayed to God to forgive her for the soldiers she'd killed, just as she caught a glimpse of a sandy uniform. Anoush gritted her teeth while she aimed, and squeezed the trigger with agonising pain! Half his face was missing so he was dead. Just then the firing abated, so Anoush crept forward while holding her rifle tightly because she may be of some use. Anoush reached the street and peered around the corner to see Khanum, Lala, Kadara, Tatush and Elsapet disarmed and being led away. Anoush pressed herself against the wall of the lane once more. She was on her own against 30 or more Ottoman soldiers and didn't have a chance. But nobody appeared; nobody at all, and after a moment Anoush peered once more to find the street empty but for fallen women. She went to Varteni and knelt to check if she was breathing, but she wasn't so Anoush closed her eyes and stood. Residents came out of their homes and did the same, closing eyes on many. Anoush didn't quite know what to do next, just as a man came to her.

"You've been hurt," he said.

"Pardon?" Anoush asked; momentarily disorientated. Then she realised that the shock of their tragedy had numbed her pain. "Yes, I've been shot," she said.

"Come with me and I will help you."

Anoush hesitated.

"Your colleagues are being cared for," he said as he opened a door to a dark room; particularly dark after the brightness inside. Anoush followed him through a courtyard; dark with shutters closed.

"What's your name?" Anoush asked the middle-aged man.

"My name's Datey Simonian."

"My name's Anoush Hagopian."

Datey Simonian led Anoush away from the courtyard to his bright kitchen. "This is my wife Zarine. Zarine, this is Anoush Hagopian."

They greeted each other before Datey Simonian asked Anoush to remove her jacket. Anoush put her rifle down and did that, and then he asked her to roll up her sleeve. He inspected her arm even though the pain was lesser. "It's a deep cut of some sort," Datey Simonian eventually said.

Anoush remembered the bullet spraying dust in her eyes. "Perhaps a bullet hit the wall and I was hit by shrapnel or chips of stone."

"Possibly," he said. "Please sit and I will wash and bind it."

He took the urn and went to the courtyard.

"You're so brave to shoot at soldiers, and be shot at too," Zarine Simonian said.

"I'm terribly worried about my colleagues," Anoush said.

"I'm afraid they're done for," Datey Simonian said.

"I suppose that's the way of war." Anoush thought of the men she'd shot and even killed, and what went around must come around. But they'd been a brigade for so long, and it was terrible that she would never see them again. Datey Simonian washed her wound and bandaged it too, and that felt much better. She pretended to aim a rifle and her pain wasn't so bad, so maybe she could play a part in her colleague's memory. Surely they weren't all dead or injured, so the surviving women fighters could reinforce another brigade. Yes, that would be the right thing to do in their memory.

"Do you want some coffee?" Datey Simonian asked.

Anoush thought that her family and especially her children may have heard what happened, and she had to get home to reassure them. "No thank you," Anoush said. "I must go."

Anoush stood and Zarine Simonian hugged her tightly. "God bless you," she murmured.

Anoush lightly hugged Zarine Simonian while thinking she had to get home to reassure her family. Surely they thought the worst.

* * *

The strategy worked. With barricades unmanned the Ottoman Army walked into a carefully laid trap, and more than 1,200 were dead. That evening the streets were quiet once more, while Anoush walked the short distance to her parent's home and let herself inside. She went upstairs to the dining room, and pandemonium broke out!

"We thought you were dead!" Mama exclaimed.

Anoush was mobbed by her children, who nearly knocked her off her feet. Papa grabbed her shoulder and she appreciated his masculine display of affection. "I escaped," Anoush said.

"How?" Papa asked.

"That's not important. Have you heard what happened?"

"A great victory, but sadly the women's brigade was dealt a bad blow."

"Khanum Ketenjian?" Anoush asked.

"She and four others were captured and told to remove their clothes, but she took a gun and shot the Turkish captain instead. They were all killed."

Anoush remembered Khanum's strychnine tablets and she would have done that. "Khanum Ketenjian was a brave woman, a capable leader, and she will be sorely missed." She felt her eyes watering and brushed the tears away. Forever, Khanum would live in her heart.

"You're giving up now?" Mama asked rhetorically.

Anoush had thought about that. "I have a rifle and I know how to use it," she said. "They will let me to continue the fight."

Chapter Eight

Anoush strode into the American Boy's School where Mgrdich Yotneghparian and Harutiun Rastgelenian were at a table, poring over a map. She went to them.

"Parev Mgrdich ist Harutiun," she said.

Mgrdich jumped up and ran to Anoush. "You survived!" he gasped while grabbing her shoulders.

"I was injured and took shelter to recover, and that saved me."

"I'm so glad, but I'm terribly sorry about the other women."

"That wasn't your fault. How many survived?"

"Knar, Maro and now you."

Anoush's heart fell. "Do you have a place for me?" she asked.

"Of course! You must return to the guardhouse you bravely captured and defended."

"That will be my honour."

"Vache Topalian is brigade commander and he will set your roster. The Ottoman Army has twelve-thousand troops and artillery on the way. This might be a matter of time."

Anoush shrugged her shoulders. "This was always a matter of time."

"But who would have thought that a few thousand volunteers could hold the line against many thousands of trained soldiers?"

"You know what happens after that time comes?" Anoush asked obliquely.

"I do."

"I will go now."

Burdened by her Mauser semi-automatic rifle over her shoulder, and her belt with three ammunition pouches around her waist, Anoush set off for the guardhouse position. There she introduced herself to Vache and his men, and was rostered for the remainder of their eight hours. Anoush settled into the routine of eight hours on and eight hours rest, but coming to the end of her second eight hours in the early hours of the morning, she heard a massive crash of thunder. Instinctively she looked up to a clear sky, when there was a terrible explosion maybe a hundred metres away. More booms and more explosions, and that was the artillery Mgrdich told her about. At the same time she heard shouts in Turkish as they came under fire. Anoush ducked below the window frame and popped her head up to shoot at soldiers quite visible in the dawn light, until her five-round magazine was exhausted. She sat on the floor, listening to Turkish voices while she loaded five bullets and snapped the magazine in place. The battle was much louder than before, from the 12,000 troops Mgrdich told her about. She popped her head up to aim and shoot, while terrible explosions battered the Armenian quarter. To her left someone fell with a dark stain on his chest, but Anoush momentarily ignored him while shot at a soldier so close she saw the veins on his forehead. She ducked down and checked on her colleague who seemed dead. Anoush sat for a moment to gain composure, before resuming firing. For many hours until Vache came close; bent over so as not to be a target. He tapped Anoush on the shoulder, the noise was beyond conversations, and indicated she should rest.

Bent low, Anoush left the guardhouse and headed to Mousali Meydan. The damaged buildings and rubble strewn across the street were something beyond her imagination, and still artillery pounded Ourfa. Anoush panicked about her children, and rifle in hand she sprinted home which was intact and everyone must be safe.

"How long will this go on for?" Mama asked.

"I don't know," Anoush said wearily. "Not for long." Anoush collapsed on a chair with her ears still ringing.

"Surely we've lost?"

"Should I lay down my rifle and let them kill Misak?" Anoush had some difficulty saying that, because her brother should be fighting instead of cowering in his home!

"No you shouldn't," Mama said quietly.

Despite their extra troops and their artillery battering their enemy, the Ottoman Army struggled to gain ground in the Armenian Quarter. Positions were overrun but rubble from damaged homes was used to build new positions, gradually squeezing the Resistance closer to the Cathedral of the Holy Mother of God. As they retreated Anoush felt torn. If they lost any more ground she would be separated from her children, but she felt obliged to the cause. When she fronted for duty on the morning of the 20th, Mgrdich was there.

"Parev Anoush," he said.

"Parev Mgrdich," she replied.

"You've been a brave and capable soldier, but we're in the last days and now it's time for your family."

Anoush didn't hesitate. She took her rifle from her shoulder and handed it to him, and unclipped the belt and handed that over as well. "Good luck," she said.

"Get rid of those clothes and dress as if nothing happened, and as a woman you may survive."

"I intend to survive." Anoush looked at Mgrdich and realised that would be the last time she ever saw him. Soon he would be dead, like Emni. She grabbed Mgrdich and hugged him tight, and felt her tears overflowing. "I'm so sorry about what's coming," she said.

He hugged her. "Go home and protect your children."

Heartbroken, Anoush turned and left him. She went home, upstairs, and removed her cap, jacket, trousers and shirt, and put them in a heap on the floor. She dressed as an

Armenian woman, and carried those clothes to burn in the kitchen fire.

* * *

Anoush sorted through the rubble that was once her bedroom. She turned over stones and pieces of timber until one piece stood out. She dug into the dust and took out her jewellery box, still intact. Outside was eerily quiet. The cathedral was overrun, the battle was over, and the last fighters had either committed suicide or were captured and hanged. Notices were put up for all Armenians to report to Samsat Gate, tomorrow morning at eight, to leave their belongings behind to be protected, and to lock their houses. Angry Armenians burned their furniture in the street so there would be no booty for the Turks, and threw gold coins into the street to dare Turks to scrounge on their hands and knees. Anoush opened her jewellery box and her gold coins sparkled in sunlight, but thought to throw those coins away was stupid. She needed those coins but she knew she would be thoroughly searched. She put her hand in her pocket, but that was too obvious. Everywhere seemed too obvious, although least obvious was her headscarf. She unfurled it and thought that she could sew those coins into her scarf, and tie it tight. Also in the box were coins to the value of a several lira, and that was obvious! She would carry some of those liras in her pocket, secret some more in the hem of her dress, and they would find them when they searched her! They would be satisfied with those lira coins and ignore her headscarf. Anoush picked her way through the rubble and went downstairs to find a needle and thread.

There, Karine, Taniel and Lilit quietly read books in the English language, and they looked so peaceful and beautiful. While Anoush sewed she thought about her options for tomorrow. First, she had to tell her children.

"Karine, Taniel and Lilit," Anoush said. "Tomorrow morning they will take us to Aleppo, and it will be a long walk. You must stay close to me and I will protect you."

"Why are they doing this, Mama?" Lilit asked.

"Because we're Christians," Karine said.

That was true.

"Do you know what this walk will be like?" Karine asked.

"It will be tough and you need to be strong to survive," Anoush said, while thinking about the deaths she'd heard about. "No matter what happens, you must never give up. I will protect you as much as I can, but you must protect yourselves too."

They all nodded and that tore at Anoush's heart.

"We have bread and cheese in the provision room, so we will eat tonight and tomorrow before we go," Anoush said. We will go to bed early so we're rested for what's to come."

"Yes Mama," Lilit said.

Anoush felt particularly sad about Lilit. Karine was their oldest and she had a special place in the family because of that. She did the more important chores and had learned to be a good cook. Taniel was the son for his father, and he often helped at the forge in times past. Little Lilit, always small for her age, fitted somewhere in the middle; helping Karine around the house more than anything else.

"Come here Lilit," Anoush said, and hugged her. "You're my special girl and I will do all I can to protect you."

"Yes Mama," Lilit said.

One other thing; the most important of all. "Don't tell anyone that I had a rifle and I fought for the resistance. If anyone asks about me fighting, tell them that I didn't. If they find out that I fought for the resistance, they will kill me."

"That's a lie," Taniel said.

"Normally it's wrong to tell a lie, but this lie is important. Have you ever told a lie, Taniel?" Anoush asked.

"No Mama."

"You're telling a lie now. Please my children; do this for me. Tell this lie if you have to."

They nodded and she hoped they would.

"I must go out for a while," Anoush said. "Tell Grandpa and Grandma when they get home."

Anoush pulled on an old headscarf and went into the ruins and rubble of the Armenian Quarter. Not far away was the home of Garnik and Lori Harutyun. Anoush knocked on the door; opened by Garnik, scowling at her.

"Parev Garnik," she said.

He bowed mockingly, and beckoned Anoush inside. "Lori is in the kitchen," he said.

"This is for both of you."

Garnik followed Anoush into the kitchen, where Lori had her children: Kadara, Tatev and Berj. Two girls and a boy like she.

"Your war failed us," Garnik said.

Anoush wasn't in the mood for arguing. "Tomorrow men will be separated, and probably taken away and executed like Emni," she said flatly. "Women and children will be marched to the south. We women need money to buy provisions on the way, and I expect we will be searched. I sewed gold coins into my headscarf and lira coins into my dress, which are easily found. I hope I can use those gold coins."

"We don't have gold coins," Garnik said. "Bakers don't earn as much as blacksmiths."

Anoush thought that some bakers were wasteful with money, but kept that thought to herself. "Gather as much money as you can," Anoush said.

"Are you alright?" Lori asked.

"No I'm not. Many friends have died these past days, and now I must say goodbye to my brother-in-law, who I will never see again." She turned and grabbed Garnik's shoulders, and kissed him on both cheeks. "Muhnak parov Garnik, and you will be in my prayers. Lori is capable as you know, and together we can help Mama and Papa."

He stood rigid and looked shocked.

"I must go," Anoush said. "Now I will say goodbye to Misak."

"I will show you out," Lori said.

They went through the courtyard. "Is it really this bad?" Lori asked in a whisper.

"I'm afraid so," Anoush whispered back. "This is worse for you than for me, because Emni was a surprise. I never expected.... Muhnak parov Lori."

"Muhnak parov Anoush," Lori said.

Anoush went around the corner and knocked on another door. Misak opened it; they greeted each other, and then went into their kitchen. There at the table was Misak's wife Vosgi. Their children were probably upstairs.

"Do you know what comes tomorrow?" Anoush asked him.

"I do," he said quietly.

Anoush hugged him. "I will miss you," she said.

"How many did you kill?" he asked.

"That's something I prefer not to talk about," Anoush said automatically.

"When they take me away, I want to know how many Turks you killed."

Anoush looked at Misak with her head tilted. "When you shoot and they fall, you don't know if they're dead or injured."

"But you must know about some of them."

"Four for certain, and probably more."

"That's good."

"Vosgi," Anoush said. "You need money to buy food on the way. I sewed lira coins into the hem of my dress which they will find when they search me, and I sewed gold coins into my headscarf which I hope they don't find."

"I will do that," she said.

"Good luck for tomorrow."

"And you."

Anoush hugged Misak again, and he hugged her tight. "I will miss you so much," she said.

"My older sister who used to tease me."

"I never did such a thing."

"So you say."

Tears ran down her cheeks and wet his shirt. There was nothing more to be said or could be said. "Muhnak parov and God bless you, Misak," Anoush said.

"Muhnak parov Anoush."

Anoush left them to walk home. She'd spoken to many women from caravans and they all said the same thing.

Despite a few gold coins in her headscarf, she knew their chances of survival were slim. But where there was life there was hope and she would never give up. For her children, Anoush had to do everything possible to survive.

Chapter Nine

It was chaotic at Samsat Gate. More than 30,000 milled about while criers called for men, and boys over the age of twelve, to go to the other side of the gate. Anoush was concerned because Taniel was already twelve. She grabbed him close and told Karine to stand in front. Criers and gendarmes went through the crowd, looking for men and older boys; grabbing them and shoving them towards the Turkish Cemetery. Gendarmes pulled husbands from the arms of their wives, crying and wailing, some with children and babies. Older men more stoic; giving their wives one last kiss before they were separated for good. Marriages that may have lasted for decades were cruelly pulled apart.

A gendarme closed on Anoush looking to his right. Then he turned his head, looked left; looked at Anoush who had her son so close. Their eyes met and Anoush felt faint, and she smiled out of nervousness. The gendarme's gaze scanned the girls with Taniel hiding behind tall Karine, and then he moved away. It seemed they got away with it. Not for the men and boys near the cemetery. A long, long line of men and boys; escorted not by gendarmes but by the army. Older men too, and Anoush then realised Papa must be amongst those men. Her heart fell and she felt sick to her core. She remembered his pride at her victory at the guardhouse which seemed so long ago. She remembered his pride at everything his oldest daughter did, and how proud he was to find a good and loving husband for her. That seemed so long ago too. Misak and Garnik of course; both in that line of men escorted by soldiers in uniform. She felt much sadder about Papa because she wasn't prepared for that. But there was nothing she could do except to vow, like so many people, to keep him in her heart. And to care for Mama and to help Lori too. Anoush looked for Mama, and spotted her alone not so far away. She took her children through the crowd.

"I will look after you now," Anoush said.

"Nonsense!" Mama said. "You have your children to care for and I'm too old for this."

Anoush's heart sank even lower. "I can't have you die too!" she exclaimed. "I will do everything I can."

Mama took Anoush's hand. "I'm proud of you, my daughter. Your happy marriage, your wonderful children, and what you did these past weeks. No matter what happens, nothing can take you from me."

Anoush hugged Mama and felt her tears welling. She held Mama tight and cried and cried and cried. She cried for everyone lost. Emni, Papa, Misak, Garnik, Mgrdich, Khanum and the other women. "We don't deserve this," she sobbed.

Mama hugged Anoush who felt lost, and didn't even know where she was. After a time of crying her confusion faded and she felt released. She wiped the tears away and took Mama's hand again. She would do all she could to get her family through.

* * *

Gendarmes pushed and prodded the crowd who surged towards Aleppo Road in a ragged, untidy mass. Anoush kept her children close and Mama close too, but lost track of Lori and her children. She looked all around but it was too chaotic! More gendarmes lined the road past the Turkish Cemetery, and the mass of humanity, women and children, became a long, strung-out line. Family bunched together when a gendarme, with a Turkish army rifle with bayonet, came to Anoush. Without saying a word he snatched her blanket away. She half expected that would happen. The Aleppo Road looped around the west of Ourfa and continued south. It was a road used by Arabs with their camel trains, and somewhere Anoush had never been. A road which crossed fertile plains, dry and wanting for rain. Mid-afternoon and about twenty degrees, but feeling hot under a baking sun. The gendarmes went from woman to woman to woman, clearly seeking money. One came to Anoush and asked her for her money, which she denied she had. He grabbed at her and found her pocket, and took her lira coins away. Mama was then searched but she didn't have anything. The gendarme went on his way questioning women and searching them too.

On and on they walked with a strange, mournful moan ahead; much louder than the crying of many babies. On and on until the caravan of humanity ground to a halt. Gendarmes shouted and swore in Turkish; whipped viciously and prodded with bayonets until they got moving again, and then Anoush saw them. Naked bodies in ditches on both sides of the road; stretching as far as she could see. Thousands, no tens of thousands of bodies; the men of Ourfa had been marched out of the city, lined up beside those ditches, and shot where they stood. Anoush felt bile rising and fought back the urge to throw up, while Mama collapsed in a heap at her feet. An ugly, scowling gendarme whipped Mama, while Anoush pulled at her.

"We have to go," Anoush said.

"Why?" Mama wailed.

Anoush pulled her harder. "Come Mama."

Mama got to her feet and plodded on, while Anoush dropped her gaze to the gravel road. Vultures swooped and swirled, almost darkening the sky, and jackals lined up beyond the bodies, watching the caravan pass. They would come when the road was clear. At Gamursh they recovered their men's bodies and gave them decent, Christian burials, but not here. Anoush kept her head down and tried to focus on her feet one step after the other, but thoughts of Papa and Misak being the meals of jackals and vultures wouldn't go away. And her children? Such a thing was almost beyond the comprehension of an adult who'd been through a lot already, but how could a child of ten cope with that? She trudged through the afternoon while wondering when night fell, would they have to camp amongst those poor men. The bodies of those poor men, and some just boys. Some the same age as Taniel, the poor things.

Eventually they left the bodies behind, and as dusk closed they were stopped by the side of the road near the village of Külünçe. There were less than half of the women and children originally gathered at Samsat Gate, and Anoush hoped the rest would be following at some time, because that meant Lori and her children. Feeling hungry and thirsty, Anoush had to put those thoughts aside while she gathered her family close on a rocky, stony road verge.

"Move as many rocks away as you can," Anoush told them. "That will make it more comfortable to sleep."

"Do we sleep here, Mama?" Taniel asked.

"Yes we do."

"Why did they do that to those men?" Lilit asked.

"Because we're Christians," Karine said.

"But why?"

"Some Turks are good, some are bad, and many are ignorant."

"I don't understand."

Anoush could never explain that. "We have to say a prayer for Grandpa, for Uncle Misak, and for Uncle Garnik," she said.

"Are they dead with those men?" Lilit asked.

"Yes they are. Please kneel and we will say a prayer." They all knelt. Anoush put her head down and closed her eyes. "Our Father in heaven, help us to honour your name. Come and set up your kingdom, so that everyone on earth will obey you, as you are obeyed in heaven. Give us our food for today. Forgive us for doing wrong, as we forgive others. Keep us from being tempted and protect us from evil. Lord, grant eternal rest to Diran Shahakyan, Misak Shahakyan and Garnik Harutyun, and let perpetual light shine upon them. May the souls of the faithful departed, through the mercy of God, rest in peace. Amen."

Anoush felt at peace, and maybe prayer and memories is all it took. She lay on the ground in the evening chill while many babies cried in the background. To be a young mother would be particularly difficult. Baby in your arms, toddlers struggling to keep up; that would be brutal. Anoush rolled onto her other side on the hard ground and doubted she would sleep. Aleppo was a long way and eventually she would sleep out of sheer exhaustion. She knew that exhaustion would take its toll and bring her relief.

The dawn sky lightened and a new group of gendarmes roused the wretched caravan. Everyone was forced to their feet, and one by one they were forced to remove their clothes and shoes: old, young and even children. Those clothes and shoes were searched for coins, and people two. Dirty fingers shoved in mouths and shoved between legs to search inside, and shoved hard. A gendarme snatched Anoush's dress from her hands, felt for the pocket, and ran his fingers around seams and the hem. He found the lira coins, ripped at the hem and pocketed them, but ignored her headscarf. He then let Anoush and her children be, but unfortunately not Mama who was searched in a most vile way. Anoush dressed and Mama was eventually able to dress.

"They took your money," Mama said, crestfallen.

Anoush came close to Mama. "I put that money there to be found," she whispered in Mama's ear. "My real money is somewhere else."

Eventually they were prodded on their way, but away from the main road and onto a donkey trail snaking across dry plains. Rocky and stony where every step was a challenge. Anoush wore her best walking boots, but such a trail was beyond the best of the best boots. The children were fine but Mama struggled, and Anoush had to encourage her, and encourage her some more.

"Mama," Anoush said. "Where there's life there's hope."

"What life is this?" Mama asked.

"This can't last forever, and if we make it through this we will be fine. You will see."

"I've nothing to live for."

"Nonsense! You have Lori, you have me, and you have your grandchildren. Surely you want to see them grow up and get married? Karine will be only a year or two."

Mama turned her head and looked at Anoush.

"That's right Mama," Anoush said. "Only a year or two."

"I will try," Mama said.

They plodded onwards, ever onwards, until they reached the village of Bildim around midday. Unlike Ourfa, the few hundred residents of Bildim didn't have the resources to provide water and food to a caravan of several thousand. There was yet another change of gendarmes, and the march was brutally efficient and well-organised. But for a moment at least, they could rest. Anoush sat in the dirt and her family sat with her. Although with a brief rest she could recover from their endless marching, Anoush sensed something. She didn't know what it was, but something didn't seem right. Some of the gendarmes were gesturing to each other and saying things that didn't quite make sense. Look at that one. No, this one. Those two. Yes those two. And then it made sense.

Up ahead they grabbed at a figure and another, bigger figure fought at them until a rifle shot shattered the quiet, and birds screeched noisily into the air. They took the smaller figure a few metres from the trail and pounced on her; she fought them but stood no chance. One and then the other and still she fought, and when the second was finished, another rifle shot. Anoush's heart raced faster and faster while she realised she was at risk, and especially Karine was at risk. A year or two from marriage, and Karine was definitely at risk. Another gendarme took a figure from the caravan but he didn't use a bullet; he bayoneted her instead. Anoush looked at what seemed like a heap of rags in the dry pasture, and hoped that bayonet had done its job. To lie alone in a field, dying, would be wretched. Anoush had to protect Karine but didn't know how. How could she protect her daughter from being raped and killed?

Chapter Ten

More women, the young and the pretty, were taken from the caravan and abused on dry fields. A great range of ages: from late twenties to as young as ten. Most were allowed to return to the caravan, but Anoush saw one young woman so distraught that she refused to get to her feet. Her abuser bayoneted her instead, and Anoush knew why. He saved a precious bullet. That taught Anoush a lesson, although it wasn't the right time to discuss family survival. One very young woman, or really a girl about ten, was raped in clear view of the caravan. After the gendarme was finished she tried to stand but couldn't, and clearly she'd been hurt by her ordeal. The gendarme shot her with the noise echoing across the countryside. Eventually the gendarmes took their share and the caravan was allowed to stumble on unmolested; as always the gendarmes beating and whipping stragglers.

It was the young and the pretty who were violated, and shot or bayoneted if they struggled, or shot or bayoneted if their ordeal proved too much. Anoush thought of a way to protect Karine, and more than one way. Fortunately Lilit was small for her age, she looked more eight than ten, and that would protect her, but Karine was tall and beautiful.

Other marches had been that way before, with bodies scattered about fields and close to the trail, and always vultures circled overhead. Anoush noticed a tiny skeleton picked clean by jackals, and she had to fight the bile rising in her throat. That skeleton was three or four years old.

The trail wound gently downhill, until they reached a small river at the base of the grade. The gendarmes moved away and the women raced to the dirty, muddy water and drank as if it was a clear, sparkling spring, despite bodies everywhere and even partly buried on muddy banks. The stench of rotting corpses was quite awful, but Anoush didn't even notice while she knelt in mud and scooped water. Mama on one side and Karine on the other side, and the other children beyond.

Anoush had her fill of the putrid water. "Karine, come here," she said. Anoush smeared mud on her daughter's face and mud on her own face too. She pulled Karine's headscarf down close to her eyes, and that looked even better. "That will protect you," Anoush said. "But if they come for you, don't fight them."

"Why Mama?" Karine asked.

"They often let their victims return, and despite what may happen, life will go on. If you fight it will hurt more, and if you fight they may take their anger out on you. If you lay still and let them have you, you should be alright."

"What if I fall pregnant?"

"You will be alive and that's what matters."

"I don't want to live amongst this!" Karine wailed.

Anoush grabbed her daughter and hugged her. "I've lost my father and brother in these fields, and I can't lose my daughter too." Anoush struggled for the right words. "I don't want you to be abandoned on this field forever," she said.

"I understand Mama, and I will do what you say."

"That mud will help."

"I hope so Mama."

Gendarmes growled at the caravan to get up and get going. One gendarme kicked Anoush in the back and she fell into the mud. She picked herself up, gathered Mama and her children together, and they plodded along once more. On and on through the afternoon, until the caravan was brought to a halt in the middle of nowhere. Anoush, Mama and the children cleared stones as best they could, while gendarmes inspected their charges. Some of the young mothers had been struggling and some of the elderly too. Thirty or forty were taken away from the main group, and there they were shot. Mothers carrying babies still crying, and their young children too. Older women ended their days in a dry field in the middle of nowhere. Anoush kept her head down and hoped that Mama would be able to keep up for however long it took to get to Aleppo.

The new day started with gendarmes inspecting the caravan while they munched on sausage, bread and cheese, and drank mugs of steaming coffee. Watching them eat stoked Anoush's hunger. She'd heard about not enough food but never expected no food. The deportees from further away, from the north and the east, had to march much further, and they would have had a terrible time. Breakfast, kahvalti in Turkish, included the resumption of abuse. The young women expected it now, and when they were violated there was little resistance. Gendarmes simply had their way and women returned as if nothing had happened. Anoush knew that sort of sex wasn't for pleasure, but she wondered what it really was. Did these Turks hate Armenians so much that they would use sex for cruelty? Was that sex a type of torture for sub-humans? Or was that sex part of the extermination of Christians? Even if they survived, once abused those women could never marry. Did they use the taking of virginity as a way to wipe out her people? Anoush wondered.

They plodded on forever and ever: Anoush's shoes excruciatingly painful, thirsty as if she never drank at that dirty river, sun beating from a cloudless sky, and hunger gnawing at her. Anoush felt like she would have done anything, anything, to satisfy her hunger pains. Always her mind drifted towards food, despite her other discomforts. She mostly thought about bread. In her mind she smelled freshly baked bread from the oven. The lack of food had another effect: she felt weaker. Despite their slow, shuffling pace it was harder and harder to keep up. Her legs no longer worked as they should, and she was out of breath with the exertion of merely walking slowly. Anoush knew, especially for Mama, they needed food soon. She had money, a lot of money, for all the good that would do her.

Weakness from lack of food was getting at other members of the caravan, with more and more stumbling and struggling to keep up. Whipping or a prod with a bayonet was usually enough to get them into line, but those who collapsed were dragged away from the trail to die. Age knew no boundaries: they could be 70 or they could be seven and relying on their mothers. If they stumbled they were whipped or prodded with bayonets, and if they collapsed they were left behind. That explained the hundreds of bodies in the fields, from previous deportees who'd collapsed from starvation and exhaustion, and were abandoned to die alone and in misery.

As the afternoon drifted by they approached the village of Boybeyi, and there they were camped. Food was critical and would even be the death of them. Anoush vowed to get food. Later, when it was dark, she would do whatever it took. Anoush lay beside Karine who would help her.

When it was fully dark Anoush gently rocked Karine who mumbled and then sat up with a start.

"We have to buy food," Anoush said.

"How?" Karine asked.

"I don't know but we have to try. Come with me."

110

Keeping low and with eyes used to darkness, they moved away from the caravan and crossed a field into a village of simple, single-storey, mud brick houses. The first house had a light on inside and Anoush lightly tapped on the door. No response so she tapped a little harder.

The door opened and Anoush was face-to-face with what looked like a Kurdish woman. "Merhaba," Anoush greeted in Turkish. "My name's Anoush Hagopian and this is my daughter Karine."

"We don't have food," the woman growled.

"Not for a gold coin?" Anoush asked.

Silence. "How do you have money?" the woman asked.

"Let me inside and we can talk."

The woman let Anoush and Karine into a living area, with her husband, two older boys and a younger girl close to the fire. "Do you have gold?" she asked.

"Do you have food that I can take to my family?"

"Bread baked this morning, olives, capsicum, lentils and eggplant."

"Enough for five?"

She nodded.

"One gold coin, and we need water," Anoush said.

"I can give you a bottle of water to share," the woman said.

"Do you have a sharp knife or scissors?"

Anoush was given a paring knife, and used that to break the stitches on one of the small pockets sewed into her headscarf. She took out the gold coin and held it for the woman and her husband to see. The woman nodded, and set to gathering the food into a calico bag, and sent her daughter to get a bottle of water from outside, which was presumably the village well. The coin was exchanged for the food and drink.

"Thank you from the bottom of my heart," Anoush said.

"My name's Adar Bashur and I wish you luck for your journey, because surely you need luck. If I could feed more I would, but this is a small village."

"I understand, and thank you so much, Adar."

"Good luck and God bless you."

Anoush and Karine crept back to the caravan, and after the brightness of the house, finding their way in the dark was particularly difficult. The only light was the fire for the gendarmes. Anoush shared the food around and they all drank from the water bottle. After, Anoush folded the calico bag and stuffed it down her dress. She may need that one day.

"You saved us, Mama," Karine said.

Anoush thought so too.

* * *

New gendarmes took over, and for that day Anoush felt refreshed and reinvigorated. Not so other women in the caravan and Anoush wondered why. Was it because she had a secret, platonic relationship with Zeki for many years, and learned subterfuge and deception? Perhaps what she learned and discussed with Zeki broadened her mind, or somehow made it easier for her to build order out of chaos, and sense out of confusion. Whatever it was, she was different to those other women in some, subtle way.

A pregnant woman went into labour and was abandoned by the side of the road, which was the cruellest thing done so far. More and more fell by the wayside, and it was particularly heart wrenching when youngsters were shot or left to die. Rather than getting used to endless, dreadful cruelty, it seemed that her tolerance to absorb cruelty had reached its limit. Every time she heard a shot or the screams of a mother when her child was killed, that tore through Anoush like a knife. The endless crying of hungry babies was a torment. The sexual abuse of women, particularly younger women and often the very young, continued.

That evening at Kobane was particularly difficult. Hundreds of Kurdish Militias rode into the caravan at dusk, raping at random and carrying women away on their horses. Those who resisted were shot without a moment's hesitation. Anoush got Taniel and Lilit to lie on top of Karine lying in a natural ditch, and as the Kurds came past, they saw two youngsters and moved on. The raping continued late into the night. Anoush, Mama and the children didn't get a moment's sleep, and the next day's walk was terribly wearisome. The food and drink was long past and they slipped into hunger once more. Anoush sensed that Mama was slipping away, and there was nothing she could say to bring her back. Promises of Karine getting married and having children no longer had an effect. Mama was beyond caring about great-grandchildren sometime in the distant future.

To add even more misery to their plight, the countryside was the bleakest and most inhospitable so far. Flat plains of scrubby grass stretched from horizon to horizon, bisected by their endless donkey trail. That night at Derbenobé Mezin, a woman went into labour, and kind souls helped her give birth to a healthy boy. Sadly but not unexpectedly, the gendarmes ordered the woman to resume her march the next day. She was beyond that of course and collapsed after just a few steps. They shot her and her baby and dragged them from the donkey trail, like so many before.

"Anoush, I can't go on," Mama said after that.

"Please Mama, for me," Anoush said.

"Why?"

"This can't last forever, and it will be better soon, I promise."

Mama put her head down and shook her head. A mother, maybe in her thirties like Anoush, had two sons and two daughters. But one of her daughters was sick with dysentery and too weak to keep going. In desperation the mother tried to carry her daughter, but a child that age was too heavy to carry and attempt to walk at the same time. The mother put the daughter down but she collapsed. A gendarme dealt with the situation by shooting the daughter.

Mama stopped dead. "What is the crime of children to suffer like this?" she admonished the gendarme. "What have they done to deserve this? How can you just kill them like that? Curses on you, shit-eating dog!"

Without a moment's hesitation, the gendarme thrust his bayonet into Mama while Anoush watched, horrified. But that didn't stop Mama, and she cursed him, his kind, the world and everyone in it. Again and again the gendarme stabbed her, and still she cursed him. Then the gendarme shot Mama three times, and she collapsed in a heap.

Anoush put her hand to her mouth in horror, and the gendarme spun around and glared at her, rifle ready. Anoush's heart beat faster and faster, but she couldn't say or do anything. That gendarme just wanted an excuse to kill her, and kill her children too.

Anoush put her hands on Karine's and Taniel's shoulders. "Come children," she said, and they left Mama to be dragged away so the trail would be free for the next caravan.

Anoush stumbled on; head down and absorbed in dark thoughts. Always she said that where there was life there was hope, and eventually things would get better. But what if things didn't get better? What if they were cursed until the end of their days? She lifted her head and had Karine at her left, Taniel and Lilit at her right, and she had to keep going. For them, for Mama, for Papa, and for everyone she'd lost. She took a deep breath and resolved to keep going with all her strength.

"Why did Grandma say those things?" Lilit asked.

"Grandma has lost a lot, and that was too much for her," Karine said.

"Mama has lost a lot too. She lost Papa and her Papa."

"Don't you worry Lilit; Mama is strong and she will protect us, and I will protect you too."

That cheered Anoush up a little. Rather than being dragged down, Karine had what it took to survive. Her oldest daughter was a special girl.

They reached the village of Cib Eiferec around dusk, where Anoush decided to get food and water. As the sky darkened to black, she roused Karine and they headed away from the caravan, guided by the light from the gendarme's fire. Stumbling across a rough pasture toward the silhouette of buildings just ahead, Anoush heard men's voices. Desperately she looked for somewhere to hide, but there was nowhere to hide. Men from the village were closing on the caravan and there was nothing around! Those men were going to the caravan at night with only one aim, and if she and Karine were caught in the open, they didn't stand a chance.

"Quick, come with me," Anoush whispered to Karine, while taking her hand and leading her away from the shortest route from the caravan to the village. Across the paddock while the men's voices were louder and louder. Louder and louder, and their shadows now visible.

"Lie down quick," Anoush whispered while she flattened herself on the bare field. The men were far too close, but they might get away with it. Maybe those men were focussed on other things and they might get away from it. The men closed talking in what sounded like Kurdish: loud and raucous and undoubtedly excited, although such excitement churned Anoush's stomach. Many poor women would suffer that night. The men were so close, so close, but they passed in the night, guided by the light of that fire. When their voices faded Anoush picked herself up and Karine got up too. They headed to the huddle of buildings just ahead.

Anoush knocked on the dark door of the first house, and it swung open to reveal a middle-aged woman in dark clothes. "Merhaba," Anoush said in Turkish.

"I don't have anything for you," the woman snarled.

"I have money," Anoush said, but the woman slammed the door.

Anoush went to the house opposite and knocked. "Merhaba," she said, "I have gold coins."

"You people don't have gold coins," the middle-aged woman said.

"I do, and for some food and water you can have one."

The woman poked her head out, looked left, looked right, and beckoned them inside. The house was empty: children grown and husband gone raping.

"My name's Anoush Hagopian," she said.

"My name's Nemal Yasin," the woman said.

"Do you have food and water for four? I have a bag." She nodded.

"Can I have a small knife please?" Anoush asked.

She sat on a chair to unpick her scarf and extract a coin. She held it up for the woman to see. Nemal Yasin nodded, and Anoush gave her the calico bag. She went from place to place filling the bag with olives, figs, persimmons, quinces and some bread. That was enough for four, for sure. Nemal Yasin went outside and came back a few minutes later with a wine bottle full of water, and handed that to Anoush.

"Thank you so very much," Anoush said while she handed the coin across. That was Nemal Yasin's coin and not her husbands, which meant much more. Anoush then wondered what to do. She had a bag, a bottle, and 100 or more men molesting the women of the caravan. She couldn't blunder into that. But she could hide to one side of the village until they returned. "I will go now," Anoush said.

"Good luck," Nemal Yasin said.

"Thank you."

Anoush guided Karine beyond the last houses of the village, and they sat on the ground to eat bread and fruit, and drink some water.

"We were lucky, Mama," Karine said quietly; almost in a whisper. "I was away when they came."

"Yes Karine," Anoush said. "We were lucky."

They left enough food and water for Taniel and Lilit, and after a time, male voices returned. Anoush waited for a while to be safe, then got up, ducked low, and picked her way across the paddock towards the light of the gendarme's fire. Using that as a beacon she found Taniel and Lilit easily enough.

"Mama!" Lilit exclaimed. "We were so worried."

Anoush knelt and hugged Lilit. "I'm sorry, but when those men came I had to wait."

Lilit nodded her head.

"I have food and water for you both," Anoush said, and handed over the bag and the bottle. It was peaceful and quiet in the caravan after the horrors just past, and with a full stomach and her thirst sated, Anoush lay on her side to sleep.

Chapter Eleven

Early the next day they reached the broad, Euphrates River, and the remnants of the caravan, a fraction of those who left Ourfa, stumbled down the bank to drink the clear, sweet water. Anoush knelt and drank, and then removed her headscarf and dunked her head to wash away eight days of grime and sweat. She rubbed the dirt off her face and that felt magnificent.

Gendarmes growled for the caravan to cross the river. Anoush wrapped her headscarf in place, removed her boots, rolled her dress to her knees, and waded into the cold water. It was icy! Breathing fast, she tried to cross as fast as possible, but it was difficult to walk against the water. Eventually the bank began to rise and she was on dry land once more. She rolled her wet dress down, pulled her boots on, hooked the laces in place and tied them, and was ready to go. Karine being tall had gotten through with wet feet and a slightly wet dress, but Lilit was drenched and Taniel in trousers particularly so. The sun would dry them soon enough, while they continued their never-ending march.

The countryside was an endless, empty wasteland. They walked from morning to night and camped in the open, and camped in the open twice more. With no villages there were no night attacks, although abuse by gendarmes continued. Beyond that the lack of food, lack of water, sickness, especially dysentery, were taking a terrible toll. Of a caravan of several thousand maybe there were a thousand left. Eventually they closed on a sizeable town; the first since leaving Ourfa, and gradually, steadily, trudged towards Al Bab. They were led taken under an arch, through a broad promenade, and like caravans at Ourfa they were taken a little further to where tents waited. Soon local inhabitants brought out food and water. Anoush kept back and let the starving women and children have their first food after twelve days of walking. After a time, Anoush took her children to the friendly locals to eat and to drink water, and she thanked them profusely even though they didn't understand Turkish. After time to eat, drink and even socialise once more, the food brightening everyone's spirits, they were able to sleep under cover for a night.

* * *

Just when Anoush thought she'd witnessed every kind of brutality; she came across something even worse. The camp was beyond the outskirts of Aleppo, with nine young women, crucified naked on crosses, with their long, black hair blowing in the breeze. Anoush stopped. Those poor, poor women, nailed to crosses to slowly die while people came and went beneath them. What barbarians would do such a thing? And then left in the open like that! Their only modesty was their long, black hair.

Past the crosses was the camp, such that it was. A dry, dusty paddock: open and exposed to the sun with a few tents or shelters of blankets supported by sticks, but where most were lying in the open, and where the perimeter was patrolled by gendarmes with rifles at the ready. The newly-arrived caravan was wasted, filthy, and some were sick. They had been driven along for almost two weeks like a herd of cattle but with little to eat, and they had nothing except their dirty, worn clothing. But the many thousands of inmates of the camp were in a much worse state: most wore little more than rags, some were nearly naked; many were emaciated, almost skeletons, and some were burned dark, almost black, by the sun. The air was thick with flies, crawling over those poor wretches who didn't have the strength to brush them away.

Anoush was shocked by the state of them, especially those with few clothes because elbows, knees and ribs protruded so prominently. They were starved almost to death. Was that to be their fates: dumped in the desert and then starved to death? Anoush sat in the dirt feeling terribly, terribly depressed while she brushed at swarms of flies. Once more she questioned her determination to survive at all costs. She honestly felt that death was inevitable, and all she was doing was prolonging the agony. At that moment she understood why Mama put an end to her suffering, there and then. But at her feet sat her children and Anoush had no other option. For them she would fight to the last, and see where fate took them.

Chapter Twelve

Paul went downstairs to the chaos of hotel reception, with many checking out and many more milling about. He handed his key to a uniformed receptionist.

"Excuse me Dr Lang," the receptionist said, and handed over a brown envelope.

"Thank you," Paul replied; noting it was a telegram. He hoped it was the reply to his telegram of many weeks before. He sat on a leather sofa and eased the flap open.

'Noted issues about possible atrocities against Armenians. Make all haste to gather evidence, take photographs, obtain survivor statements. Book own travel and accommodation and arrange local interpreters. Withdraw CHF 2000 to cover expenses.'

Even though it was brief, Paul read it again. He was to go alone to find as much information about deported Armenians as he could, take pictures, and then notify Geneva. His head spun. He opened his notebook and pulled out his fountain pen. He wrote: Train to Alexandria. Damascus by boat? Inland or a port? Hotel at Damascus. Ask at hotel for an interpreter. Travel agent for bookings and maps. How to get to camp? Taxi? Film camera and rolls of film. Mail rolls of film to Geneva, with transcripts. How to send mail?

Practice with camera and develop a roll to check before leaving.

Paul put his notebook down and wondered what else. He was going to be travelling to far-away places, and he needed to be dressed for that. How? Open neck shirt, trousers, and a hat to shade his face from the intensely bright sun in that part of the world. He'd seen Western men wearing cotton hats with large brims, and decided to buy one of those. And if it was cool, a pullover would be more practical. He had black and dark grey trousers, so a blue or black pullover would suit. He wrote: Hat and dark pullover.

Paul tapped the edge of his notebook while he wondered what else he had to organise, but that seemed to be it. Damascus was Turkish-occupied so there was a possibility that representatives of the Imperial German Army would be there, and of course such barbarism would be abhorrent to most Germans. He might be able to use those Germans for assistance, because he had to locate the camp and get to it. But first he had to go to the prisoner of war camp to tell Asil that he was leaving Cairo straight away, and then go to the travel agent outside the hotel to book his journey to Damascus.

Paul snapped his notebook shut and strode outside.

* * *

Gendarmes wheeled carts into the camp, and immediately were stampeded by deportees. Anoush watched those

125

gendarmes beat the deportees back with clubs, and clearly they were used to such behaviour. There were barrels of water with battered tin cups, and large cauldrons with battered tin plates. Anoush edged close and managed to get a cup of water and a plate of what looked like grains of fried wheat. She sipped the water and gave it to Karine, and asked her to share the mug with Taniel and Lilit. She gave the plate to Lilit and asked her to share the wheat with Karine and Taniel. No wonder the deportees were starving. Anoush had two gold coins but felt that bribing gendarmes would be a waste of money. She decided to leave things be for a few days, and sneak away to Aleppo at night to buy food. She thought that with so many deportees and so few gendarmes, it would be possible to sneak away for good, although she wondered what she would do after that.

Dusk settled for yet another night of sleeping on hard ground. The following morning, Arabs in their robes and ghutrahs, and other men were escorted into the camp by gendarmes. They sought out the new arrivals and it was clear what they were after. The surviving young women were stripped naked; then poked and prodded like at a cattle market. Inspected from top to toe. Some of them were too young: not yet developed breasts and no pubic hair either, but that didn't prevent a sale. A swarthy Arab accompanied by a gendarme came to Karine. Anoush moved close, except a gendarme's rifle blocked her way. The Arab roughly pulled

Karine's headscarf off, literally ripped her jacket and dress apart, and tore her underwear too. Naked but for her boots she was inspected closely, the Arab nodded and the gendarme moved towards Karine.

"Karine no!" Anoush shouted, and the gendarme thumped her stomach with the butt of his rifle. Anoush collapsed to the ground struggling for breath while the gendarme escorted Karine away. For sure she was destined for sex slavery. Anoush took a deep breath. "Don't fight them!" she shouted, and Karine looked over her shoulder. Their eyes met and Anoush knew that would be the last time she would ever see her daughter. Anoush cried and cried and cried while two men took her daughter away.

Anoush didn't know how long she lay like that, curled up in a ball. Eventually she realised that Taniel and Lilit needed her, and they would be confused about seeing their sister taken away like that. But what to tell them?

Anoush sat up. "Taniel and Lilit," come close," she said. "Those men have taken Karine away."

"Why Mama?" Lilit asked.

How to explain sex slavery? How to explain sex? "Do you remember the women from the caravan who were taken to the fields?" Anoush asked.

"Yes."

"Like that, only not in a field. Somewhere in the city."

"When will Karine come back?"

"She will stay in the city now," Anoush said. "They will feed Karine and look after her."

Lilit nodded her head in understanding while Anoush hoped they really looked after Karine. Clearly Armenian women were bought and sold, which was just another example of the brutality of it all. Brutality, inhumanity, cruelty, barbarism; there were not enough words to describe what was happening to her people. The food and water cart came later in the afternoon, was stampeded as usual, and with that Anoush vowed to slip out of the camp that night to get food and water from Aleppo. Dusk faded to darkness relatively early, as expected in November, and it was cool when Anoush set off. The lights of the city guided her but it took quite a while to walk that distance.

Aleppo bustled with Arabs in their robes, Ottoman Army soldiers, other soldiers in grey uniforms of a type Anoush had never seen before, and other men, probably Kurds. The city was much bigger and much busier than Ourfa, while the crush of men in the city centre was quite astonishing. There were many cafes and the smell of their food stoked Anoush's hunger. Anoush walked along Baron Street through the city centre to see what she could get out of Aleppo, but the further she went the less promising it felt. There were cafes still open, food shops closed at night, butchers, fabric merchants, cobblers, and everything expected in a large city; all closed at night. Like Ourfa, she knew there was no place for a woman to work at those shops, especially an escaped Armenian woman in dirty and torn clothing. She had two children and two gold coins, and within a week they would be starving and destitute.

Anoush returned along Baron Street until she heard a man shout "who are you?" in Turkish. She spotted four Ottoman Army soldiers; rifles at the ready while they closed on her. Anoush turned and tried to run, but her long dress got in the way! How she wished for trousers! Several soldiers in grey uniforms, probably German soldiers, were spread across the footpath; all but blocking it. Anoush crashed through them and they spread to let her pass. Just to her left was a dark lane and she ducked down there, and hid in a doorway a bit further along. It was a busy lane with men coming and going, and at any moment Anoush expected to be found. But she wasn't found and after a time returned towards Baron Street and peered around the corner. Still bustling and no Ottoman army, so Anoush continued into the crowds. On and on she walked until she sensed something, and saw two Ottoman soldiers checking her, before they crossed the street. Anoush wondered where to go when a group of Arabs headed into a cafe. Anoush squeezed amongst them and went into that cafe, but hid behind the open door. Moments later those soldiers casually poked their heads in to look around, and once more she'd escaped detection. Although it was easy to sneak out of the camp, she would be found and sent back. There were too many Ottoman soldiers and she stood no chance.

Anoush noticed those Arabs were at a table, so she sat at a small table near the corner, where a waiter dressed in white over black poured a glass of tea. There was a list of dishes in Arabic and in Turkish, and when the waiter came back Anoush greeted him with "Merhaba," and the waiter responded.

"I would like some kubbeh dumplings, some kibbeh bll salenh, and some dolma please," Anoush said in Turkish. "Can I also have a bottle of water and a sharp knife?"

Dark looks from the waiter showed he either didn't want a dirty Armenian woman in his cafe, or didn't want to give her water and a knife, but both appeared regardless. Anoush ate some of the food and it was delicious, and finished another glass of tea, before packing the remaining food in her bag. Then she unwrapped her headscarf, picked at the stitches to retrieve a gold coin, and paid for her meal to get four lira and some kurus change.

With a bag of food and a bottle of water in her hands, Anoush peered out the door of the Kazar Cafe but saw no Ottoman soldiers. She joined the bustling crowd to make her way out of Aleppo unmolested. After a long walk she saw the silhouettes of those terrible crosses, and used that to find her two children. The food in the calico bag made a good meal for Taniel and Lilit, and that food and water would keep them going for a few more days.

Anoush lay on her back and wished for a solution, but a solution wouldn't come to her. With the Ottoman Army on the lookout there was no future in Aleppo for an escaped Armenian woman with two children, but there was no future in the camp either. Anoush didn't know what to do to protect her family.

* * *

A bedraggled group of women and children were escorted into the camp by weary-looking gendarmes. Anoush watched them closely, and recognised Maro from Ourfa, and she recognised others. But not Lori or her children. Then Vosgi came into view with her son Davit; both looking dirty but healthy, and Anoush went to her.

"Parev Vosgi," Anoush said.

"Parev Anoush," Vosgi replied. "This must be the camp?"

"It is. We've been taken here to die."

"I'm sorry about Lori. We stayed together but...."

"Sickness?"

"For all of them. And Nare too."

"I'm terribly sad for your loss.

"Your children?" Vosgi asked.

"I have Taniel and Lilit here, but Karine was taken away yesterday."

"What for?"

"She's young and beautiful," Anoush said flatly.

Vosgi put her hand to her mouth. "That's terrible."

Anoush sighed. "She's alive at least."

"Of course she is."

"They bring food and water in the afternoons, but little of each, although you will get some water. Other than that, there's nothing." Anoush pondered, and the answer was obvious. "You must stay with us."

Anoush took Vosgi and Davit to Taniel and Lilit, who didn't know them that well. They shared water and a little food that afternoon, and slept when the sun went down. The next day was windy which blew dirt all around. As dirt blew into the air, bones were revealed. That was quite horrible. Many were left where they died, and Anoush didn't realise they were camping on graves. All around were hundreds and thousands of bones. Indeed, there wasn't a square metre in the paddock without bones beneath the surface. Anoush was quite shocked that so many had died at the camp, after surviving the ordeal of their marches. It seemed as if not one Armenian would be left alive once this was over. What had they done to deserve such treatment?

Chapter Thirteen

Paul leaned against the mudguard of the taxi, watching Hassim negotiate with an uncooperative Turkish gendarme with a rifle. About 300 metres away, maybe 500 bedraggled specimens tried to huddle under the shade of a single, scraggy tree. Closer, there was much waving of arms and shaking of heads, but even if he were allowed close enough to take photographs, Paul didn't think that 500 Armenians in the desert north of Damascus indicated a major problem. Hassim eventually gave up and returned to the taxi.

"I am sorry Dr Paul," he said, most apologetically.

"That's alright Hassim," Paul replied. "Do you know of any other camps?"

"I have heard of camps far from here at Kahdem and Nebek."

Paul contemplated that, but it seemed vague. "I will return to the hotel and find out what I can, and if I need you again I know where to find you."

"Yes Dr Paul."

Hassim spoke with the taxi driver while Paul climbed into the back, and soon they were on their way to the bustling city of Damascus. It was a strange place; like an oasis in the desert. Quite bare, rocky, sandy and bleak; except for the city itself. They arrived at Hotel Victoria; a rather odd building next to a canal. Quite large and three storeys, but with an unusual, stepped roof, and a surprisingly small entrance with a simple sign above. There Paul paid the taxi driver and went inside, grabbed his key from reception, and went upstairs to wash the sweat from his face. He went to the balcony, and leaned against the rail with the vista of the city spread before him. He needed information, but where to find it? More than likely, Kahdem and Nebek would be two more small camps.

Paul went downstairs to the bar and noticed three German officers in immaculate grey uniforms; drinking beer at two sofas. Paul ordered a beer and went to them.

"Guten tag," Paul said, and decided his title could be of advantage. "Mein name ist Dr Paul Lang."

They all stood.

"Guten tag Dr Lang, mein name ist Captain Karl Müller, und bei mir ist Lieutenant Richard Bauer und Lieutenant Ernst Ludwig."

Paul shook hands with each in turn.

"Would you like to sit with us?" Captain Müller asked in German.

"Thank you," Paul said, and they all sat.

"Where are you from?"

"Switzerland, Bern."

"I thought I could pick an accent. And why are you here?"

Straight to the point, as expected. "I'm from the Red Cross in Geneva and I'm investigating reports of atrocities against Armenians."

"Ah yes; that's very bad."

"I went to a camp outside the city but it wasn't what I was looking for."

"You know something about this, Ernst?"

"I do," Lieutenant Ludwig said. "They take civilians to a number of camps, with the ultimate destination being a camp in the desert at Dier el-Zor, which the Turks call either Der-el-Zor or just Der Zor."

"If I was to go to Dier el-Zor, I would find what I was looking for?" Paul asked.

"You would and it's particularly bad, but Dier el-Zor is difficult to get to." Lieutenant Ludwig frowned. "What are you investigating?"

"I've been asked to find evidence, take photographs and obtain witness statements."

"For relief work?"

"I'm not sure. The Red Cross is a voluntary organisation, so before relief comes fund raising, but before fund raising would come evidence of an issue that requires our attention."

"Yes, I do understand. I recommend the camp at Aleppo. It's quite large and Aleppo is easily accessible from here. Catch a train to Beirut, there's a regular ferry to Tripoli, and catch a train from there to Aleppo. Ask a taxi driver to take you past the airport and you will find the camp there."

"Thank you very much, Lieutenant Ludwig."

"My pleasure."

Paul barely believed his luck.

"Dr Lang," Captain Müller said. "Would you like to dine with us this evening?"

"Thank you Captain," Paul said. "Yes I would."

They all stood and Paul stood too. To the dining room and as a bonus, Paul was going to have company for his meal. He couldn't have asked for more.

Chapter Fourteen

Lilit got very sick very quickly, of a sickness similar to many on the walk from Ourfa to Aleppo, but much more severe. Lilit had terrible diarrhoea but very watery, and was weak and feverish. Anoush felt helpless while she tended her sick child, because she could only hope and pray that Lilit would recover. Vosgi helped, but there was nothing that could be done. Lilit got weaker and weaker, her breathing became shallower and shallower, and then she stopped breathing. Anoush closed Lilit's eyes and said a prayer in her mind. Gendarmes carried the body away to where Anoush knew not. It was too sudden, only a few hours, and Anoush had difficulty understanding how a child, fed every few days and seemingly healthy, had died so fast.

"Come with me," Anoush said to Taniel, to find a place of privacy. She knelt and Taniel knelt too. "Lord God, from who human sadness is never hidden, you know the grief that we feel at the loss of our beloved Lilit. As we mourn her passing, please comfort us with the knowledge that she now lives in your loving embrace. We ask this through Christ our Lord. Amen."

"Lilit has gone to a better place," Taniel said quietly.

Anoush put her arm around her son. "She has. Now it's just you and me, and you need to protect me."

"I will Mama," he said seriously.

Anoush hugged her little man. "I will look after you my son," she said. He was all that she had left in the world, and she would protect him with her life.

"It's terribly sad when they die too young," a woman said.

"Yes it is," Anoush agreed. "My name's Anoush Hagopian."

"My name's Kohar Simonian."

Anoush turned her head and looked up into the sun. "What should I do?"

"Do whatever it takes."

"I have."

"Then keep doing it."

"How do we get out of here?"

"From time to time they take caravans to Der Zor, but you don't want to go there. It's many days' walk across desert, and a death sentence."

Anoush thought she must go before then. "Thank you," she said.

"Knowledge is power."

Kohar left Anoush to ponder her options. A march to Der Zor was a march to their deaths, but she didn't know what to do. After all that happened that day, it was too hard to think of a solution! Anoush decided to do what she always did. She would sleep, and in the morning the answer would come to her. When the food and water came she got a mug of water at least, and shared that with Taniel, Vosgi and Davit. Later as darkness came, she curled up in the open and fell asleep.

* * *

Anoush woke suddenly, with the sun beating down and flies swarming, as always. She rubbed her eyes and checked Taniel sitting beside her, with Vosgi and Davit sleeping to the other side. She looked around the camp as some slept and some stirred. Something caught her eye. Not far away was a gendarme with a shortish man in dark trousers and a dark jacket. There was only one reason for a man to be in the deportee camp at Aleppo, and that could be their escape from a march to Der Zor. Anoush rubbed her eyes again, got up, and casually crossed the dusty field while keeping her eyes away from them. The young women from Ourfa were long gone; there were a few other women from Ourfa, while the other deportees had suffered badly from their longer treks. She closed on the two men and turned her head to face them. He was lined with age, had a hooked nose, and shorter than she which was to her advantage. When their eyes met, Anoush casually unwrapped her headscarf and then unbraided her hair to let it fall to her waist; something a husband would only ever see. He stopped to study her closely and then talked with the gendarme in Turkish.

Anoush moved closer and heard the words 'ten kurus' from the gendarme, and was insulted that was all she was worth. The man nodded and Anoush moved much closer.

"I can be good for you," she said in Turkish in a soft voice. "If you buy my son as well."

"I don't need your son," the man said abruptly.

"He's young and healthy and he can help in your business. What business do you have?"

"I have a goat farm."

"Check him out. He's healthy like me and he can help you."

"Alright."

Anoush beckoned Taniel to come to her. He stood beside while shading his eyes from the sun.

"He's very young," the man said.

"He's healthy and he can work for you," Anoush said. "Chop wood, help on your farm; just for his meals." Anoush lightly touched the man's arm. "I will make this worth a few meals," she said softly.

"How much?" the man asked the gendarme.

"Five kurus," the gendarme replied.

The man reached into the purse at his waist and extracted two coins. And with that it was done.

"My name's Anoush Hagopian, and my son is Taniel."

"My name's Merdim Hardi."

Anoush bowed. "Merhaba Bayim Hardi."

He nodded in acknowledgement. "We must go; we have a long way to travel."

"I would like to say goodbye to a relative."

Merdim Hardi nodded. Anoush went to Vosgi, now sitting on the ground. "That man is buying us," she said.

"Buying you?" Vosgi asked; clearly confused.

Anoush bent close. "They march deportees to a place called Der Zor, but that's a march to your death. Avoid that at all costs."

"By being bought?"

"That's one way," Anoush said. "Muhnak parov Vosgi ist Davit, and good luck to you both."

"Muhnak parov Anoush ist Taniel," Vosgi said. "Good luck to you both."

Anoush returned to Merdim Hardi while she braided her dirty hair, and then wrapped her dirty headscarf in place. They walked to a donkey munching on grass past the crosses, where Merdim Hardi rode off with Anoush and Taniel trailing. His donkey carried two fair-sized bags and he let it walk at a modest speed. They left Aleppo behind and crossed the dry wasteland of that part of the country. Unlike the deportation they kept to the main roads which made walking much easier, stopped at the village of Baznatrah for tea and some bread, and shadows were getting long when they reached the town of Andzara. Merdim Hardi went to a cafe with a sign in Arabic; which had men sitting out the front at tables: talking loudly, drinking coffee and smoking hookahs. There Merdim Hardi led his donkey to a barn at the rear.

"Excuse me Bayim Hardi," Anoush said respectfully. "Is there a bathhouse where we can wash?"

"There's no time for that," he said grumpily. "There's a wash basin in the barn; you can use that."

He went into the cafe while Anoush told Taniel to wait outside. She stripped and washed, and felt much better after. She told Taniel to quickly wash, and by the time they entered the cafe, Merdim Hardi had already ordered. It was dark inside with rough tables and rougher benches, and more raucous Arabs drank coffee and smoked hookahs, which gave an overpowering, pungent odour. An open doorway led to a corridor, with the kitchen on one side and two doors on the other side. After their meal of tepsi, a tasty casserole washed down with tea, Merdim went outside to his donkey and returned with one of his bags. He led the way to one of those doors which opened to a small room, barely big enough for a single bed with a stuffed, straw mattress covered by a dirty sheet. It was grubby, smelled of bad feet, and had a small window giving a view of the wall of the house next door.

"Take off your clothes," Merdim said to Anoush. "Now we fuck."

Anoush recoiled in horror. "Not in front of my son."

"You," Merdim said to Taniel. "Go outside."

Taniel left the room.

"Now we fuck," Merdim said again. "Take off your clothes."

Anoush removed her jacket, released the clasp of the belt at her waist, removed her dress, and removed her underwear. She looked up at Merdim already naked on the bed: dark, hairy and scrawny.

"Get on your hands and knees," Merdim ordered.

Anoush got on the bed and knelt as he asked, and got the greatest surprise when she felt a slippery, oily finger at her arse. He slid his finger in there for a moment, and then she felt his hard, erect penis pressing at her arse. Oily and slippery, he pushed that into her and it stung! Anoush put her head down and breathed deeply. The stinging went away but it felt peculiar to have him going into there, especially when he grabbed her hips and fucked her. Huffing and puffing her fucked her for a bit, and then he grunted when he came. Slowly for a moment longer and then he pulled out, and she felt his juices running down her thigh.

He slapped her bottom. "That was good," he said proudly.

Anoush was shocked. It was like nothing, no attempt at pleasure for her, and she felt dirty being fucked there. Anoush sighed, but at least she wouldn't fall pregnant. She looked over her shoulder at Merdim already dressed and calling for Taniel, so she quickly pulled on her clothes before he returned. That made her ordeal worse. Her son knew that she had just fucked that horrible man for the past few minutes, which was as long as it took. She lay on the bed squashed against Merdim, and couldn't look her son in his eyes. Taniel lay on the dirty, grubby, floor while Anoush felt so ashamed.

* * *

The next day they walked further north across rolling hills, now with bare, rocky mountains to the east. Anoush wanted to talk with Taniel in Armenian which Merdim wouldn't understand, but realised he would hear them and know that they were using Armenian so he wouldn't understand. So she kept silent while they walked for quite a few hours, until they reached Deir Semaan by mid-afternoon. Deir Semaan was a small village of simple, mud brick houses all painted white, and all single storey with flat rooves. Three shops were grouped together; each with signs in Arabic. One was a cafe, with five Arab men at tables outside smoking hookahs. Anoush wondered if Arab men did anything more than sit at cafes all day, drink coffee and smoke hookahs, until it was time to go home to their undoubtedly hard-working wives.

It was a small cafe: two tables, each with four chairs, a counter, and a kitchen where the cook was visible through an opening. Dark with a small, grubby window, and most of the light falling through the open door. Once more Merdim ordered their meal, this time mujaddara which was lentils with onions, and glasses of tea. After that was finished, Merdim went outside to his donkey, and Anoush watched him lead it away.

"Taniel," she said. "This isn't what I want but this is what we need. We have food, we have drink, and I can get by with this."

"I understand," he said.

She put her hand on his hand. "I wish your father was still alive."

"I wish he was alive too."

"I loved him," and she felt tears in her eyes. "We can survive now," she said quietly.

"Yes Mama."

Merdim returned, and beckoned them outside. Behind the cafe was a barn, and inside were straw mattresses with blankets, and his donkey in a stall.

"Taniel," Merdim said. "You can go away."

He did, and Anoush went inside and removed her clothes. With the donkey watching curiously, Merdim fucked her in the arse again. After, he called Taniel back. They lay down to sleep on rough, straw mattresses, while Anoush wondered if her future was to be abused like that for the rest of her life.

* * *

After another day walking further north, still with those rocky mountains to the east, they approached Merdim's village of Bassouta, tucked into a valley. Rows and rows of olive trees lined the road, reaching as far as the buildings of the village. Further north and to the west, Anoush saw more rows of olive trees. The houses of the village were quite small; all made of stones fitted together, and all with ramshackle flat, thatched rooves. Brown stone houses surrounded by dirt were far less attractive than the whitewashed mud brick houses and gravel roads of most other villages. There was a village square around a stone well with a windlass, surrounded by a couple of shops and a cafe, each with rough, timber balconies. The village was quite different to the Arab inhabited country further to the south, with men in conventional clothing and women dressed in bright colours; mostly red and orange, and looking more like Armenian clothing.

They had walked for days with barely more than a few words spoken. They were to spend a lot of time together, and Anoush felt it was time to get to know each other. She came to beside his donkey. "This is your family's village?" she asked in Turkish.

"Yes it is," Merdim said abruptly.

"You have children and they have grown up?"

"My family is of no concern to you," Merdim said firmly. "I bought you and your son, and both of you will serve me, serve my wife, and serve my mother. You," he said, turning to look at Anoush, "will make yourself available to me, whenever and however I desire you. In turn, I will provide food and lodgings for you both. Is that clear?"

"Yes, Bayim Hardi," Anoush said, quite shocked. She let him move ahead while she contemplated her situation. She was his slave, his concubine, and for the rest of her days, or until he discarded her, he would use her and abuse her, and he would use Taniel too. In order to survive the annihilation of her people, she was consigned to the most wretched existence imaginable. But at least she and Taniel would survive.

A donkey trail led out of the village to the west, past more olive groves until they reached his farm on the side of a small hill. The pastures were rocky and stony with tufts of green grass here and there, and fenced by low, stone walls. Surrounded by pastures was a simple, square, stone house with a flat, thatched roof; with two glass windows and a rough, timber door. Standing on the front step was a short, dumpy woman, seemingly as wide as she was tall, with arms crossed while she glared at the new arrivals. Beside her was an old woman, hunched over and dressed all in black. Anoush and Taniel were taken past the house to a small, stone barn. This had a pitched roof of thatch, and a single timber door. Inside was piled with straw and had a few, basic farming implements. They were led inside, where Merdim dismounted his donkey.

"You two will sleep here," he said. "I will bring out some blankets."

"Is there somewhere I can wash?" Anoush asked.

"At the bottom of the hill is a stream. You can wash there."

"I will wash shortly."

"Do that, and tomorrow you start work. Cooking, cleaning, washing clothes and milking goats. You," he said to Taniel. "You can repair fences to start, and milk goats too."

He left them and went to the house. Taniel looked out the door. "This is alright, Mama," he said.

Anoush joined him. "Yes it is, my son."

Chapter Fifteen

Paul stepped from the taxi and looked up, horrified. There were nine crosses each with naked, young women who'd been crucified. Who would do such a thing? Obviously a mockery of the key symbol of Christianity, but to actually strip young women naked and nail them to crosses to die in the open like that? Paul didn't want to but it was a powerful image. He walked about 10 metres away from the first cross while opening his camera. He rotated the focus ring for 10 metres, centred the line of crosses in his viewfinder and pressed the shutter. Paul put his head down and walked past, and then took a picture from the far end. He closed his camera and looked up at those poor women, hanging from nails in their wrists. *Rest in peace whoever you were. My prayers are with you.*

Further beyond, the camp was huge. Thousands and thousands of victims, in dirty, torn and ruined clothing, only skin and bones, in a dirty, open paddock with a few tents or shelters of blankets propped by sticks, but where most were left in the sun and the rain. It was inhuman and barbaric, but not possible to photograph with clarity from where he stood, and the gendarmes with rifles wouldn't let Ferhard, his translator, any closer. He would write about the camp, but photographs would be more powerful. Paul sighed: it was late and maybe something would come to him.

"Come Ferhard," Paul said. "Take me to a hotel."

"Yes Doctor," Ferhard said, while they walked to the taxi.

"What do you think?" Paul asked as they walked past the crosses.

Ferhard spat on the ground. "They are Turks," he said.

They climbed into the taxi, and about 20 minutes later Paul was deposited at the entrance of the small but lovely Baron Hotel, close to the railway station. He paid the driver and told Ferhard he would contact him when he needed him. Paul entered a small reception with a towering ceiling, surrounded by columns and arches. He went to a desk set into a small, timber-panelled recess, and which had a table covered with papers behind.

"Excuse me," Paul said to the young man in a white shirt and black tie. "I need a room and I'm not sure how long I will be staying."

"Certainly sir," the young receptionist said. He ran his finger down the register and nodded. "Room one-ten is available."

He spun the register around for Paul to write his details, and sign. He was given a brass key attached to a block of metal engraved 'Baron Hotel' and '110'. The receptionist came from behind the counter, grabbed Paul's suitcase, and led the way up a narrow, timber staircase to a narrow corridor. He opened double white, panelled doors to a compact room: double bed with a dark-stained timber bed

150

head, a dark-stained wardrobe opposite with dressing mirrors set into two doors, a timber cabinet beside that, and a timber desk and a timber chair. There were French windows which opened onto a balcony with a good view of many beautiful buildings. Paul gave the young man a tip, and set to unpacking his case. While he hung his clothes, he decided to take advantage of that lovely street and the pleasant weather, and find a nice cafe or restaurant. It was Saturday night and he would take a break on Sunday, to be fresh for his challenge on Monday.

Paul locked his room, went downstairs and outside to lovely Baron Street; more like a piece of Paris than anything else. Aleppo was substantial; much bigger than famous Damascus to the south, and a busy and prosperous-looking city with beautiful buildings in the city centre, including many apartment buildings; lovely gardens a little further away, and many houses of various ages and sizes beyond that. Like Cairo the smell of Aleppo was of smoke, food and waterpipes, but not so overpowering. Mingling with the crowds, Paul walked two blocks past a couple of cafes, and decided to return towards the hotel by walking a block to his left to see if there was a restaurant there. Only Paul found himself in a narrow street lined by commercial-style buildings, but still very busy. If men calling for business and men entering and leaving anonymous doorways didn't give those premises away, then red lights surely did. Paul continued to the end, and turned left to emerge at Baron Street once more. On his right was the Kazar Cafe, and Paul went inside to a sharp scent of food, cigarettes and waterpipes. An olive-skinned waiter in a white tunic showed Paul to a table, and returned moments later with a teapot and a glass. Paul poured himself a glass of tea, when the waiter returned to him.

"Sprechen Sie Deutsch?" Paul asked.

The waiter shook his head.

"Do you speak English?" Paul then asked.

"A little," the waiter said, holding his fingers about a centimetre apart.

"Please bring me what you think would be nice."

The waiter nodded and went away. Shortly after, Paul was presented with a veritable feast. Flat breads with smooth, tasty dips, fried dumplings of meat and vegetables, tasty vegetables wrapped in leaves, grilled meat on skewers with onions and capsicums. It was the loveliest meal he'd ever enjoyed. And while he ate he thought. If Turks were cruel enough to crucify young Armenian women purely to mock Christ, surely they would do barbaric things to other Armenian women. The American missionaries said that Armenian men are killed, while women, children and the elderly are deported. What would happen to these Armenian women, beyond being abandoned in a field outside Aleppo, or perhaps crucified? Perhaps while he ate, some of those women were just a few metres away.

The waiter came to take the dishes away.

"Superb," Paul said, and it was. The waiter merely nodded his head in acknowledgement.

Paul went to the counter to settle the bill which was extraordinarily cheap, and retraced his steps to that seedy street. While he walked the answer came to him. That would work for sure.

Swarthy men, many with trimmed, black beards, spruiked for business. Paul went to the first.

"Do you have an Armenian woman?" he asked.

"Yes, yes," the pimp said. "Plenty Armenian. Two kurus. Come this way," while grabbing Paul's arm and guiding him inside. Paul felt dirty being taken into a brothel, despite his motives being honest. He was led to a door.

"Two kurus," the pimp asked.

Paul reached into his change pocket and took out two coins. He handed them across and the door was opened for him. Paul went into a small, cream-painted room where the only furniture was a double bed covered by a grubby sheet. She was young, tall, slim, naked with an olive complexion, dark eyes, long, black hair, and lying on her back.

"Do you speak English?" Paul asked her.

She grimaced.

"Please?" Paul asked.

"I speak English," she said clearly and precisely; with an accent.

"My name's Paul Lang. What's your name?"

Again she grimaced.

"I only want to talk," Paul said. "What's your name?"

"Karine Hagopian."

"Are you Armenian?"

"Yes I am."

"You can sit up."

She did.

"Can you tell me your story?" Paul asked.

"Why do you want to know?" Karine asked him.

"I'm from the Red Cross and we want to help."

"My story will take longer than the time you've paid for."

That was true.

"You can buy me," she said.

"Pardon?" Paul asked; surprised.

"They bought me from the Turks for one lira, so you can buy me from them. Then I will have time to tell you my story."

"You will do this?"

"On one condition."

"What's that?"

"Buy me first and I will tell you."

"I will do that now."

"Don't pay too much. Not more than a few lira."

Paul went to the street. "I want to buy Karine," he said to the pimp.

"You cannot buy her."

"You bought her for one lira, so I will buy her for five lira."

"She will make a lot of money for me."

"Seven lira."

"Alright."

They went to Karine's room, and the pimp spoke with her in what sounded like Turkish. So she spoke English, Turkish and almost certainly Armenian.

"I need clothes," Karine said.

"I can't take her into the street like that," Paul said.

"I will find clothes," the pimp said. He left the room.

"How much did you pay?" Karine asked.

"Seven lira," Paul said.

"That was too much," she said flatly.

The pimp returned and threw a dirty-looking blue dress at Karine. She got up and pulled it on. "Başörtüsü?" she asked and he went away, before returning with a green scarf. She wrapped that over her head and around her neck. "Now we can go," she said.

They went into the street. "I'm so sorry about what's happened to you and to your people, and I really want to help," Paul said. "I don't know what we can achieve, but I must try."

She nodded her head silently. They reached the Baron Hotel and Paul led Karine to the reception desk. The same young man was on duty.

"Excuse me," Paul said. "I need another room for my friend. Close to my room if possible."

Then young man checked the register. "Room one-eleven next door."

Paul signed the register and was given the key, which he gave to Karine. They climbed the stairs to the first floor.

"Do many Armenians speak English?" Paul asked.

"Only if they went to American missionary schools in larger towns and cities," Karine said. "And not all of those."

"Do you want to bathe?"

"Yes please. Then I will tell you my story, on one condition."

"What's that?"

"That you help me find my mother."

Paul looked into her big, dark eyes, and my word she had beautiful eyes. "I will help you find your mother, if you help me to translate."

"I can do that."

They reached Paul's room. "This is my room, and that's your room," Paul said. "Bathe, and knock on my door when you're ready. At some time I need to buy you clothes."

She looked at her grubby dress two sizes too big and nodded.

"I hope we can make a difference, Karine," Paul said.

"I hope so too," she said.

* * *

Paul heard faint knocking on his door and let Karine in. In the meantime he worked out how he wanted to do this.

"I feel better after a bath, thank you," Karine said.

"Do you want to tell your story now, or tomorrow?" Paul asked.

"We used to sleep during the day and – you know, at night, so now is fine."

"Sit on the bed, and dictate slowly to me so I can write it down."

"I can write in English."

"If anything doesn't make sense, I can clarify it when I write."

"Alright." Karine sat on the bed. "My name is Karine Hagopian, age sixteen from the Armenian village of Gamursh in Anatolia. In July this year the Ottoman Army recruited all Armenian men in Gamursh from the ages of eighteen to forty-eight, including my father and two uncles. These men were taken to a forest, shot in the head, and found in an open grave a few days later. We buried them and then my mother took me, my younger sister and my younger brother to her city of Ourfa, which Turks call Urfa, where we lived with her

157

parents. There we heard stories of deportations, murder and starvation of Armenians, so a war was fought between Armenians and the Ottoman Army for two months, until we Armenians were defeated. The next day, all men and boys over the age of twelve were lined up either side of the road to Aleppo, and shot or had their throats cut. This included my grandfather and two uncles. I, with my mother, my sister, my brother and my grandmother, were put in a caravan of many thousands of women and children, and we were marched along that road past these men, towards Aleppo. This march took almost two weeks, and of about seven-thousand, only one-thousand survived. We were fed and given water only once, and the only other water was at rivers we crossed every few days. Women were searched for any money, but my mother managed to hide gold coins...."

"How?" Paul asked.

"I won't say in case other women use the same way. My mother used her gold coins to buy food and water at villages at night, and that's how we survived. We were escorted by different groups of Turkish gendarmes, who raped many women. Sometimes they killed these women and sometimes they didn't. Sometimes, gendarmes would let villagers rape women in our caravan, while one night Kurdish Militia raped many women in the caravan and carried those women away. Most days, gendarmes would shoot women and children who were sick, and those who collapsed from sickness were left behind to die. Women who went into labour were left behind to die, while those who gave birth were expected to march, and were shot when they couldn't march. Once my grandmother got upset when this happened, and then a sick girl was shot, so my grandmother was stabbed and then shot to death. The first food for most of the caravan was at Al Bab after eleven days. After thirteen days we reached the camp at Aleppo where there was little food or water. The next day Turkish gendarmes allowed Arab and Kurdish men to buy women, and I was bought for one lira. My clothes were taken from me, and I was locked in a room in a brothel where I was abused by many men every day. After more than a month of this I was released by Mr Paul..."

"It's Dr Paul Lang, but I don't use that title very often."

"I was released by Dr Paul Lang of the Red Cross. The other women sold by the Turks will still be in brothels or harems."

"Thank you Karine," Paul said automatically, until he realised the extent of what he had just written down. "This is terrible," he said quietly. Every single male relative, except her younger brother, had been shot. Her grandmother had been shot. They only survived because her mother smuggled some gold coins. And even then she ended up in a brothel, and was only released by a random good fortune. "We need to stop this," he said.

"It's almost too late," Karine said.

"It's never too late. We can help women in brothels and harems, and we can help people in camps."

"Through my story?"

"Yes, and I want to take pictures in the camp."

"I can get you into the camp, if you have money."

"How?"

Karine leaned right forward; close to Paul. "I need to buy clothes, and I also will buy a black Arab robe so I don't look Armenian. We will change some of your money for gold coins, and use that to bribe gendarmes to let us into the camp. You can take your pictures while I search for my mother."

Paul thought there was little food or water, and it was more than a month. It was far from certain Karine's mother or anyone from her family was alive. More likely Karine was the only survivor.

"I know what you're thinking," Karine said. "If anyone survived it would be my mother."

"Well then, we will find her."

Karine looked at the floor. "Part of me wants to be hugged and feel love just for a moment, and another part of me can't stand the touch of men anymore." She looked at him. "I feel really bad."

"It wasn't your fault and you survived," Paul said.

"That's what my mother said and she was right. But now it's hard. I want to write something," she said.

Paul turned over a fresh page and got up. Karine sat at the desk. She frowned while she wrote, and when she finished she handed the notebook to Paul. He'd never seen anything like it! Big, loopy characters with many Ws and Us.

"That's Armenian," Karine said.

"Can you read it for me?"

She did and it was totally different to anything Paul had ever heard before. It sounded strangely ancient.

"How old is your culture?" Paul asked.

Karine nearly, nearly smiled. "Almost three-thousand years," she said. She got up. "Goodnight Paul, and thank you for letting me tell my story."

Karine slipped out of his room and Paul felt a strange ache in his heart, for her strength, her suffering and her vulnerability.

Chapter Sixteen

The sun was barely up when Dilsa came to the barn and shouted at Anoush in Kurdish, and the message was clear enough. Time to get up. Anoush shook Taniel who mumbled for a moment before sitting up. Anoush climbed out of her bed, such that it was: a coarse blanket laid on straw with two blankets over. She pulled her clothes on while Taniel turned away to dress. With headscarf wrapped in place, Anoush went to the shelter while Merdim gathered the goats. As always it was semi-dark and cold when Anoush led the first goat onto the platform, put a bucket in place, and sat on the stool. She milked while Taniel worked opposite; both in silence and emptying their buckets into the barrel, until the 30 goats were dealt with. Then Taniel sealed the barrel so that Merdim could carry it onto the donkey cart for Taniel's ride to Bassouta. While that was happening, Anoush went into the warm house to bake bread for breakfast. When cooked, she took the bread with honey and glasses of tea to their dining room, and then returned to the kitchen to eat her food. At some time Taniel would return and have his breakfast before he cleaned the milk barrel returned from the day before. Anoush took the dining table dishes to the kitchen to wash in a dish filled from the well.

Dilsa came to the kitchen with hands on hips and frowning. "We şuştin, cilên," she ordered abruptly, which

Anoush knew meant to wash their clothes. Anoush gathered dirty clothes from the two bedrooms, and took them in a basket to the stream to scrub, and that was terribly cold. Cold outside in the open and very cold water. When clean she brought them back, and as always Dilsa picked through the basket to make sure they were perfectly clean. Dilsa loved finding the smallest speck of grime, and throwing the garment in Anoush's face. Anoush had learned not to give her that opportunity. Taniel was in the shelter shovelling manure, while Anoush prepared lunch. Dilsa told her to make koftë, which always took a lot of preparation. In silence Anoush cooked, and finished with making coffee, which she took to the dining room. She took her lunch and Taniel's lunch to the barn. They ate in silence, before Anoush returned to the house to clear the table and wash the dishes. Taniel headed off where he must have been given a job by Merdim, while Anoush went to the stream to bathe.

Feeling clean and fresh, Anoush returned to the shelter where Merdim had gathered the goats for the afternoon milking. She worked alongside Taniel until that was done, and then went to the house where Dilsa ordered her to make kulki or vegetable pies for dinner. Once more the family ate in the dining room while Anoush and Taniel ate in the barn, food washed down by tea, before Anoush returned to the house to collect the dishes from the dining room, wash them and put them away. In darkness she returned to the barn having barely spoken two words all day.

Outside a light approached, and Taniel knew to go outside. Merdim hung an oil lantern on a post while Anoush removed her clothes and got onto her hands and knees. As always her stuck his finger into her arse before fucking her there, and when he was done he left without saying a word. Taniel returned and slipped into his bed, while Anoush felt dirty when she climbed beneath her coarse blankets and said "bari gisher" to Taniel, who replied with "bari gisher" to his mother.

Chapter Seventeen

Paul watched Karine, dressed in black, talking with a Turkish gendarme; rifle over his shoulder. He scowled at her but she stood her ground. She reached into her pocket and Paul saw a gold coin glinting in the sun. The gendarme grabbed for it, but Karine put her hand behind her back and they talked some more. The gendarme's antagonistic stance eased; she brought her hand out and he snatched the coin from her. Karine turned and beckoned Paul to her. Together they entered the camp.

Paul took a moment to deal with the horror around him. He never imagined that people could be so thin, nothing but skin and bone, and still be alive. The doctor in him thought that such a state wasn't possible, but there they were. He fiddled with his camera. He didn't want to take pictures of their suffering, but for a greater good he should. He unfolded the camera, set focus for 3 metres, and took pictures of women in bright sun, some emaciated children, an old woman although perhaps she wasn't as old as she looked, more children, more women, a woman with a gendarme in the background with his rifle clearly visible; until he finished the roll of film. That would be enough and it wasn't possible to change his film in the sun. In the background, Karine went from person to person, with no success it seemed.

Paul went to some children and spoke with their mother, but she didn't understand English. He knelt and checked their pulses; very slow not surprisingly. Their bodies conserving energy. He wished he could help in some small way. He sensed something and turned around to see Karine. He stood and she didn't have to tell him.

"Mama, my sister Lilit and my brother Taniel aren't here," Karine said. "Nobody remembers them. My aunts and their children aren't here either, and nobody remembers them."

"You didn't mention aunts," Paul said.

"We got separated at Ourfa."

She looked very downbeat.

"I do thank you for getting me in here," Paul said. "My other translators never got that far."

"They weren't Armenian," Karine said. "Did you take your pictures?"

"I did."

"We will go to the post office where you can send your mail."

They walked past those crosses to their black taxi. Karine spoke with the driver before climbing in the back. She frowned while she played with the sash around her waist.

"We need a picture of Mama," she said. "We will go to Ourfa to get a picture of Mama. Do you need to take more pictures?"

"Of what?" Paul asked.

"Of a massacre of fifteen-thousand men; or more."

That was staggering, as everything associated with this tragedy was staggering. "I don't really need to take more pictures," Paul said. "But that will help."

"Good. Mama had a wedding album, and it should be in my grandparent's house. There are pictures after she took off her veil."

That was odd for a wedding, Paul thought. "She took off her veil?" he asked.

"Armenian women dress modestly by wearing headscarves," Karine said. "At a wedding her headscarf would be a lace veil, with a second veil to cover her face. That second veil is removed after the service, and the headscarf later with her husband."

That was interesting. "How can we get to Ourfa?" Paul asked, and then the answer came to him. "I will check at the hospital if they have a car or a truck for a doctor and his translator."

The taxi rattled along the unmade road, trailing a cloud of dust. Paul felt he was with someone from a past age of headscarves, veils and rituals. At the same time she was independent and really bright. Brighter than his other translators for sure. Karine was an interesting mixture.

* * *

Paul sat at the table in the kitchen beside the fireplace, which in times past would have been cosy but was now abandoned. He pulled out his notebook and fountain pen.

'As you approach the city of Urfa, nothing can prepare you for what you will encounter. On both sides of the road are ditches many kilometres long, with ten thousand or more naked bodies laying where they were shot, or where their throats were cut through. The sight of this defies any attempt at description, as does the stench of rotting corpses. It churns your heart, it hits you in the stomach, and it leaves you so shocked that you cannot think anymore. It's much worse when you walk amongst them. Old men, boys, teenage boys, middle-aged men, men in their twenties. Tens of thousands of men dead. Some look happy, some look frightened, especially their eyes, some look in pain, as if they took time to die in agony. Many look peaceful. Some faces have been all but removed by vultures, jackals and all manner of vermin. Emboldened jackals feed off corpses, and are not the least bit frightened while you walk close to them. Vultures fly above or pick at eyes in particular. The air is thick with flies and thick with the smell of it. The massacre of the men of Urfa is an evil act committed by monsters.

'The city of Urfa is large and initially seems
prosperous. Go to the Armenian quarter and things
are different. Many houses have been bombed and
damaged, and all houses have been abandoned, their
occupants either shot alongside the road, or their bodies
strewn along the length of the walk from Urfa to
Aleppo. In abandoned streets papers swirl in the
breeze, while the ghostly Cathedral of the Holy Mother
of God keeps a silent sentinel for its Armenian
congregation long gone.'

Karine entered the room and Paul handed his notebook to her. She sat in the chair opposite and read while Paul watched her. She wiped tears from her cheeks, before handing the notebook back.

"Your grandfather and uncles are there," Paul said.

"We said a prayer for them on the first night," Karine said. "That was their funeral." She put a weather-beaten folder on the table and opened it. The pages were damaged by water but the pictures had survived. Inside were pictures of a happy wedding from years past. In one picture the bride, face veil removed, smiled at the camera. "That's the one," Karine said.

There was more than a passing resemblance between mother and daughter.

"Thank you for writing those nice things," Karine said.

169

"I can't put words to it, but I had to try." Paul said. "A camera can't capture even a fraction of the magnitude of that tragedy, even though I took many pictures."

"We should go. I took more clothes from our old bedroom, and my medallion for coming first in English." She shrugged her shoulders. "My sister Lilit was clever at maths and she used to help me, but I was better at English and I helped her. I hope we find her."

They went outside and walked through Samsat Gate to where the ambulance waited. Karine wore a Red Cross coat over her dress, which did well to hide her identity. Paul climbed in beside the Arab driver, Karine climbed in and sat beside the door; with a bundle and the folder on her lap. The driver started the engine, crunched first gear and they were on their way for the five-hour drive to Aleppo.

"I will mail another letter when we get back," Paul said. "This film and my description, as inadequate as it is."

"Your description is good," Karine said. "Brief and emotional."

"How did this happen?"

"American missionaries came to Anatolia, and because they're Christian and we're Christian, the first Christian church in the world, they adopted us. They built schools, they taught us in Armenian and in English, they taught us that Christians are better than Muslims; they filled Armenian heads with ideas of an Armenian homeland."

"Surely you deserve a place where you can live with your culture and practice your religion?"

"If things stayed as they were, if we lived peacefully side-by-side and went to our churches on Sunday, then none of this would have happened. Compared to most I'm lucky. I survived and most didn't. They died wretched deaths, beside the road here or in other, terrible ways. None of this would have happened if heads hadn't been filled with ideas that could never be."

Karine flicked through the pages of the wedding album. "This will never happen to me," she said quietly.

"What?" Paul asked.

"Getting married. Nobody will want me after what I've been through."

Paul was shocked. Karine was the most amazing woman he'd ever met. "I would marry you," he said, and he really meant it.

"Would you?" Karine asked.

Paul looked deep into her big eyes. "You're tough, smart and beautiful."

"Would you marry me?" she asked again.

"In a moment."

She put her head down. "I'm not ready for such things," she said. "Maybe one day I will be, but not now."

Paul didn't want to pressure Karine in the slightest, because she was right. She'd been through a terrible, terrible time. "When you're ready," he said. "It will come to you."

She nodded her head in understanding.

* * *

Dressed in black once more, Karine showed the picture to the gendarme closest to the crosses. He shook his head so she held up a coin, tempting him. He said something and reached for the coin, but she put it behind her back, out of his reach. They talked and she nodded, and then she handed over the coin. She came to Paul.

"He remembered my mother," she said. "She and a boy were bought by a Kurd with a donkey, but he doesn't remember a girl. I don't know what happened to Lilit. If the Kurd had a donkey he's probably not from Aleppo, so we will ask at Kurdish villages."

"How does that work?" Paul asked.

"The races have their own villages: Turk, Kurd, Armenian and Assyrian. They share towns and cities but in different quarters, like you saw in Ourfa. I must find which are Kurdish villages, and perhaps we will hire donkeys. And buy rifles too, because I don't trust Kurds."

Paul couldn't just abandon his job, as much as he wanted to help Karine.

"You're thinking about something," she said, ever observant.

172

"I have a job and responsibilities, and riding donkeys across the countryside isn't the right thing for me to do."

"You said you would help," she said indignantly. "I told you my story, I got you into the camp; I did more for your job than anyone else could."

That was true. "Yes I did agree and yes you're right. If we devote two weeks...?"

"Three weeks," Karine interrupted.

"Three weeks to search for your family."

She nodded in agreement, but it was clear she wasn't happy. Paul admired her single-minded determination and her ability to get things done. They were very attractive qualities. Even her simmering anger was attractive.

Chapter Eighteen

They rode north on donkeys, on a cloudy day threatening rain. Never in his wildest imaginations would Paul have pictured himself crossing plains north of Aleppo, riding a donkey while accompanied by a young Armenian woman. If found Karine's mother, and given she was bought from the camp that was possible, the mother's story would add an extra dimension to what Paul had already sent.

It was quite obvious that Karine was one step away from a total breakdown, and she was keeping herself together by sheer force of will. She had been through a lot although her mother, Anoush, had suffered much more.

"Tell me about your country?" Karine asked to break into Paul's thoughts.

"It's small and mountainous, and cold with snow in winter. Many people live there and it's quite crowded. You can't go anywhere without crossing paths with other people, not like here. Life is busy, and at times nobody seems to have time for anybody else. Just getting through the day takes all your energy. I live in a part of the country where they speak a German dialect, while other parts of Switzerland speak French or Italian."

"You don't normally speak English?"

Paul shook his head. "I normally speak Bernese, and I also speak High German."

"If people are always busy, how do they find time for their families?"

"Men in my country don't have so much to do with their children and leave that to their wives."

"You're not yet married?"

"I'm twenty-four and not married, because I haven't yet found the right woman."

"Your families don't arrange marriages?"

"Tell me how that works for Armenians?"

"Family is everything. Mothers prepare their daughters for the responsibilities of looking after a husband, managing a house, and raising children. Fathers prepare their sons to support a family, and to look after a wife. At the right age, families consider which sons and daughters will fit well together, and the decision is made. You saw my parent's wedding photos, and now it's my turn to be made ready to be a wife."

"What age do you marry?"

"Sixteen or seventeen for women, and nineteen or twenty for men."

"When you say made ready to be a wife?"

"Cook, clean, sew, weave, be intimate with your husband; raise children. Women's tasks."

"And men have their tasks?"

"That's right."

That was simple, and in some ways that seemed superior to life in Europe. Rather than getting married more or less unprepared, they'd been taught. And when children came, they would be prepared for that too. Also, although women were still the home makers, they seemed to have a greater degree of independence than women in Europe.

"When a woman gets married she moves to her husband's household and comes under the charge of his mother," Karine said. "When she has her first child, she may move into her own home or become independent in the family home, depending on circumstance."

That made sense. "This is why your mother is from Ourfa, but was living in a village?" Paul asked.

"Yes. I didn't know my grandparents, or my uncles and aunts from Ourfa very well. But Mama left Gamursh because she was worried about the army coming for the women there. That eventually happened at Ourfa though."

"I like the way your culture works," Paul said. "It sounds like it hasn't changed much for many thousands of years."

"The basic reason for life is family, and that can never change," Karine said.

He also liked the way she was so sure of herself, and he suspected that was more common amongst Armenian women than Swiss women.

"You're a doctor?" Karine asked.

"I am, and I worked in a public hospital where I could do a greater good for ordinary people."

"That's worthy."

"I thought so. When this is over I will return to the public hospital. I suppose."

"Will this ever be over?"

"It will be over one day, and I hope with the defeat of the Ottoman Empire."

"We can never go back to Ourfa or Gamursh. If they hate Armenian Christians so much to try to kill every last one of us; we can never fit together again. Even here is dangerous for me, as you know."

"Is this because you're Armenian or because you're Christian."

"Some Armenians were agitating for independence, and even joined Russia against the Ottoman Empire. As minority Christians in a predominately Muslim country, we were always going to lose in any form of conflict. Only small numbers of Armenians were involved, but all of us have been targeted."

"This means that you and the survivors of this won't have a country anymore."

"First comes survival, Paul."

That was true. They plodded on in silence, and late in the afternoon reached Andzara, a busy, Arab town. Karina found a cafe with many Arabs out the front, and inside was quite crude and pungent with the smoke from waterpipes. Karine talked with a waiter before guiding Paul outside again.

"There's a barn for our donkeys," Karina said. "We can rent rooms here as well."

They put their donkeys in a pen in the barn, and went into the cafe once more. Again Karine spoke with the waiter before returning to Paul at one of the rough-hewn tables.

"I ordered our meal," she said. "What's food like in your country?"

"Not as good as here!" Paul exclaimed. "We eat a lot of meat: grilled, roasted or fried, with vegetables like potatoes, cabbage and carrots, usually boiled. Here the food is tastier, there's more variety, and it has a lovely texture to it. I suspect there's more effort in preparing your food than grilling a steak or boiling a potato."

"Some dishes are complicated and some like stews are quite easy. It's a woman's job to choose what to cook and to make sure she has provisions for her meals. Armenians drink wine with meals, but they don't drink wine here."

"I noticed that. In my country they usually drink beer, but I prefer wine."

Paul sipped his tea.

"Armenians invented wine," Karine said.

Paul nearly choked. "Really?" he exclaimed. But then he thought nearly 3,000 years. No, that wasn't right.

"Our ancestors, maybe ten-thousand years ago, invented wine."

Every day was a new discovery of the ancient past of his companion. Fascinating.

The food, as always, was superb, missing only Armenian wine as accompaniment. It had been a long ride; Paul was weary and looking forward to a good sleep. Karine stifled a yawn and she was as weary as he.

"We should sleep," Paul said.

"This way," Karine said, leading Paul to a corridor with the kitchen on one side, and two bedrooms on the other side. She opened the door and led Paul inside, and closed the door behind her. She looked up into his eyes. "Can you hug me please?" she asked.

Paul did, and she hugged him while burying her head into his shoulder. They held each other for a long time in silence, until she eased away and looked into his eyes once more.

"I love you," she said quietly. She kissed Paul lightly on his cheek. "Goodnight Paul and sleep well."

Paul left and went to his room.

Chapter Nineteen

Paul woke in the early light of dawn. In a barn behind a cafe in the village of Deir Semaan, they slept side-by-side on straw mattresses with blankets. He listened to Karine sleeping soundly; her gentle, regular breathing. He rolled over and admired her olive complexion, and her long and braided jet-black hair; not often revealed. He turned again to lie on his back to give her privacy. They were close to Kurd Mountains, and she had a map of villages and roads. They were close to the first Kurdish village, Barad, and Karine had plotted a route which looped through most of the villages.

Karine stirred and sat up.

"Good morning," Paul said.

"Good morning Paul," she replied. "We will eat breakfast; then start."

"I will dress first to give you privacy."

"Thank you."

In the cafe they had freshly baked bread with honey, and strong, black coffee. Then they rode to Barad, which was quite sizeable in fact, with a white mosque, and many streets radiating from the centre of town like a spider's web. Karine first asked at the cafe, she professed to speaking a bit of Kurdish, and then at the mosque, with no success.

Next was Burj Abd Allah, back on the main road. This was much smaller, perhaps sharing facilities with the larger village of Bassouta a few kilometres away. After asking at the cafe and the grocery store, Karine came out looking downcast.

"I'm not Kurdish and they know it," she said. "Why should they help me? Mama could be here, she could be in one of these houses, and we would never know. We could walk right past her and never know."

She was right and Paul didn't want to be facile with her. "Let's go to the next village and check there," he said.

They rode off and soon were amongst olive trees. The olive trees didn't relieve the drab nature of the village itself, which was quite a bit larger than Burj Abd Allah. It was getting late and Paul suspected they would spend the night in Bassouta which looked large enough to have accommodation for travellers. They reached a village square surrounding a stone well, and there they left their donkeys. Paul followed Karine into a dark cafe, with several men drinking coffee and playing draughts. Karine went to the proprietor and spoke with him while showing the photo, which the man glanced at before shaking his head. She spoke sharply and he looked at the photo for longer, before returning to drying the plate in his hand. Karine then went to men not playing the game and asked them, insisting they take a good look at the photo, but with no success.

She went to the other shops while Paul waited near the well, and returned looking downcast once more.

"We have enough time to check at Kerzayhel," she said while she climbed onto her donkey.

Paul got on his donkey while wondering if there was a better strategy. Could she bribe them to take her seriously? That would cost too much. Could she offer a reward? *If you lead me to this woman I will pay you a gold coin.* That might work. Paul rode off when suddenly a woman came from behind the cafe and went to Karine. This woman was agitated; tense and nervous while she looked all around, clearly concerned that someone would see her. Karine fished the picture from inside her dress and showed it to the woman, who nodded and pointed. Karine bowed to the woman while the woman touched Karine's hand, before disappearing from where she came.

"That woman recognised my mother," Karine said.

Paul barely believed that. "That's great," he said.

"She said to take the trail to the west, to the goat farm of Merdim Hardi."

Karine turned her donkey around and threaded past basic, stone houses on paths of dirt and mud, until they were amongst olive trees once more. On and on towards a ridge a few kilometres away, with the village and the olive groves set in a valley. The land was poorer quality closer to the ridge, with scrubby, weedy pastures fenced by low, stone walls.

"There are some goats," Karine said.

182

There were goats on a farm on the side of a hill dropping away, fenced in by stone walls which were in need of repair. Towards the centre of the farm was a pathetic-looking stone house, similar in style to houses in the village but in poor repair. They left their donkeys to graze on weeds beside the trail, and Karine led the way to the house with Paul following. She knocked on a weather-beaten door which opened to reveal a short, dumpy, middle-aged woman in brown and black, frowning. Karine spoke with this woman and showed the picture, but the woman shook her head and pointed at the trail to leave.

Paul reached into his pocket and fished out two gold coins. "Offer these if we find your mother," he said while handing them across.

Karine offered the coins but the woman slammed the door in reply. Clearly that wasn't the farm, because they wouldn't turn down two gold coins. The farm was nearly derelict and they really needed that money.

"There must be another goat farm," Paul said.

They headed to their donkeys which still grazed on weeds.

* * *

Anoush overheard Dilsa with another woman, which was unusual given nobody, not family or friends, ever visited. Anoush popped her head around the corner and Dilsa was at the front door, arguing in Kurdish with a woman dressed in bright clothing, but who was hidden by the part-opened door. There was more argument before Dilsa slammed the door hard. Anoush looked out the window, and gasped with shock. The other woman speaking Kurdish was Karine! There, just metres away was Karine with a tall man in Western clothes. Anoush never knew Karine spoke Kurdish. Anoush ran towards the front door until Merdim grabbed her arm and twisted it behind her back. Oh, that hurt so much! Anoush tried to pull free, but he was too strong.

"That's my daughter," she gasped.

"You're my property now," he growled, and pushed her. Anoush fell and hit her head on the sharp edge of a chair. That hurt even more, and she felt woozy and saw strange, black and white chequered patterns; swirling.

"Get to work," he snarled.

"My daughter...," Anoush tried to say, but the words wouldn't form.

He kicked her. "Get back to work," he said; this time slowly and deliberately.

Anoush rubbed her head. "I can't, not yet. My head feels strange." Karine was so close but leaving, and once she'd gone she would never come back. Her one chance was leaving. What to do? "I can pay you a gold coin," Anoush said, looking up at Merdim, arms crossed.

"The labour of you and your son is worth more than a gold coin to me. Where do you have a gold coin?"

Her money was well-hidden. "I don't, but that woman, my daughter, will pay you."

"She offered two gold coins, but my wife knew what to say."

He kicked Anoush again.

"Get back to work," he ordered.

Still feeling woozy, Anoush used the chair to get to her feet, and then one foot after the other went to the kitchen to continue preparing dinner.

* * *

Paul rode with Karine towards the ridge in the near distance, but he saw no more goats. Scrubby pasture deteriorated into rock and stone, and there were no goat farms there. Karine stopped her donkey.

"Something wasn't right at that farm," she said. "We should check it out."

She was right, and with shadows lengthening they retraced their path to that farm, to leave their donkeys grazing on weeds once more. Karine climbed over the low, stone wall, and kept low while she crossed a pasture, such that it was. Paul followed for protection just in case, and kept as low as he could. They went as far as a stream, and then to a barn with straw, a few tools and a donkey, but nothing else. There was a covered area with a couple of platforms and a barrel, he assumed for milking goats, and apart from the house that was it. Still keeping low Karine went to the house

185

and peered into a back window, and then went to another back window to peer inside. She came back to Paul near a cart beside the barn.

"I can see a man, that woman and an old woman," she said. "No sign of Mama. She's not here."

"Let's go," Paul suggested.

"There might be another trail to the west that we can check tomorrow."

Paul thought there must be another trail, while they kept low and crossed another pasture. They mounted their donkeys, and with dusk approaching they set off for town. They should find rooms at the cafe.

* * *

"Your daughter and her friend are persistent," Merdim said. "But they're gone now, so you and your son can stand up."

Anoush stood from her position beneath the kitchen window, as did Taniel. Merdim threw their blankets at them.

"Get your bed ready; I will be out shortly," he said.

Anoush walked to the barn and knew she had to do something, after Merdim was finished with her.

"I'm getting us out of here," she said quietly in Armenian.

"How Mama?" Taniel asked.

"Leave that to me. Stay outside for now, so this will be over quickly."

"Yes Mama."

Anoush laid their blankets on the straw and quickly removed her clothes. As soon as Merdim entered the barn and hung his lantern, she got onto her hands and knees. As always he stuck an oily, slippery finger into her arse before he put his oily penis in there, and then he huffed and puffed for a few minutes until he came, and moved some more before he finished. He got up, dressed, and went to the house. Anoush just finished dressing when Taniel returned.

"I'm going to find Karine to get us out of here," Anoush said in Armenian.

"Yes Mama," Taniel replied.

Anoush kept low while she crossed the pasture to the donkey trail, relying more on her sense of direction than what she could see. The stone wall was darker in the darkness, and she felt for it before climbing over. Beyond, the gravel trail was lighter than weeds, and she used that lightness to guide her. It was late when they left which meant they had to stay overnight in town, and this trail went to the square with the well. Anoush stumbled on lumps and bumps a couple of times but didn't fall, until she saw lights from the window of a house. Now it was easy, and soon she was in the square. Now what? When she travelled with Merdim they always stayed in rooms or barns at cafes. Which one of those shops was the cafe? Anoush went to the road from Deir Semaan, the road they originally entered the square from, and there she pictured it. Second shop on the right, closed and locked.

Anoush peered through the window, but all was dark and still. She hoped Karine and that man were there, but she would go to every house in Bassouta if she had to. She used a narrow lane between the cafe and the building next door to go to the back, and spotted a barn. She went to that barn, eased a timber door open, but only saw two donkeys. She then went to the shuttered rear windows of the cafe and tapped. Nothing. She knocked louder. Nothing.

"It's me, Mama!" she shouted in Armenian.

Moments later the door opened, and Karine fell into her arms. "Mama!" she exclaimed. "You found us!"

"Yes Karine my love; I found you."

"I missed you so much."

"I missed you my love. If I could take all this away, I would, but...."

"I know Mama, but I never gave up. I knew you could do it."

Anoush was so proud of her daughter.

They hugged each other for so long, even though Anoush was aware of another person. That man that she saw. She eased away from Karine and saw him at a distance, watching.

"This is my friend Paul Lang," Karine said in English.

"Good evening," he said in a deep and masculine voice while shaking Anoush's hand. "I'm glad we found you."

"Paul rescued me," Karine said.

That made sense, but now came the bad news. "Karine my love, we need to rescue Taniel," she said in Armenian. "But Lilit didn't make it."

* * *

Paul watched Karine crumple in a heap and cry hysterically. Her mother Anoush knelt and held her, while Paul moved away to give them space. One or both of the children were dead, and that was tragic. Tragedy upon tragedy. But crying like that would be good for Karine. She'd been keeping it in for too long, like pressure building against a dam wall, and she needed to let it out before her wall collapsed. That wouldn't bring her family back, but she needed to release that emotion before she broke from the stress. She cried and cried and eventually it was all gone. She stood and her mother stood too.

"Her sister is dead," Anoush said to Paul.

"My condolences," Paul offered, as banal as that was.

"She got sick, like so many. But we need to get her brother now, before Merdim finds out."

"Yes. Where is he?"

"In the barn at the goat farm."

It was dark at the back of the cafe despite light spilling around, and darker beyond the village. "We need light. Karine, you should ask the wife of the proprietor, who told us about your mother."

Karine went inside, and a few minutes later she returned carrying a kerosene lantern, burning low. They set off with Karine leading the way along the gravel trail until they reached the farm, easily identifiable by light glowing from that decrepit house. Paul wondered what to do. Anoush had to be part of this, because she knew where the son was, and she could get him away without any drama or delay. Paul would accompany Anoush for protection, while Karine should keep a distance and fetch help from the village if necessary. That was best.

"Your mother and I will fetch your brother," Paul said to Karine. "You stay here with the light to guide us. If anything happens, go to village and get help."

"Yes," Karine agreed.

Anoush climbed over the low, stone wall and crossed the pasture. Paul followed her, and on a dark night the kerosene lamp at the trail did help. Past the house and around the back, where the dark shape of the barn was clearly visible. Anoush went to the door and eased it open. She went inside with Paul following into total darkness.

Anoush spoke quietly and a boy's voice spoke back; probably in Armenian. He saw movement, Anoush put her hand on the boy, and then light came through the door. Either Karine had followed or something else was happening. Anoush and the boy backed away while Paul looked around.

He stood at the door holding a lamp: short, ugly with grey hair and a hooked nose, dressed any old way. But he was broad, not fat but broad. Broad with muscle. He hung the lamp on a hook on a post and stood with hands on hips. He snapped at Anoush who snapped back at him, and then he went for her. Paul had to deal with this man and he wasn't a fighter, which this man probably was. He glanced around and just behind were farming implements, including a shovel with a short handle. Paul grabbed that and swung at the man, who ducked to avoid the blow and grabbed the blade. He pulled hard, almost pulling Paul off his feet, and easily pulled the shovel out of Paul's grip. Ignoring Anoush and the boy, the man advanced on Paul, hemming him to the corner of the barn. Anoush stood to one side, watching with the whites of her eyes clearly visible. The man turned the shovel around, clearly to use it as a weapon, just as Paul backed into something low on the ground. He reached down and had a three-legged stool in his hands. He threw the stool to hit that man hard on his head. The man dropped the shovel and reeled away as if dazed. Paul grabbed the shovel and hit the man on the back of the head, and he groaned and fell to the ground.

"Quick; we must go," Paul said.

Paul led the way outside to confront that dumpy woman clearly visible in the light from the barn. Anoush threw a coin at that woman, glinting in the light, and said

191

something sharp at her. The woman retorted before they were gone. Down the paddock, guided by light from the open door of the barn, and Karine's light just beyond the wall. Paul followed Anoush and the boy over the wall, where mother and daughter spoke for a moment.

"We can go now," Anoush said.

They returned to the village guided by Karine holding the light. Eventually they were at the rear of the cafe, where the proprietor's wife waited, smiling brightly.

Karine handed the lamp back while they spoke, which Anoush seemed not to understand. The woman beckoned them inside.

"How do you speak Kurdish?" Anoush asked Karine in English.

"When I was young we used to play with Kurds at Mishacerk," Karine said. "I don't know much but I know enough."

Paul contemplated their situation. It was late and unfair on the proprietor's wife not to bed down now. There were two rooms; both decently sized. "Karine; ask the woman if your mother and brother can share your room, and we can sort things out in the morning."

"Her name's Hana and I will do that."

They spoke and clearly Hana agreed.

Anoush shook Paul's hand. "Thank you very much for helping us," she said.

"We came here to rescue you," Paul said. "I'm glad we could. It's late and we should sleep now, so goodnight to all of you."

Paul went into his room, stripped to his underpants and collapsed into bed. He was exhausted.

Chapter Twenty

Anoush woke to an empty room. She opened the shutters to see Karine, Taniel and that man, Paul Lang, outside on a bright, sunny morning. She quickly dressed and wrapped her headscarf in place, and went to meet them.

Paul was with Taniel; on his knees so he would be shorter and not imposing. Paul shook Taniel's hand and said in English, "My name's Paul Lang and I'm a friend of your sister, Karine."

Taniel said, "My name's Taniel Hagopian."

"Pleased to meet you Taniel. I know you have been through many bad things these past few months, and from now on I will protect you. I will make sure that nothing bad will ever happens to you, your sister, or your mother, again."

Taniel nodded.

"He's a good man," Karine said in Armenian.

"He is," Anoush replied in Armenian.

"I love him and one day we will marry."

Anoush was shocked and turned to look her daughter in her eyes.

"I'm not ready and he knows this, and he will wait for me."

Anoush looked back and he was a good man. She was pleased that some good came out of their tragedy.

"He's here to record stories of our suffering," Karine said. "I told our story up to the camp at Aleppo, and you can tell him your story after that."

Anoush's stomach knotted and she felt flushed.

"You have nothing to be ashamed of, Mama," Karine said. "All of this was out of our control."

"I flaunted myself to that Kurd so he would buy me," Anoush said while feeling ashamed. Feeling worse than ashamed.

Karine took her hands. "You did that to survive, Mama," she said. "If you didn't do that, then you and Taniel would be in that camp starving, or you both would be dead. You saved your son and that's nothing to be ashamed about."

Anoush looked at Taniel now talking with Paul about his school. If she hadn't gone with that Kurd, she and Taniel would have been marched to Der Zor. They would have died. "You're right," she said. "I will tell Paul my story."

"When I told Paul my story it was like a big weight was lifted from me. I was suffocating and then I could breathe once more. When you let it out, it releases you."

Anoush hoped that if she told her story to Paul, the same thing would happen to her. At that moment she felt terrible shame for what she did, and for surviving when many good people didn't.

"We need to know what happens now," Karine said. "Paul," she called. "Can you come here?" she asked in English.

He came.

"What do you think we should do?" Karine asked.

"I was working in Cairo when I heard about this," Paul said. "They sent me here to get information and photographs, which I have. It's dangerous for you and your family as Armenians in the Ottoman Empire, and I think you should return to Cairo with me. There you will be safe."

"What about the people here?"

"A war is being fought, and I believe the Ottomans used the cover of war to do what they did. We can't help the people in the camps and those yet to come, because we have to deal with the Ottoman Army to rescue them. When they're defeated, then we can help the survivors."

"What about women in brothels and women captured by Kurds?"

"That's hard. I bought you, but they won't sell me every woman because that will put them out of business."

Anoush felt sick that the terrible suffering of Armenian woman was 'business'.

"If you rescue a woman from a brothel, they will buy a woman from the next caravan," Karine said.

Paul sighed. "We can only help when this war is over and the Ottoman Empire has been defeated. I'm a doctor and I can help the sick and the starving, and there will be many orphans and many women from brothels and other places, and they will need our help too."

Karine grabbed his arm. "You will come back to help my people?" she gasped.

"They're our people, Karine," he said.

Anoush felt a sudden glow of warmth, and she understood why her daughter loved this man.

"It's going to be hard to leave my people behind," Karine said glumly.

"When we can, we will return," Paul said.

"Paul is right," Anoush said. "We have to wait. When this war is over, then we can help."

"You will help too, Mama?" Karine asked.

"Of course I will." Anoush knew why. "This will give purpose to my life."

"Mama will tell her story to you," Karine said.

"That will do you good," Paul said to Anoush. "If you keep emotions bottled up inside for too long, they do harm. But if you let them out; that's good for you."

"I know what we should do!" Karine exclaimed. "When we come back we should write down the stories of the survivors. We can help our people in a way that outsiders can never do."

"That's a brilliant idea, Karine," Paul said. "Then we can translate and publish those stories, so that this thing never happens again."

"Yes, that too. Another thing," Karine said. "While we're waiting I will teach you Armenian. When you come back, you can help them in their language."

"Yes, you're right. As a doctor speaking Armenian, I can help them better."

Anoush was proud of her clever daughter. If only her father was there to see her. But his memory would always live in his surviving children.

"We should eat now," Karine said.

They went into to the cafe where Karine spoke with Hana before joining them at a table.

"Hana remembered you," Karine said. "She knew Merdim Hardi would treat you even worse than he treats his wife."

Anoush nodded in understanding. That explained Dilsa behaving as she did. She'd been abused for decades. Hana brought fresh bread, cheese, honey and glasses of tea. Anoush was still coming to terms with Karine being rescued, and she being rescued too. That seemed almost unimaginable.

"We have two donkeys," Karine said. "You and Taniel can ride and we can walk."

"Nonsense!" Anoush exclaimed. "We will take turns riding, leaving after this lovely breakfast. If you don't mind, I would like to leave here soon."

"Of course Mama. We will ride to Aleppo where I'm sure Paul has business to do. Then...?"

"We need to buy clothes and I have money for that," Paul said. "Then we will catch a train to Tripoli, and a ferry to Cairo."

Anoush ate more bread. That sounded good.

* * *

They reached the busy Arab town of Da Ta Izzah late in the afternoon, where Paul guided them to a cafe. Anoush overheard Karine speaking with the proprietor in Turkish, and they had rooms and they had a barn for their donkeys. That was quickly settled, although the rooms were rather small.

"Taniel can sleep with me," Paul said.

"I couldn't ask that," Anoush said.

Paul got onto his knees. "We're friends now, Taniel," he said.

"Yes we are," Taniel replied.

Paul looked up at Anoush. "There, it's done."

Paul really was wonderful. Taniel had been through terrible horrors and he needed a good man in his life. Now he had one.

"There's a bathhouse nearby," Karine said. "It's women's day today, Mama."

That sounded good, after many weeks of quick splashes in the stream.

"Sorry men," Karine said. "We women have more important things to do."

"We will be fine," Paul said. "Won't we Taniel?"

"Yes Paul," Taniel replied.

The bathhouse was close to the cafe; nondescript on the outside but lovely on the inside. Black, red and white diagonal tiles on walls, ornate columns; the large, rectangular bath itself, in green-blue tiles and with several women bathing and talking quietly. Anoush had always found nakedness comfortable, because man and woman were made naked by God, and everybody came into the world naked. Normally they were burdened with layers of clothes and headscarves, but not in a bathhouse. She slipped into the water and Karine slipped beside her. Karine poured water over Anoush's unbraided, long hair, and Anoush did the same for her. Then Anoush lay back to enjoy the moment.

"I love Paul," Karine said in Armenian.

"I don't think I can ever have a man touch me again," Anoush said.

"I once felt that way. When Paul first met me I was in that place, and I just wanted him to get out of my life. Only he wanted to talk instead. After we talked I felt better, and after a few days with him I felt better still. Now I love him and he loves me."

Anoush was surprised that Karine could go from that to love.

"That Kurdish man, Merdim Hardi, used to fuck me in my arse almost every night," Anoush said.

"Kurdish and Arab men often did that to me," Karine said. "I don't know why."

"It's something their wives won't do, but other women don't have a choice."

"That sounds right."

"You could go from that to loving a man?"

"That Karine was just surviving. This Karine has her whole life to come, and her Mama, her late Papa, and especially her late sister, would tell her to live her life as it should be." Karine turned her head to look at Anoush. "It's only been one day, Mama. Don't say I could never have a man touch me, because you're too young to be in widow's black for the rest of your days. If Papa was here, he would tell you that."

Anoush was about to say 'I can't' until she replayed those words. Karine was right. "When the time is right...."

"Paul and I hugged the other day and that was good. It will come to me."

"I'm proud of you my daughter."

"If it wasn't for you Mama, I wouldn't be here. Your hidden coins, the way you protected me, the advice you gave me. If you hadn't done those things I wouldn't be here."

Anoush was about to say all mothers protect their children, which they do, but Karine meant more than that. She did things that other mothers didn't do, and that's what Karine meant. Anoush lay back, relaxed, and let the hot water take away some of her pain.

Later they dried, dressed and returned to the cafe where Paul and Taniel played draughts, which surprised Anoush. Paul must have taught him. They were just finishing a game.

"Do you want to hear my story?" Anoush asked.

"If you don't mind?" Paul asked.

"This may unburden me."

"Come to my room."

They went into the room where Paul closed the door.

"What should I call you?" Paul asked.

"I would be proud for you to call me Mama," Anoush said.

"Thank you Mama. Please sit on the bed and tell me your story, as much as you want, and I will write it down."

Anoush sat on the bed and Paul sat beside her. She wondered where to start. "One day in July, the Ottoman Army came into the village of Gamursh," she said. "They conscripted all Armenian men of fighting age, including my husband, and we would never see them alive again."

* * *

Paul screwed his fountain pen closed while he considered what he'd just written. It was more detailed than Karine's version, and more powerful as a result. He decided to send it to Geneva in its entirety.

"Karine was right," Mama said. "I feel better now. I'm not healed and maybe I will never fully recover, but I do feel better."

Paul was pleased. "The survivors of this atrocity won't be from camps at Aleppo or Der Zor, but women from brothels or women held as sex slaves. If this process helps; then when we come back, Karine and you will not only be well-placed to help these women because you're of their culture, but also because you've been through the same things."

"Yes you're right. Karine was also right about you learning Armenian. Those survivors will be more comfortable dealing with a doctor who speaks their language, rather than through an interpreter."

"I know you've lost a lot, Mama, and I can't begin to comprehend what you've been through. But you do have a very special daughter who has risen to the challenge, rather than being ground down by it."

"I know and I'm proud of her, and the part her father and I played in making her what she is. When your time comes and you have children, you will discover that raising children can be hard at times, but your children are worth the sacrifices you make, ten times over."

Paul thought that must be true, despite his own past. Everything Anoush, Mama, had done over the past months of horror was driven by her love for her children. His parents had it wrong, but Mama and Karine knew what family meant.

* * *

Anoush leaned against the rail of the ferry, watching the brown-green smudge of land recede into the distance. She sensed Paul coming alongside to lean against the rail beside her.

"I have mixed feelings about this," Paul said. "I achieved what I set out do, and I hope that did some good. But it doesn't feel right to leave them, even though we can't help them."

"I know what you mean," Anoush said. "We have to leave because we're in danger, and there's little we can achieve at the moment anyway. But it doesn't feel right to leave my people, even if I have no other option."

"We will be back," Paul said.

Paul left her. It was Monday, February the 14th, 1916, less than 10 months after April 24, 1915, and the commencement of the extermination of the Armenian race.

PART TWO

Chapter Twenty One

The deportation camp at Aleppo was gone, and deportees or refugees as they were officially known, were under the care of the British Army in a camp closer to the city. Anoush wandered past rows of tents, while a larger tent with an open side, manned by soldiers in uniform with aprons over, smelled of food cooking. Those who survived and there were many, looked healthy, especially with new clothes, even if those clothes were Western dresses or Western children's clothing. Anoush wandered through her people, although Armenians were far from homogenous so really 'her people' were Western Armenians of the Apostolic faith. Another legacy of American interference was the rise of Western Protestantism. Americans preached their Protestant faith was a superior form of Christianity, which made little sense given Armenian Apostolic was the first Christian faith, but which succeeded in dividing Armenians beyond the language differences of East and West.

A woman, older than Karine but younger than she, with two children, an older boy and a younger girl, queued for water, now freely available.

"Parev," Anoush greeted this woman.

"Parev," the woman replied.

"My name's Anoush Hagopian."

"My name's Talin Sarkissian."

"Once I was here," Anoush said. "I've been in Egypt these past years, and it's good so see my people being cared for."

"Once the Ottoman Army was driven out, the British came with food, water, clothes, tents and medical aid."

Anoush nodded. "Do you know what comes next?"

"They want to send us back."

Anoush wasn't surprised. "Where's that for you?"

"Near Sivas."

Sivas deportees were once driven past Ourfa, and always were camped there. "What do you think about that?"

"Can we go back? But can we stay here?"

Staying 'here', Aleppo, posed challenges; maybe not insoluble. "Where's home for you, Tikin Anoush?"

"Near Ourfa, but I won't be going back. I'm working for the Red Cross."

"Can the Red Cross stop us from being sent back?"

"The Red Cross can try. Muhnak parov Tikin Talin."

"Muhnak parov."

Anoush left the camp and returned to their apartment of two bedrooms, a kitchen and a living room.

"I found out," Anoush said to Karine and Paul. "You both were right; they want to send them back."

"Superficially that makes sense," Paul said. "The reality is they should stay here, and perhaps be settled in this region away from Turks."

"I want to do something about this," Anoush said. "I will meet with the British Army commander."

Paul reached into a bag and pulled out three pages stapled together. He gave it to Anoush. "This is the typed version of your story," he said. "Give this to the commander to read first, and that puts context to the principle that Turk and Armenian can't be re-joined."

* * *

Anoush sat with Karine, while a middle-aged soldier in uniform typed slowly and deliberately using two fingers. The door opposite opened, and a tall, dark-haired officer came out.

"Mrs Hagopian and Mrs Hagopian-Lang?" he asked.

Anoush stood with Karine, and he shook their hands. "I'm Captain Holmes. Please come inside."

It had once been a professional's office; a lawyer or something of that sort, and retained the furniture and feel of such a past.

"Please sit," Captain Holmes said, and they sat. "What can I do for you?"

"Thank you for seeing us," Anoush said just as she'd practiced. "Please read this and then we can talk."

She handed over the typed pages and Captain Holmes frowned. He read it while Anoush watched his face change, and change some more, and change even more. He read it quite quickly and then put it down.

"This is your story?" Captain Holmes asked.

"This is our story," Anoush said. "As you know Talaat Pasha, Enver Pasha and Djemal Pasha, who attempted to exterminate my race, escaped from Constantinople last month. Their deputies are still in power, while their masters live overseas under different names. I think that when the occupation of Anatolia ends, Armenians living alongside Turks will be threatened once again."

"You're saying the Three Pashas will return to power?"

"That could happen, or they could rule through their former deputies. This is a risk if refugees are sent back."

"If the Three Pashas were found and arrested?"

"Armenians will still be under threat from Turks."

"Surely not all Turks are bad."

"Some of my best friends were Turks. We had many common interests, which is how we shared Anatolia for many centuries. But we have reached a point where that's not possible, as my story shows."

"Some Turks are good, some are bad and many are ignorant," Karine said. "A Turkish man told me that, and it's the ignorance of how similar we are which drives hatred and murder."

"They think you're the enemy, when you're not?" Captain Holmes asked.

"That's right," Anoush said. "We can live together and worship God in different ways, but now they think we're an enemy to be eliminated."

"Your experiences show extraordinary hatred which I wasn't aware of. I saw starvation and mistreatment which was horrendous, but the brutality of your experiences goes far beyond that. Unfortunately I'm under orders."

"Like the Turkish soldier who shot my late husband in the back of his head," Anoush said dispassionately. "But you're a captain who can tell his superiors about this hatred."

"I will do that, although I don't promise anything. This would require a major change in policy."

Anoush smiled at him. "I hope for the best and I prepare for the worst, which might be how I survived."

He stood. "I thank you both for making me aware of this situation, and I hope I can achieve something."

Anoush stood, as did Karine. "We can try," Anoush said.

"What are your plans?"

"Many young women were kidnapped to brothels, harems and other places. We're associated with the Red Cross to rescue these women, and to help them after rescue."

"Good luck with your mission. Goodbye to you both."

"Muhnak parov Captain Holmes," Anoush said, while amused by his smile.

"Muhnak parov," Karine echoed.

"Escaped from Constantinople!" Karine fumed when they reached the street. "The German navy took them away in a boat, along with Dr Bahaddin Shakir, Dr Nazim Bey, Cemal Azmi and Bedri Bey. The worst of the worst."

Talaat Pasha had been the de-facto leader of the Ottoman government since the 1913 coup, and the mastermind behind the extermination of Armenians; supported by Enver Pasha, Djemal Pasha and others, especially Shakir and Azmi. It was unforgivable that Germany, the former ally of the Ottoman Empire, knew about these atrocities, and yet helped the men most responsible for them to escape, before they could face justice for their crimes. Anoush and Karine reached home and climbed the stairs to their apartment, where Karine unlocked the door.

"How did the discussion go?" Paul asked.

"Captain Holmes was shocked by Mama's story and he understood our logic," Karine said. "He will tell his superiors."

"Maybe something will come of that."

"At least we tried," Anoush said. "It's late and I should cook lunch. I will cook a dzhash."

"I will help," Karine said.

The kitchen was cramped for two. "You don't have to help," Anoush said.

"Mama makes a good dzhash," Paul said.

211

Karine punched him lightly on his shoulder. "And I don't?"

He kissed her cheek. "I didn't say that."

In a moment Paul was cradling Karine with her legs wrapped around his waist while they kissed. Anoush backed away to give them privacy, and went to the kitchen. There she laid ingredients on the table, while thinking that she loved Emni, she truly did, but not with the intensity of passion between Karine and Paul. It was wonderful for her daughter to be so much in love, and she missed that. She missed feeling wanted, loved, adored, and more. She chopped pumpkin while thinking that she missed being ravished, especially living so close to love and passion. It had been almost three years since her rescue, well over three years since Emni was taken from her, and that was a long time. She was only 36, and she didn't want to live another 36 years just as 'Mama'. She needed more than that, but where was she to find love in a city of widows and orphans?

Anoush let the stew cook in the cauldron on the fire, and returned to the living room where Paul was in the armchair with Karine sitting on the arm, to be as close to him as possible.

"Mama," Paul said. "Who are we meeting this afternoon?"

"The priest here; Ter Grigor Hakobian," Anoush said.

"That will test your Armenian," Karine teased.

212

"Is he the permanent priest of Aleppo?" Paul asked.

"I don't know," Anoush said.

"Do you know what Ter means?" Karine asked.

"He's a married priest," Paul said.

"Very good."

Anoush returned to the kitchen where Karine helped her set the table, serve lunch, and clean up afterwards. Then with the help of a map, they headed to the northern part of Aleppo and the al-Jdayde district beyond the city walls. Aleppo was a big city, many times larger than Ourfa. Many, many times larger than Ourfa; crowded and bustling. Towards the centre of al-Jdayde was a lovely square decorated by a gurgling fountain. Around the perimeter of the square were the Greek, Syrica and Armenian Apostolic churches, as well as a bathhouse. The priest lived in a home nearby. Anoush wished she'd known of the al-Jdayde district years before, because she could have sought refuge there. But she had little chance of finding an Armenian district, hidden beyond the north of the city. Paul knocked on the door which was opened by a grey-haired man with a long, grey beard, dressed in a plain, black robe.

Paul shook hands. "Muhnak parov Ter Grigor," he said. "My name's Bjishk Paul Lang," he said in his accented Armenian.

"Muhnak parov," the priest replied.

They greeted each other in turn, before being taken to a neat, tidy, and well-organised study, with many books on shelves on two walls. Those books took Anoush's attention.

"Please sit," Ter Grigor said in Armenian.

They sat on three, simple wooden chairs, with Ter Grigor behind his desk with no papers and no clutter.

"We three are from the Red Cross in Geneva," Karine said. "We're here to help women held in brothels, and women held as concubines, in forced marriages, and any other form of sexual slavery. We will also help children of these women, probably held as slaves. The Armenian National Union estimate between twenty-thousand to thirty-thousand women and children are being held against their wills. We will start here in Aleppo, and work outwards from this city. Others will work from Dier el-Zor."

"This is tragic for our women," Ter Grigor said. "The Armenian community here will do all it can to assist you, and to assist the Red Cross. We have a house belonging to the church which I hope you can use."

"Thank you very much for that," Karine said. "These women and children will need medical examinations and possible treatment, but more importantly they will be traumatised and they will need our help to recover."

"How do you intend to rescue these pour souls?"

"The Red Cross has given us fifty-thousand Swiss Francs which we will change to gold coins, and we will buy as

214

many women and children as we can. When the deportations were taking place, rescuing sex slaves wasn't possible, because one would be replaced by another. Now there are no replacements and the cost will be considerable. But we will do our best."

"Every woman you rescue will be a victory," Ter Grigor said.

"That's true."

"Excuse me Ter Grigor," Paul said. "You do have a permanent Armenian community here?"

"We have more than eight-thousand Armenians living in Aleppo."

"Do you have any doctors for your congregation?"

"We have one. Are you interested, Bjishk Paul?"

"I will be busy for a while, but maybe later."

"We would be pleased to have you as part of our community."

"Thank you."

"Now that you have offered us use of a house," Karine said. "We will make it ready with beds and whatever else we need."

"How will you do that?" Ter Grigor asked.

"We know the commanding officer of the British Army, and we will ask him if we can have some of his beds and medical supplies."

The priest smiled. "You have been busy."

"We speak English, which helps."

"Do you speak other languages?"

"My mother and I speak Turkish, and we all learned Arabic before we came here."

"That will help a lot." Ter Grigor stood. "I wish you luck," he said.

"I was once held like these women," Karine said. "I know what they went through, and I hope that will help. It's a feeling of helplessness, despair and hatred. Hatred is inevitable, but I hope we can shine a light for their futures."

They all stood and departed with muhnak parov all round, before heading to the apartment.

"You have something planned, dear husband," Karine stated rhetorically.

"I wouldn't plan anything without discussing it with you first, dear wife," Paul said. "I thought that we will be here on this rescue mission for some time; maybe even years. After that I could stay on as a doctor here. We could buy a house now, and make Aleppo our home."

Karine stopped walking and looked at Paul. Anoush contemplated what he'd just said.

"What do you think, Mama?" Karine asked.

"This is your decision," Anoush said automatically.

"What's your feel for it?"

"I think it's good," Anoush said. "It's a good-sized community and there would be a future here for you, and for your children when they come." Anoush thought a sharing a house was better than sharing a small apartment, and she could get Taniel educated in Aleppo rather than in a boarding school in Cairo, although she didn't want to burden her daughter with her son; her responsibility. Perhaps she could have a future in Aleppo outside of her daughter's home. "I think this is a very good idea," Anoush said.

"Then that's what we will do." Karine looked at Paul. "Where do you have the money to buy a house?"

"My grandfather left me an inheritance in a trust," Paul said.

Karine nodded her head slowly. "I'm sorry to hear about the death of your grandfather."

"He lived a good age to eighty-two."

"Your father's father?'

"Yes. He was a lot like my father."

"I understand."

Anoush wondered what Paul meant, but clearly Karine knew from their time in Bern. Regardless of that, buying a house was a good idea, and she was pleased her family would make their home in the lovely city of Aleppo.

Chapter Twenty Two

Paul and Karine turned off Baron Street and headed to the red light street that ran parallel. There, big, swarthy men touted for business, and little had changed despite the passing of many years.

"It feels strange to be on this street once more," Karine said.

Paul thought it must be.

"When you first met me, I wasn't interested in rescuing the Armenian people," Karine said. "All I wanted was to get out of my misery, and rescue my family. But you were good and kind even though you were a man, and I felt much better after telling you my story. That horrible pimp took my virginity, and then all those other men; but even after that, I was able to like you. Perhaps I remembered the good men of my past: my Papa, my uncles and the men of my village. Later you talked about marriage, and I don't remember exactly but I didn't say no."

"You said you weren't ready to think about marriage, which was true," Paul said. "Marriage was something that came up in a conversation."

"By then I knew you were in love with me, and I liked you too. Later I was lonely and I asked you to hug me. You hugged me for a while, and when I wanted you to go, you left. I loved you by then."

"You were in a bad way."

"I was. I knew you wanted to marry me and in a strange way I loved you, and in a strange way you loved me too, even though I was in a bad way."

"You were so determined and so strong."

"Mama showed me how to be strong."

"I had never met anyone like you, and I knew when you were ready, we would be good together."

Karine looked into his eyes. "I knew we would be good together too."

They reached that brothel with the same, swarthy pimp out front.

"You paid too much for me last time," Karine said. "You leave him to me, and stay here with the money."

"They're expecting to pay fifty or even sixty gold coins for each woman," Paul said.

"We will see."

Karine came close to the pimp. "Ahlan," she greeted formally in Arabic. "I want to buy your Armenian women. How many do you have?"

"I have six Armenian women, and I will sell them for seventy gold coins each."

"I don't have that much money," Karine said. "I have thirty gold coins."

He gave a despairing look. "Fifty," he offered.

"Where's your business?" Karine asked rhetorically while looking around. "Where are the men for your women? I don't see any. Who will pay more than thirty gold coins for your Armenian women?"

"Will you leave them here?"

"I will if I can buy women from other brothels for thirty gold coins. If I can rescue twelve women for the price of six, then I will do that. You're a businessman so you understand."

Karine turned to walk away and he grabbed her arm. "Forty," he said.

"Thirty-five."

"Thirty-five," he agreed, and they shook hands.

Karine beckoned to Paul who brought the money bag.

"First we will check these women," Karine said.

The pimp led the way inside and Karine paused for a moment. Paul knew what it was. Then she followed him while he opened three of the four doors off the corridor, and went upstairs to open more doors. One by one, Karine greeted them and asked them their names in Armenian, and they all replied to her in Armenian. Paul was horrified to see them: young, beautiful, naked, locked in rooms which just had double beds, where they'd been abused for years.

"I want clothes, shoes and headscarves," Karine said in Arabic, and the pimp went upstairs. He returned a few minutes later, and threw the articles to each woman. Silently they dressed while Karine watched.

"Paul, now you can pay him."

Paul had a bigger velvet bag containing six small bags of 100 gold coins each. He gave the pimp two small bags and ten gold coins from a third.

"Shukraan," the pimp said. Thank you.

Karine gathered the women around her. "My name's Karine Hagopian-Lang and with me is my husband Paul Lang, but you can call him Paul. We have a refuge where you can stay, and where we will feed you and care for you. I know what you've been through because I was once here like you. Do you want us to care for you?"

The women silently nodded.

"Good," Karine said. "Now we will go to your new home."

They left, and bunched together they trooped silently through the streets of Aleppo. While they walked Paul thought they were more traumatised than Karine was. They'd been in that brothel for much longer than she, and that showed. In the refuge they had camp beds with sheets and blankets from the British army; they had food they'd purchased, and they planned to buy clothes once they knew sizes. Paul has his medical bag and planned a general check-up, watching for signs of tuberculosis, and a necessary gynaecological examination, but only when those women were ready for that. They'd arranged for Karine and Mama to prepare meals and care for them during the day, and for volunteers from the Union of Armenian Women of Aleppo to stay with them at night. But they were so traumatised! Those women were six out of maybe 20,000 or even 30,000. What a task!

Over the next few hours the women bathed, while Mama bought new clothes to replace the dirty rags from the brothel. Lunch followed in silence as the women adjusted to their new surroundings, or adjusted to their unexpected good fortune. Paul recorded their names, ages and family details, and how they were purchased for the brothel, which took a few hours. At dusk, they handed over to Kohar Petrosyan from the Union of Armenian Women of Aleppo. Then followed a walk to their apartment, and while walking Paul thought that he should buy a house in the Armenian quarter close to the refuge, soon.

There was one big question though: what next for those women?

"I was pleased with that," Karine said. "There are five brothels in that street, and if they have similar numbers of women to be rescued, we will have many gold coins left over."

"Could there be brothels in other parts of Aleppo?" Paul asked.

"There could be," Karine said. "I will ask that when I buy from the last brothel in that street."

"One thing we haven't planned is what happens next for rescued women, and for rescued children later."

"Those women were like me: bought young and never married, and they have no children. Probably there's no surviving family, but that's not certain."

Paul had the answer. "The British are repatriating survivors, which may include mothers, brothers and sisters. I will visit Captain Holmes tomorrow and give him the details of our women and their families, and see if any of his survivors from the camp correlate."

"If they haven't survived, which is more likely, what do we do?" Karine asked.

"The United States is pressuring for an Armenian homeland in the east part of Anatolia, but agreement on that is many months away. Even when agreed, it will take time for them to be able to take refugees."

"We won't send them to live with Turks, and they don't have homes there anyway. We can't rely on the generosity of the local Armenian community to support these women forever."

"Do you have any ideas, Mama?" Paul asked.

"I do," she said. "Many Armenians have emigrated, mostly to America but also to France. There, these women will have the support of community in a safe environment, and even marriage when they're ready for that."

That was an excellent idea. "Mama," he said. "You should write to the Armenian Nation Union, give them details of our survivors, and ask that they be resettled in America or France, when they're ready."

"This is now a French colony, so I think they should be settled in France," she said. "I will write to the Armenian National Union and ask if they can help us."

They reached home, and having eaten already there wasn't much to be done. They bid each other 'bari gisher' and went to their respective rooms.

Karine sat on their bed and looked at her feet. "Today brought back memories for me," she said softly. She looked up at Paul. "Can you hug me?"

He sat beside her and hugged her, and she rested her head against his shoulder.

"Our love started with a hug," she murmured.

Paul remembered.

"Can you make love with me?" Karine asked. "To remind me that God gave us the gift of love, so that two become one."

Paul let her go, and watched as she undressed for him.

* * *

Anoush took a break from the refuge and wandered through the streets of al-Jdayde, which was the Christian quarter of

Aleppo. Armenian mostly, but also home to Assyrians and Greeks. Ancient stone houses lined narrow, winding streets and lanes. Close to the square containing the churches was a busy shopping street, with Arab, Armenian, Greek and Assyrian shops all squashed together. Women bustled in and out, taking no heed of the stranger in their midst. Further along was a small mosque beside a Muslim school, and away from that was a covered textile market with Muslim and Armenian traders. It was enlightening that Christians and Muslims could interact peacefully side-by-side in such a manner. This was to be her home, perhaps forever, and it was a good home. Anoush wondered. Surely there were Armenian widowers. There might be many, but how to find out? There was one way to find out.

Anoush retraced her steps to the refuge but went to the home of Ter Grigor instead. She knocked, and moments later he opened the door.

"Muhnak parov Ter Grigor," she said.

"Muhnak parov Tikin Anoush," he replied.

"Do you have a moment to talk?"

"Please," he said, and beckoned her inside. They went to his study lined with books, and Anoush couldn't help but scan the spines.

"You have a wonderful library," she said.

"Do you like reading?"

She turned to face him. "Very much. I had a Turkish friend with a bookshop in Ourfa, and we often used to read and discuss books. In Cairo they had a library where I borrowed books."

"You're welcome to borrow my books," Ter Grigor said.

Anoush turned and ran her fingers over the spines of some. "Thank you very much," she said. "Reading takes you far away to other places, other times and other adventures." She turned to face him once more. "One day the Ottoman Army came to my village and conscripted all Armenian men of fighting age, including my husband. A few days later we found their bodies in an open grave. Some months later I was here, but fortunately I was able to escape with my daughter and my son. Now we're back as you know."

"And doing good work."

"Yes we are. But I need more than good work in my life."

Ter Grigor nodded his head. "I understand," he said.

"Do you know anyone?" Anoush asked.

"I do. Saro Agopian lost his wife to influenza about a year ago. He's older than you but a good man. He's a lawyer."

"Does he have an office I can visit?"

"Parin Saro has an office amongst the shops."

Anoush thought that was good. "Thank you very much Ter Grigor. I will speak with Parin Saro and see if we have things in common."

"I hope things work out for you Tikin Anoush."

"Thank you again. Muhnak parov Ter Grigor."

"Muhnak parov Tikin Anoush," he said.

Anoush went outside and pondered. If she thought about it for long enough she wouldn't, so she would now! She returned to the retail district, took a deep breath, and climbed the stairs to the lawyer's office. Inside was cool, hushed and musty, with a man in a dark suit; head down at a desk showing his thinning hair, grey at the temples.

He looked up, and he was somewhat lined and haggard. "Can I help you?" he asked in Armenian.

Anoush swallowed. "My name's Anoush Hagopian," she said. "I'm new in Aleppo and I hope this will be my home. Ter Grigor Hakobian suggested that I speak to you."

"About...?"

"Well, my husband died a while ago now, and I heard your wife died a while ago too."

"I understand. Well Tikin Anoush; please take a seat."

Anoush sat. "It's terrible when our loved-ones are taken from us," she said. "But life goes on."

"That it does. What brings you to Aleppo?"

"I was brought here during the deportations, but I was rescued. I've come back with my daughter and her husband to help women who weren't so fortunate to be rescued."

"That's good of you to do that."

"Thank you. You have lived long in Aleppo?" Anoush asked.

"Armenians have a long history in this city. I was born here and we had two children, both married."

"Congratulations for your children."

"Congratulations for your daughter."

Anoush decided not to talk about Taniel for now, but wondered what came next.

"There's a cafe at the square if you would like to have lunch with me, and we can talk some more."

"I would like that," Anoush said.

"Come back here at midday."

They departed with muhnak parov each. Anoush walked slowly to the refuge, which was in the capable hands of Karine and Paul so they didn't really need her. She tried to remember what it was first like with Emni, but that was long ago and muddied by memories of their good life together. His pride at the way she managed their house and raised their children, his encouragement that she should visit her friends in Ourfa and read in her spare time, and especially the way his eyes lit up whenever he saw her. That memory would always stay with her. But how was it when they were new together?

Shy and awkward, but from the first she felt he would be good for her. She always felt he would be good for her. Anoush thought that would be the feeling she would look out for, when she had lunch with Parin Saro.

Chapter Twenty Three

Paul laid his head between Karine's breasts while she stroked his hair. That felt nice. She said that making love was when two became one, and she was right.

"It's been two and a half years for us now," Karine said. "Surely something's wrong."

Paul got himself tested in Cairo and he was fine. But there was clear evidence that prostitution often led to infertility, perhaps through an infection with no other symptoms. "This might be from your time in that brothel," Paul said.

"Oh no!" she exclaimed.

"I'm speculating, but we know there's a linkage between one and the other."

"What can I do?"

"I don't know." Paul lifted his head and looked into her big, dark eyes. "We can adopt orphans in need," he said.

"Let me think about that," Karine said. "Are you sure there's a linkage?"

"There is."

"You shouldn't have married me," she said, turning her head away.

He kissed her cheek. "I married you because I love you, and lack of conception won't change that. Many couples suffer this fate."

"I suppose you would know."

"I will always love you, and there are ways for us to have a family."

"Through adoption?"

Paul nodded.

"I will think about that," Karine said.

"We're young and there's time," Paul said.

"I know. I think Mama's trying to find a husband."

"That will be good for her."

"She's a special woman and not because she's my mother. Papa was kind, hard-working, and he loved us dearly. Mama was the driving force of our family and she loved us too, but in a different way. You always knew you were the centre of her life, and everybody else was the centre of her life too. It was uncanny that she had so much time and love for everyone, and still had time for herself."

"I wrote her story including her role in the Ourfa uprising." Paul tried to put words around that. "She was brave, tough, and she had the courage of her convictions."

"I hope this man is good enough for her."

Paul ruffled Karine's hair. "You don't need to worry about that my love. She won't accept anyone less than she deserves."

* * *

Anoush knew that Saro Agopian wouldn't be good for her. He looked older than his years, but worse that he acted older

231

than his years. He was too set in his ways, and he didn't approve of her volunteer work outside of a home. They ate at the cafe twice and she cooked a meal at his house so they would have more time together, but that didn't help. As she spent more time with him she realised that she didn't love him, and she could never love him. She would do the right thing though. She would go to his office and tell him that she thought they weren't suited to each other. Then what? She couldn't go to Ter Grigor and say that Saro Agopian wasn't good enough, and did he know another? Anoush sighed. Someone would come up. Surely some good man would come into her life.

* * *

With care, attention and love, the first group of six were ready for the next stage of their lives, a journey to France. Paul escorted them to Tripoli, and with new passports with visas, they boarded the ferry. At Alexandria, a representative of the Egyptian Armenian community would meet that ferry and help the women to board a ship bound for Marseilles. There they would be met, and helped to settle in their new homeland.

The next day Paul escorted Karine to that street and they purchased eight women from another brothel, and it was sure to be easier the second time. By then there was discontent over the French colonisation of Syria, particularly in one Arab newspaper: Al-'Arab. This was understandable, given that King Faisal was promised independence if he joined the Allies against the Ottoman Empire, which he did, and which led to the successful capture of Damascus. In fact there was still an Arab Army in addition to the British Army. Despite that, the Allies had no intention of an Arab homeland and had previously carved Arabia amongst themselves, with France already ruling Syria. This discontent somehow became a campaign against Christians and Zionists, and the Al-'Arab newspaper was promptly closed down. Over the next days rumours swirled through Aleppo of massacres committed by Armenians against Arabs in Cilicia, which were probably false. On February 23, a protest demonstration was announced to take place on the 28th.

"This demonstration on Friday could go bad if the authorities aren't careful," Karine said.

"I've never seen such a thing," Paul said.

"Nor I, but it could go bad if they turn on Christians and Jews. Our women are almost ready which is good, because they will be better able to cope with whatever happens. I think we should lock all doors and keep out of sight."

Friday closed and there was a palpable tension in the air. Christian shopkeepers barricaded their shops as did Arab traders, showing the sentiment for trouble was confined to a small number of Arab radicals rather than the majority. Groups of Arabs roamed the streets, especially in the evenings, while the Arab Army had a much bigger presence than ever before, armed as they were with British-supplied rifles.

The morning of the 28th was dead quiet in al-Jdayde, unusual at any time and especially unusual for a Friday, which was the busiest shopping day of the week. The demonstration was scheduled for ten, and then it erupted. Crowds swarmed through the streets of al-Jdayde, accompanied by rifle fire

Karine cowered low beneath a window. "This brings back memories," she moaned. "This sounds like Ourfa all those years ago."

Paul sat beside her, while Mama came across the room bent low. "Keep away from windows," she said. "Glass can shatter and hurt you. I will tell the other women."

She left the room while Paul considered what she said. They would be safest sitting against the wall facing the street, but not opposite that wall. So that's where they sat for two or three hours, until the noise dropped away. Later in the afternoon they went outside to quiet streets scattered with rubbish and debris.

Karine angrily kicked an upturned packing case. "Will they ever learn?" she lamented. "I've seen too much of this."

Around the corner, bodies were laid in front of the Apostolic church in two rows. Paul didn't count but he thought about 50, mostly men. In the background, Ter

Grigor kept watch over the departed members of his congregation. Paul put his arm around Karine's shoulder and guided her home.

Chapter Twenty Four

Paul walked through the door of his new home, to be grabbed by Karine who hugged and kissed him as if he'd been away for weeks, rather than a few hours taking their next group of women to Tripoli to catch the ferry. He hugged Karine and she always felt good in his arms.

"I have something for you," he whispered in her ear.

Karine backed away and he gave her a copy of The Times from a week previously, on July five 1919. She read the article with her face changing from interest to dark anger.

> *The Court Marshal taking into consideration the above-named crimes declares, unanimously, the culpability as principal factors of these crimes the fugitives Talaat Pasha, former Grand Vizir, Enver Pasha, former War Minister, struck off the register of the Imperial Army, Cemal Azmi, former Navy Minister, struck off too from the Imperial Army, and Dr. Nazim Bey, former Minister of Education, members of the General Council of the Union & Progress, representing the moral person of that party. The Court Martial pronounces, in accordance with said stipulations of the Law the death penalty against Talaat Pasha, Enver Pasha, Cemal Azmi, and Dr. Nazim Bey.*

She handed the newspaper back and sighed deeply. "They're living somewhere secret, obviously with new identities, and never will be punished for their crimes."

"If they're found, they will be executed."

"There will be important people protecting the worst criminals in human history." Karine sighed again. "How did it go today?" she asked.

"Excellent," Paul said. "I won't say these women are healed because I don't think you're ever fully healed from what these women went through, but we've been to every brothel in Aleppo and helped forty-five women to be ready for new lives. Perhaps they will find love, marriage and children."

"I was a month in a brothel, and I healed in time. You're not what you were before, but in some ways you're better. Once you've been to the depths of despair you're more appreciative of the good things in life."

Paul thought that was an interesting perspective.

"Now we start on the villages," Karine said.

"Do you know how that works?" Paul asked.

"Sit down because this is a story."

Paul sat and Karine sat opposite.

"The Old Testament allows men to have multiple wives, and to have concubines too," Karine said. "Christianity changed marriage into one man and one woman, but Islam still allows multiple wives and also concubines, who are sex slaves. Muslim women can't be held as slaves, so the only concubines are non-Muslim. Also, Muslim men can't marry non-Muslim women."

"So Armenian women will be concubines."

"Mostly, but if they've been converted to Islam, either by choice or through force, they could be wives. Sometimes second or third wives, but it's possible they could be first wives."

"Some of these men literally bought their wives?"

"They could have; yes. Now, the concept of harem is misunderstood. Harem comes from hareem...."

"Forbidden?" Paul asked.

Karine nodded. "Forbidden to men, or the women's part of an Islamic household, where wives, concubines and their children live."

That made more sense when Armenians talked about rescuing women from 'harems'.

Paul thought about this while on the train. "This will be like our ride into Kurd Mountains," he said. "So it's not possible to use a car."

"That's right," Karine said. "We will use donkey trails, and there has to be two of us in case of an accident."

"I thought we should ride horses."

"What?"

"Ride horses."

"Why not camels?"

Paul hadn't thought about that.

"I'm only joking," Karine said. "Camels are horrible creatures. Noisy, smelly and hard to ride. Why horses though?"

"It will seem more imposing when we ride into a village on horses rather than on donkeys."

Karine nodded. "We will be in a better position to negotiate."

"Yes. Can you ride a horse?"

"No; can you?"

"It can't be that hard."

"I suppose not," Karine said. "We will find two horses which are easy to ride, and buy saddles and other things, and learn how to ride them."

"And care for them."

"That too. We can ask Ter Grigor if he knows a reliable horse-trader."

"Starting tomorrow, so we're ready for the first villages perhaps next week."

"This countryside is like where I grew up, so there will be hundreds of small villages of a few hundred people each."

Paul thought about that. "We can go from place to place, and Mama can look after women in the refuge while we find more."

Karine sighed. "God didn't make us to be alone, and I really want Mama to have a good man in her life. But until that happens, she will get great satisfaction looking after these women while we scour the countryside."

Paul hoped so. He always went back to her story, where she was courageous, practical, and even brilliant at times. She had much to offer any lucky husband, but she was limited to the Christian community of Aleppo, where there seemed to be few single men her age.

Karine went to the kitchen while Paul went outside to the courtyard and sat in the shade of the jacaranda tree. It was a lovely house, quite ancient, and modest from the outside. There were six rooms: living room, kitchen and bathroom downstairs, and three bedrooms upstairs, all with French windows overlooking the courtyard which was closed off by the side wall of the house next door. The upstairs rooms were stepped back from the downstairs rooms, which allowed balconies with iron rails. With all French windows open to the courtyard, especially at night, heat in the house was moderate. Karine called him for dinner and Paul returned inside. Tomorrow he would visit Ter Grigor and then arrange horses for the next stage of their rescue mission.

* * *

Anoush was tucking the last of the freshly-washed sheets onto the camp beds when she heard firm knocking downstairs. She went down the narrow staircase to greet a tall and handsome man, not Armenian, Kurd or Arab, and particularly well-dressed in a suit but no hat.

"Bonjour Madame," the man said. "Est-ce que vous parlez le Française?"

That was some, strange Western language. "I don't understand," Anoush said in English.

"Ah, you speak English," the man said. "My name's Henri Durand, and I'm a journalist for Le Figaro, which is a newspaper in France."

Anoush took a moment to digest that. He worked for a French newspaper, and that was an opportunity to publicise their cause and get donations. That was good. "Good afternoon Mr Durand," Anoush said. "My name's Anoush Hagopian. Would you like to come inside?"

"If that's no intrusion."

"Of course not." Anoush stood aside and allowed Mr Durand into the refuge.

"I heard about your program and I would like to tell my readers in France about your success."

"This refuge is owned by the Armenian Apostolic Church, and they made this available to us. My daughter, her husband and I are from the Red Cross in Geneva, and we're rescuing Armenian women sold into brothels and harems, helping them, and arranging for their settlement in France, assisted by the Union of Armenian Women of Aleppo and the Armenian National Union. We have rescued forty-five Armenian women from brothels here in Aleppo, and now we're preparing to rescue women from nearby villages. My daughter and her husband are buying horses for this."

"They intend to ride horses to villages to rescue women?"

"That's right. We don't have women here at the moment, but I can show you around."

Anoush took Mr Durand from room to room and explained the beds, sheets and blankets were originally supplied by the British Army, and when they get new women they feed them, buy fresh clothes, and help them to recover from their ordeals. Passports and visas are obtained, and then they contact the Armenian community in France. That all takes six weeks or more.

"This is quite fascinating," Mr Durand said. "Do you know how many women need to be rescued?"

"In total about twenty-thousand," Anoush said. "These women are spread throughout Anatolia and northern Syria. We don't know how many women are held near Aleppo, but possibly a few thousand.'

"That's a big task."

"It is," Anoush agreed. "The more donations the Red Cross in Geneva receive to rescue these poor women, the more women we can rescue."

Mr Durand smiled, and he had a lovely smile. "Can I take pictures of the house?"

"You can," Anoush said. He took his pictures, and that was much less complicated than when her wedding pictures were taken.

He finished his pictures and came to Anoush in the kitchen. "Can I make you a cup of coffee?" she asked.

"Oh, that would be lovely."

Anoush set to making coffee, and felt this man, Mr Durand, was a lot like Paul. Kind, polite, decent and very handsome! Tall like Paul; a firm, masculine jaw, thick dark hair nicely trimmed, and sparkling eyes which smiled brightly. She gave him his coffee and joined him at the table.

"I would like to take pictures of your daughter and her husband on their horses," Mr Durand asked.

"You can come here tomorrow for that," Anoush said.

"I will." He finished his coffee. "Thank you so much for today, and for your hospitality. Now I must find my way back to the Baron Hotel."

Anoush wasn't going to let this man go just like that! "I can show you the way," she said.

"That would be too much, Madame Hagopian."

"My name's Anoush, and I would like to show you."

"My name's Henri, and thank you."

They went outside; Anoush locked the door, and then they headed from al-Jdayde to the city centre.

"Are you from Aleppo?" Henri asked.

"I'm from Ourfa to the north of here," Anoush said. "My husband was killed and I was lucky to escape the atrocity with my daughter and son. I decided to help women who didn't have the luck to escape."

"I understand. That was a terrible atrocity."

"The more donations we receive, the more women we can rescue."

He laughed. "I will write that, Anoush! Through the Red Cross in Geneva."

Anoush smiled and looked him in his eyes. "That's right."

They talked about Henri's impression of Aleppo and of Syria, all the way to Baron Street. They reached the hotel, where Henri took Anoush's hand and kissed it. "Thank you so much for a lovely afternoon," he said. "Now I must eat alone." He looked at Anoush with his head tilted. "Unless you could accompany me for dinner?"

Of course she could! "Yes please," Anoush said.

"The Kazar Cafe is just down here," Henri said. "I'm sure you will like their food."

Anoush went with Henri to that cafe, a place where she'd once eaten and something she was used to after her experience with Saro Agopian. But unlike Saro Agopian, she knew in her heart that if it came to that, Henri Durand would be good for her.

* * *

Anoush heard firm knocking on the front door, and knew who it was.

"I will get that," she said.

"Bonjour Anoush," Henri said, and then he kissed her hand.

"Good morning Henri," Anoush said. "Come inside and I will introduce you."

Anoush took Henri to the kitchen and introduced him to Karine and Paul.

"I took pictures here yesterday," Henri said. "I'm impressed by the good work you're doing here. Anoush told me that you bought horses to rescue women from villages."

Anoush glanced at Karine who raised her eyebrows when Henri used her first name.

"Yes we did," Paul said flatly.

"Could I take pictures of you on your horses?" Henri asked.

Paul frowned. "Alright," he eventually said.

"My readers will be impressed by your work. And to think that in this day and age, you're going to ride horses to rescue these poor women. This is like another world."

"This is another world," Paul said. "We have our horses stabled about ten minutes away. Come with me."

Anoush went to Karine. "You go as well," she whispered in her ear in Armenian.

"Why?" Karine asked.

245

"Because you're beautiful, and when men see your picture they will donate lots of money."

Karine nodded her head slowly.

The stables weren't so far away: with two horses in a pen, along with saddles and blankets on a stand. It took Paul and Karine a while to get their horses ready. Then they led them out into the sun, and Paul mounted his. Anoush was surprised how big horses were, especially when Karine mounted hers. They were side by side holding their reins against their saddles, while Henri took his pictures.

Henri thanked them both, before they put their gear away and penned their horses once more.

"When do they head out?" Henri asked Anoush.

"Monday for the first villages," Anoush said. "There are many villages in this area, so this will take a long time."

They returned to the refuge, where Henri thanked Paul and Karine once more.

"I can show you to your hotel," Anoush said.

Henri laughed. "If you want to, Anoush," he said.

They headed outside. "This is like another world," Henri said, yet again. "I suppose it doesn't seem that way to you."

"I like to read," Anoush said. "I know about other countries from what I have read, but sometimes it's hard to picture these places. I know in our world we have donkey trails leading to small villages, and those are not for cars."

246

"I understand. What do you like reading?"

"I like stories with strong characters." She looked into Henri's eyes. "I like love stories," she said.

"Many women like romance."

Anoush wanted more than reading about romance. "How long will you be here, Henri?" Anoush asked.

"A few days," he said.

Anoush stopped walking while she thought about that. She had little time with this nice man, and she had to make the most of that time. "Could there be a future for us?" she asked.

"Us?"

"Us together."

Henri frowned. "I do like you, Anoush" he said quietly. "You're nice, you're friendly, and you're a good person." He paused. "You're beautiful," he said even more quietly. "It's rude to ask your age."

"I'm thirty-six."

"I'm thirty-two."

"Have you ever married?" Anoush asked.

"I spend too much time travelling."

"Could you marry?"

"That's hard with just a few days. We could write letters and see where that takes us."

Anoush was disappointed. "Yes, we could write," she said. She wanted more than writing, even if that was wrong.

She wanted that look when you close the door, when you take off your clothes, when he climbs onto the bed, when he kisses you, when he ravishes you. That was what she wanted, even though that was wrong. She liked Henri: he was friendly, cheerful and handsome. Anoush knew he would be good for her, if that happened. "We will write," she said to Henri.

Chapter Twenty Five

They plodded east in silence, across the flat, featureless and fertile plains surrounding Aleppo. Towards Fah, about an hour from Aleppo. They entered a village of maybe 50 houses, all of whitewashed mud brick, and most with tall, dome-shaped rooves made of mud. The village was a jumble of dirt streets branching from a main, north-south trail. Some of the houses were a simple square with a single window beside an arched door, but most consisted of something like three to six square buildings joined together, where each square had a separate dome-shaped roof. Paul thought their quest was like searching for Mama in Kurd Mountains. First they needed information.

"We will find a cafe and ask," Paul said. "I think we should offer a reward?"

"A gold coin for information about Armenian women," Karine suggested.

The mosque and a cafe were towards the centre of the village: the mosque being of stone with a copper, dome roof, and the cafe being almost as large with a flat roof. Karine went into the cafe first but Paul thought he ought to ask.

He went to the counter and ordered two coffees. The proprietor poured them and handed them across. Paul put two kurus coins on the counter for the coffees which the proprietor took, and then he put a gold coin on the counter but kept his finger on it.

"I'm looking for Armenian women," he said in Arabic.

"You're not Armenian," the proprietor said.

"If you tell me where Armenian women are, you can keep this coin."

"I will tell you."

Paul took out his small notebook and a pencil. He drew the zigzagged north-south trail, and a cross. "We're here," he said.

The proprietor drew two lines. "Dabir Hussain is here, and Akil Ali is here."

"Shukraan," Paul said, and released his finger. He drank his coffee and some water before going outside to where Karine waited. Taking the reins of his Arab gelding Ira, he led the way to the home of Dabir Hussain. That was medium-sized with four domed rooves, which Paul assumed to be four rooms. Living, kitchen, bedroom and harem perhaps.

"We will do this together," Karine said. "These are my people and I don't care if Muslim men don't think much of women like me."

Money talked, and Karine had a way of getting what she wanted. They went to the unpainted timber door and knocked. Moments later it swung open to reveal a paunchy,

middle-aged Arab man in a white robe but no ghutrah.
Karine bowed to him.

"Ahlan," she greeted in Arabic. "My name's Karine
Hagopian-Lang, with my husband, Paul Lang."

"Ahlan," he replied.

"You have Armenian women in your household and we
will buy them from you."

"Come inside."

Paul and Karine removed their boots before entering a
cool space, especially noticeable after the morning heat.
Clearly the tall roof was effective at keeping that heat at bay.
The room had a large green carpet from wall to wall, and
several contrasting lighter green cushions. Beyond the
window beside the front door, there was an arched doorway
to the other rooms of the house. A woman in black with a
black headscarf entered carrying a tray of glasses, which she
placed on the carpet. Keeping low, she removed herself from
their presence. Paul pondered that. An Arab man was free to
come and go and to receive visitors, while his wives or
concubines subserviently served him and his guests, while
avoiding eye contact.

"Please drink," Dabir Hussain said, while he took a
glass of tea.

Paul drank some tea as did Karine.

"You wish to buy my Armenian women," Dabir
Hussain said.

"We will negotiate a price for your women," Karine said. "How many do you have?"

"Two."

"Concubines?"

He nodded.

"I offer twenty gold coins for each of your women," Karine said.

"That's too little. I need a hundred gold coins."

"You paid maybe a lira each, and they have given you good service. Twenty gold coins each is a good profit."

"Why should I sell my women?"

"Because it's time for them to go home, and because twenty gold coins is a good profit."

"I want a hundred gold coins," Dabir Hussain said.

"I don't have that much money. I can offer thirty."

"Eighty."

"Forty, or else I will leave. If your women are too expensive I will buy women from other villages."

"Fifty."

"Forty."

"Forty," he said, and extended his hand. Karine ignored that.

"First I see the women, and then we agree the price."

Dabir Hussain snapped his fingers and the woman in black came into the room. He whispered in her ear before she went away. A few moments later two young women in black robes appeared at the doorway; both carrying babies. Paul was shocked. The robes hid their form, but they were small and their faces were young and not yet fully formed. He would guess early teens. And yet they'd been concubines for maybe three years and had children each. Did that mean they were sold at age ten?

"You didn't say they had children," Karine said. "This makes them worthless to you."

"I can still get pleasure from them," Dabir Hussain said.

"And keep their children as your own? I think not. I offer twenty gold coins each."

"You agreed forty."

"Would you get twenty gold coins if you sold them at a slave market with those children?"

"Alright; twenty," and he extended his hand. Karine shook and the deal was done.

"Do you remember Armenian?" Karine asked.

They nodded their heads with their eyes dropped low.

"We will take you from here and look after you and your children," Karine said. "My name's Karine and this is my husband Paul. We will care for you and protect you, and especially protect your children."

They nodded again with eyes down.

Karine stood so Paul stood with her. "I will get the money," he said.

He went to his saddle bag and returned with the big velvet bag. He took a small bag and counted forty gold coins into the greedy hands of Dabir Hussain. In the meantime Karine guided the two young women outside.

"Ma'a as-salaama," Paul said flatly.

"Ma'a as-salaama," Dabir Hussain repeated.

Paul went outside and put his bag into his saddle bag and buckled it.

"Paul, these are Mina and Astrid."

"I'm pleased to meet you, Mina and Astrid," Paul said in Armenian. "We have to visit one other household. Then we will go to another village before returning to Aleppo, where we have a refuge where you can stay."

"How do we do this?" Paul asked in English.

"You stay with these girls while I meet with Akil Ali," Karine said.

"How do you know about concubines and children?"

"Mama spoke with Arabs in Cairo and she told me."

"How old are these women?"

Karine's shoulders dropped. "It's possible they were about ten. Sometimes gendarmes raped ten year olds, and they sold them too. My sister Lilit could have been at risk but she was small for her age; more like an eight year-old." Karine stood straight. "We will go to the home of Akil Ali and do more good work."

254

Paul checked his notebook while he led the way across the village. They reached a house also with four domed rooves. Paul gave Karine a small money bag and waited with his young charges. Astrid's baby cried and she turned her back to feed it, protected from sight by the horse. Paul's heart was broken by that.

After a while, Karine emerged from the house with a young woman clutching a bundle. Karine introduced Yeva to all, and gave Paul his money bag which he put away. He wondered what to do next.

"Do any of you want to ride a horse, and we walk?" he asked.

Mina and Astrid shook their heads while Yeva looked horrified at the prospect.

"We will ride at walking speed and you stay with us. We're going to Rasm Al Abd and then home to Aleppo."

Silent nods all around, Paul swung himself onto his gelding Ira as did Karine onto her mare, and they headed along the trail to the north. Paul looked down at Mina and Astrid, eyes low while they trudged along, babies clasped tight. He'd seen traumatised but nothing as bad as those two. He knew what the problem was. They should have been playing dolls with their friends and told stories by their parents before sleep, instead of being sexually abused. Their childhood was turned into hell.

"Don't worry Paul," Karine said in English. "I know they're young, but this isn't the end of life. With help and with love they can recover, and in time find a man who loves them, and who will adopt a child as his own. Mama is good with children and she will be good with Mina and Astrid, because they're still children after all."

That was true. Ahead was Rasm Al Abd, where the main trail circled around the eastern perimeter of a small village, again with houses with tall, domed rooves. Away from the trail there was no obvious cafe, so Paul offered a gold coin to the proprietor of the grocery shop. He was directed to the home of Jamel Maloof. Paul walked Ira in the general direction of what was described as the largest house, which stood out with a roof of six domes. They tied their horses to a tree; one of a few trees in the village.

"Yeva," Paul said. "Can you stay outside with Mina and Astrid?"

She nodded her head. Paul went to the front door, painted bright blue, and knocked. A younger-looking Arab in white robes, but somehow smartly-dressed, greeted them both with "Ahlan".

"Ahlan," Paul greeted in reply. "My name's Paul Lang and I have my wife Karine Hagopian-Lang."

"You have Armenian women in your household," Karine said. "We will buy them from you."

Jamel Maloof seemed quite shocked by that. "Come inside and we can discuss this," he said.

They removed their boots and went into a cool house, particularly cool after the ever more intense heat outside. That coolness was refreshing. The room was carpeted in dark red with two lighter red suffahs against two walls, and their host asked them to sit. For some reason Paul felt confident about Jamel Maloof, although he didn't quite know what it was. He'd bought a woman or perhaps women which was wrong, and they were there to buy them back.

"Now what's this about my Armenian wife?" Jamel Maloof asked.

Paul grasped the significance of that. "Has she converted to Islam?" he asked.

"She has."

"Do you have another wife?"

"I have two other wives."

"Can we speak with your Armenian wife?" Karine asked.

"You can."

Jamel Maloof got up and left the room. Moments later he returned with a young woman in a lovely green silken dress with a darker green headscarf.

"Mar Haban," she greeted.

"This is my third wife Amani," Jamel Maloof said.

"We're here to take you away and to protect you," Karine said in Armenian.

"I don't need to be taken away," Amani replied in Arabic. "I'm pleased with my life here."

"Were you forced to become Muslim?" Karine asked, again in Armenian.

"I chose to be a wife and to have children," she again replied in Arabic.

Karine didn't look convinced. Paul was convinced though. Not totally convinced, but Amani, who'd taken an Arabic name, sounded positive.

"I believe Amani is better here," Paul said to Karine in Armenian.

She glared at him.

"She has taken on a new religion and a new life," he said. "There's no point rescuing women who don't want to be rescued."

Karine frowned and eventually nodded her head.

Paul pondered what to say. "During our travels we've found many Armenian women in terrible situations," he said in Arabic. "This is not one of those. I do apologise for inconveniencing you both."

"No need to apologise. Amani came to me through someone who was treating her badly, and here she's treated as an equal."

"I understand, and I'm pleased for Amani's new life." Paul stood. "Ma'a as-salaama," he said.

"Ma'a as-salaama," they both replied.

Karine stood and wished them both ma'a as-salaama as well.

"I'm not sure about that," Karine said outside.

"This makes sense to me," Paul said. "She doesn't need our help, but there are many others who do. We only have money to rescue less than half the women in this area, if that, so let's concentrate of those.

"Yes, you're right."

"We will leave now for Aleppo," Paul said to Yeva, who nodded in acknowledgement. He checked his notebook for the directions and mounted Ira. Soon they were on their way, in intense summer heat. After a time Paul glanced at his watch and it was half-twelve. He dismounted and grabbed the canteen from his bag. He took a swig and handed it around, and Karine followed his lead and shared her water too. She talked quietly with the three women, but time was slipping away and they had to be on their way once more. Slowly they plodded across the endless plain while the two babies got ever more restless. Eventually they reached Aleppo. At the stables, Paul paid the boy two kurus to unsaddle the horses, brush them down, and pen them with fresh straw and water.

Mama had food ready for a late lunch, and then she guided the women to bathe which was necessary after a long, hot walk. After that, Paul recorded their names, ages and family details, and how they were purchased. He then wrote a letter for the Neutral Home in Constantinople, who were coordinating the identification of survivors. Later, they handed over to Garobed Pztikian from the Union of Armenian Women of Aleppo. It had been a long, hot day, and Paul was looking forward to bathing followed by a good sleep.

* * *

On their horses once more, to Soran, Shamer and Marran, once more under intense, summer sun. They were directed to Azzam Isa, who had two Armenian women. Yet again it was a mud-brick house with a tall, domed roof, in four parts as many houses in that part of Syria were. At the front door Azzam Isa was quite a sight: maybe about 50, almost as wide as he was tall, scruffy, black beard; lanky, black hair; bloated face, hooked nose, and a mouth of twisted, yellow teeth. He invited them to a room with a stained, brown carpet, and threadbare, black cushions to sit upon. He clapped his hands and a skinny, deeply lined and aged woman brought a tray with three glasses of tea.

She left discreetly, as Arab women invariably did.

Karine sipped her tea. "You have Armenian women in your household and we will buy them," Karine said.

"I have two women and I will sell them for three-hundred gold coins," Azzam Isa said.

"I can only offer thirty gold coins each."

"That's not enough." He clapped his hands, and when the old woman came into the room, he asked her to bring the 'other women'. Shortly after, two young women, tall and beautiful, entered the room and stood near the doorway. Undoubtedly Armenian, with olive skin, aquiline noses and big, dark eyes. "See; they are beautiful."

"That's not my interest," Karine said. "I'm buying Armenian women to return them home, and nothing more than that."

"If you want to buy my concubines, then you will have to pay me three-hundred."

Karine put her glass down. "I have limited money, so if I pay you three-hundred gold coins, I will have less money to rescue other women. But just for you I can offer forty, but no more."

"Two-hundred and fifty," Azzam Isa said.

Karine sighed. "One-hundred for both is as far as I can go. You only paid maybe a lira each, so that's a handsome profit for you."

Azzam Isa waved his hands dramatically. Paul looked at the two women holding onto each word. Their futures literally in the balance. "Meet his offer," Paul whispered in English.

"I can't," Karine whispered back. "If word gets out that we paid one hundred and twenty five each, we will be finished."

Paul glanced at those young women, and they deserved better than to held as slaves primarily to be fucked by that horrible, ugly man, and ruled by his old, haggard wife. But Karine had a powerful point. If word got out, their rescue mission would be ruined.

Karine stood. "I will pay you one-hundred gold coins, and you can buy new women at a slave market and still have a profit. You only paid a lira each, so that's a good profit."

"These women are more beautiful than African women at the slave market," Azzam Isa said.

"Is their beauty worth one-hundred gold coins?"

"It is to me."

Paul looked up at Karine and saw the angst in her eyes. "I'm sorry for wasting your time," she said to Azzam Isa. "Ma'a as-salaama."

She left the room.

Paul quickly stood, mumbled "ma'a as-salaama," and chased after his wife. He found her holding the reins of her horse with tears running down her cheeks. She wiped her face with the back of her hand.

"We have to go to Shamer," she said. "We will have better luck there."

Paul mounted Ira, but he couldn't leave the looks of despair from those women behind. For the sake of 150 gold coins, their lives were cursed.

* * *

Paul sat at his desk in the bedroom and slit the envelope. It was a letter from Hayk who fortunately wrote in English, because Paul didn't read or write Armenian as well as he spoke the language. Beyond those who studied at American mission schools, some Armenians had spent time in America and were multi-lingual with English. The English language bound Armenians to the rest of the world, which they needed more than ever before.

> *'Dear Paul. The rescue mission of Ruben Heryan goes well and we have rescued many women and children. We have particular success with marrying rescued women to our volunteers, which Ruben encourages. Many of our volunteers come from America, and these married women will eventually reside in America with their husbands. It is particularly satisfying to rescue underage girls from their situations which are always appalling, but this can be expensive. Just the other week we paid 1,800 gold coins to rescue 12 girls from a Bedouin tribe. At the moment Ruben is raising more funds, but the massive scale of our task is taking a toll on his health. It's taking a toll on his finances too. He has put all*

his money into the Liberation Mission and even
borrowed money. While we have many successes I fear
for the future of our mission. I was pleased to read
about your successes in your last letter. You have a
small operation and yet are making good progress in
Aleppo. These rescue missions are the future of my
people, although I should say our people because you
are one of us now, and every woman we rescue is
another victory. I wish you good luck for the ongoing
success of your mission. Hayk.'

Paul re-read the short letter. Funding was always the problem, and the priority was to stretch those funds to rescue as many women as possible. Although 12 underage girls held by a Bedouin tribe was a particularly wretched situation. How could you ride away and leave that many girls to their fates? That was a decision he hoped he never would have to make.

They were doing well: they had stretched their money to rescue many women and had funds to rescue more, and were receiving more donations after the publication of the newspaper article by Henri Durand. But they would run out of money well before their task was complete. He wondered if there was another way, beyond buying women.

Karine came into the room carrying a cup of coffee, and she sat beside the desk. "What did Hayk write?" she asked.

"They have rescued many women but are running out of money," Paul said.

"How are we doing with money?"

"We can rescue maybe one-hundred and fifty more."

"That's not enough."

"How about what we did with Mama?"

Karine sipped her coffee. "That nearly went bad for us, and you ended up fighting with that man. Breaking into harems is much too dangerous."

Paul wondered about other options. "What about some of the men helping Ruben Heryan? If we get several of his men, they could break into harems and rescue women."

"They could. You should write to Hayk and ask if they have volunteers to help us. We know of two women who need to be rescued."

Paul took a pad and his fountain pen and pondered what to write.

"Even if we run rescue missions like that," Karine said. "We will only rescue maybe a few hundred women. That's not enough."

"Every rescue is a victory," Paul said.

"I know, but it's not enough."

Chapter Twenty Six

At the village of Hazwan it was claimed there were no Armenian women, despite Paul offering three gold coins. Next village was Sousian in the midst of a dry, desert-like landscape. There, at the cafe, Paul was told that Mahir Awad had an Armenian wife. That meant the woman involved had converted to Islam, or she was forced to convert in order to move from concubine to wife.

The houses in Sousian were conventionally mud brick with flat rooves, while the house of Mahir Awad was modestly sized. On a hot, dry morning, already about 30 degrees and baking under the sun, the white house shimmered with heat reflected off sand. Everywhere was sand, and Sousian was a most bleak and miserable place.

Paul knocked on the door; greeted Mahir Awad with "Ahlan," and middle-aged Mahir Awad responded with his greeting.

"My name's Paul Lang and with me is my wife Karine Hagopian-Lang. We're buying Armenian women to take them home."

"I don't have an Armenian woman," Mahir Awad said.

"We were told you had an Armenian wife," Karine said. "If so, we can offer good money for her. This will be a good profit for you."

Paul wiped the sweat off his forehead. "Can we come inside please?" he asked.

Mahir Awad nodded, so they removed their boots and went into a room with a sealed mud floor, a dark blue carpet and raised blue suffahs. Stifling hot inside, but better than outside.

"We were told you had an Armenian wife," Karine repeated. "We will offer good money for your wife, and you can make a good profit on her."

"My wife isn't for sale," Mahir Awad said.

"Do you mind if I ask how many wives you have?" Paul asked.

"Yes I do mind."

"Can we speak with your wife?"

Silence.

"Please," Paul asked.

Mahir Awad left the room and returned with a young woman dressed in dark brown. "This is my wife Fatima."

"Parev Fatima," Karine said. "Are you Armenian and do you want to stay here?" she asked in Armenian.

"I'm Armenian but I can't leave," Fatima replied in Armenian, although clearly that wasn't her real name.

"Are there other wives?"

"She died."

That made sense.

"What are you saying?" Mahir Awad asked.

"Your wife is Armenian," Karine said in Arabic. "She needs to be with her people now."

"I'm not selling Fatima."

"Forty gold coins."

"You must leave now."

"Fifty gold coins."

Mahir Awad grabbed Karine and Paul by their arms, and firmly dragged them to the door, which he opened. "You must leave and never come back."

They took the hint and left.

Paul was resigned. "His wife died, before or after he bought Fatima. He's forced her into Islam, or else she would have been like Amani and wanting to stay with him. I don't think we can do anything though."

"Imagine buying your wife!" Karine exclaimed.

"I know. I will put this in my notebook, and if we get help to break into houses and rescue women, this will be one of those."

"If we get that help." Karine mounted her horse. "Let's go. This has been a long morning and we haven't gotten anything but disappointment."

Paul mounted Ira, and they plodded out of Sousian, heading west to Hazwan. Hazwan had a hole in the wall cafe where they bought maraq and chilled ayran, yoghurt and water, both kept in a bucket of ice, and most refreshing on a hot day. After lunch, Paul offered a gold coin and was told of

Munir Khouri who had an Armenian woman, probably a concubine, and Tariq Bitar who had Armenian children.

The home of Munir Khouri was extraordinarily plain, being a rectangular box with a single window and nicely varnished double timber doors, surrounded by sand. The mud bricks were coated with an additional layer of mud, making the building look like a solid, dried mud structure.

Paul contemplated where to tie Ira in the bleak landscape, but there wasn't anywhere. Fortunately he was unlikely to wander off.

"Unless this man is really attached to his concubine, or he really prefers a white concubine to an African; he's likely to accept our money," Karine said. "It looks like he needs it."

Karine knocked on the door, to be greeted by a short man in black robes and a black ghutrah.

"Ahlan," she said. "My name's Karine Hagopian-Lang and with me is my husband Paul Lang. We would like to talk with you about your Armenian concubine."

He beckoned them inside, so they removed dusty boots and entered a room of white-painted packed mud with a worn floral carpet, and a black suffrah. It was quite dark given the single window, and even darker when their host closed the door.

"What's this about my concubine?" Munir Khouri asked.

"We're paying good prices to buy Armenian women to send them home," Karine said. "I offer thirty gold coins for your concubine, as long as I can speak with her first."

Munir Khouri clapped his hand and a woman in a dark robe came through the internal doorway. They spoke for a moment and she went away, to be replaced by another woman much the same age, maybe thirties, and also in dark clothing.

"Parev," Karine said. "Are you Armenian?" she asked in Armenian.

The woman nodded. "I am."

"We're from a rescue mission, and we want to take you home."

"Where's home? How can we go home when they did such unspeakable things to us?"

"Home is with your people in somewhere safe like France, where you can have an independent life. Would you like this?"

She nodded.

"Munir Khouri," Karine said. "I offer thirty gold coins for your concubine."

"Alin is worth more than thirty gold coins to me. She's worth at least forty gold coins."

"I will give you thirty-five gold coins."

"I agree. Please sit. Alin, please bring us some tea."

They all sat on the suffrah, and after a time Alin brought a tray of tea glasses. It was time to drink in the Arab tradition.

"Alin has been good to me," Munir Khouri said. "I have cared for her, but now it's time for her to go home."

"If you hadn't protected Alin," Karine said. "She might have died at that camp."

"Yes, the camp was very bad. Other men bought young women and even girls, but I was more comfortable with Alin."

Karine nodded.

Paul finished his tea and put his glass on the tray. "I will get your money," he said. He went outside, took a small bag from the saddlebag, and returned to count thirty-five coins to Munir Khouri.

"We should go now," Karine said. "Shukraan for your hospitality."

"Ma'a as-salaama," Munir Khouri said.

"Ma'a as-salaama Munir Khouri," Paul said. "Alin; please get your things and we will leave now."

She left for a moment and returned with a small bundle. With another round of 'Ma'a as-salaama', they left the decrepit, little house.

"He was good and he saved my life," Alin said.

"I can see that," Paul said. "But now it's time for you to be with your people."

"What future do I have?" she asked. "All our men are dead, and who wants a woman my age?"

Paul didn't know what to say. She was about the same age as Mama, Anoush, and she was right. "We have to go to another home," he said. "Then, we will return to Aleppo.

Paul checked the sketch map in his notebook, grabbed the reins of Ira, and led the way to the more substantial home of Tariq Bitar. There was even a tree where they could tie their horses, and which would provide shade for Alin. After greetings, they were in another living room.

"I was told at the cafe that you have Armenian children," Paul said.

"Yes I do," Tariq Bitar replied. "I was in Al Bab when a caravan came through, and there were two children struggling to keep up. They seemed to be alone, so I offered to buy them."

"That was good of you," Paul said.

"No, not at all. Any decent person would have done the same thing."

"Do you want any money for your trouble?"

"They're my children and are free to go, if they want to."

Paul understood. "Bring them out and we will ask."

Tariq Bitar went into another room and returned a moment later with an older boy and a younger girl, around eight to ten years old. That would have made them quite young at the time of the caravan.

"This is Abdul and Hadya," Tariq Bitar said.

"Ahlan Abdul and Hadya," Karine said. "Do you remember your Armenian names?" she asked in Arabic.

They shook their heads.

"Do you remember this language?" she asked in Armenian.

"A little," Abdul said.

"I will speak in Arabic for you. We're from the land of your parents, and we will take you to the people of your parents, but only if you want us to."

"Are our parents alive?" Abdul asked.

"No, they're not alive, but you might have relatives who are alive. I know this is a big decision. Either you can stay here, or you can come with us to the people of your parents."

"What should we do?" Abdul asked.

"You should go to your people," Tariq Bitar said.

Paul was glad that Tariq said that, because he wasn't so sure if that was better for them.

"We will go with you," Abdul said to Karine.

"I will get their things," Tariq Bitar said.

He came with a bundle which Paul took. "They should be where they belong," he said.

"I'm not so sure they don't belong here," Paul said. "But you can be assured we will do our best for them."

"You look like you will. Ma'a as-salaama."

"Ma'a as-salaama Tariq Bitar."

Outside was hot, and after telling Alin they were heading to Aleppo, he picked up Abdul and swung him in the saddle and told him to hold tight. Then he swung Hadya behind, and told her to hold tight to Abdul. He grabbed the reins for the walk to Aleppo, which was a long walk. After leaving the horses at the stable, they arrived at the refuge late in the afternoon. Mama was pleased to have children to look after, as Karine guessed. She arranged bathing while Paul and Karine headed home. There a letter from Hayk waited, with the good news that he and friends would help with the rescue of the two women they had to leave behind.

"What did Hayk write?" Karine asked.

"He's coming early next week with friends to rescue those two women by force," Paul said. "While he's here we can rescue Fatima as well."

"You said 'we'," Karine said, ever observant.

"I did," Paul agreed. "They're helping us and it's only fair that I be part of this."

"Do you want me to help?"

"Only if you want to."

"I will leave this one to the men! You need a gun or a rifle, and you need to practice before they get here." Karine smiled brightly. "I know someone who can teach you how to shoot a rifle!"

Paul chuckled.

"You should have seen the rifle Mama stole from the Turks," Karine said with her eyes wide. "It was like what the gendarmes had at the camps, but without a bayonet. If you speak with Ter Grigor, he can help you to borrow a rifle."

Paul planned to do that tomorrow, and then take shooting lessons with Mama. Momentarily he wondered how many men had a mother-in-law like Anoush Hagopian. It was no wonder that Karine turned out as bold as she did.

Chapter Twenty Seven

Paul heard knocking on the door, and he opened it to greet who he knew was Hayk along with another man; both holding saddlebags and holding rifles. Both men perhaps mid-twenties and just a few years younger than he. Introductions were made, before Paul invited Hayk and Aren into the living room where he introduced them to Mama and to Karine. Luggage was left to one side while they sat.

"I'm impressed with what you've achieved here," Hayk said.

"Our priority is to make our limited money go as far as possible," Paul said. "Karine is good at negotiating prices, but unfortunately we weren't able to negotiate affordable prices for the two concubines held by Azzam Isa in Soran."

"I'm worried that if we pay too much, word will get around to other villages," Karine said. "Since then we found a woman named Fatima held by Mahir Awad in Sousian, and he wouldn't sell Fatima to us."

"We will help with Fatima as well," Hayk said.

"My Armenian isn't good enough to describe the wonderful job done by Mama," Paul said. "We spend a lot of time away now, while Mama runs the refuge, cares for our women and keeps this rescue mission going." Paul glanced at Mama who nodded but didn't say a word. "We also have help from the women of Aleppo, who watch over our women at night."

"You are achieving a lot with limited resources."

"Thank you. Now for tomorrow, I can show you a map," Paul said.

Paul led Hayk and Aren to the table and laid out their map. He pointed out the two villages.

"This will take two days, with rest for our horses," Hayk said. "You will to dress warmly, because it's cold on the plains at night."

"That's very true," Mama said.

"You were part of the deportation?"

"Karine and I were."

Hayk bowed to Mama.

"Paul; you will need food, water, and a rifle," Hayk said.

"I have a rifle and I practiced with Mama," Paul said.

Hayk looked at Mama, Anoush. "I was part of the Ourfa Resistance," she said.

Hayk paused for a moment before holding her arms and kissing her cheeks. "I'm honoured," he said. "That's a great part of our history. It took eighteen thousand trained Ottoman soldiers to defeat two-thousand Armenian militia, and only when they brought in artillery. The Ottoman commander, Ömer Türkkan, said 'what would we have done if we had a few Urfas to deal with?'"

"We hoped for a widespread Armenian uprising, but the Ottomans knew that was a risk so they killed our leadership in Constantinople before they began deportations. Even so, it was better to fight than to be meekly led to our deaths."

"I'm honoured," Hayk said again.

"We can prepare dinner, if you want," Karine said.

"Yes; that will be much appreciated. We will sleep early for an early start tomorrow."

Mama and Karine went to the kitchen to cook, while Paul showed Hayk and Aren to the unused bedroom.

* * *

There were times when Paul missed the green mountains of Switzerland, but not that morning. It was cool and crisp under a muted, morning sky, with mist rising from the endless and desolate plain. Truly magnificent. They rode in silence, well laden with bulging saddlebags and rifles slung over shoulders. On and on while mesmerised by the steady sway of Ira.

They reached Soran late morning after a three and a half hour ride, where Paul led Hayk and Aren near to the home of Azzam Isa. They dismounted in the shade of a tall, conifer tree.

"You and I will knock on his door with our rifles ready," Hayk said to Paul. "Aren will stand guard outside. When this man opens the door we push our way in, and I will detain him while you search for our women. You know who you're looking for, and they should recognise you. Then we leave, and outnumbered three to one we should be alright."

"How do we leave?" Paul asked.

"One woman rides behind you, and the other woman rides behind Aran. When you mount your horses I can help the women to climb on."

"His front door opens onto a living area with one window, and an opening to the rest of the house, which I assume to be bedroom, harem and kitchen."

"Good. Let's do this."

They tied reins to the conifer and marched to the front door with rifles at the ready. Paul held his rifle in his left hand while he knocked, and moments later the door swung open to reveal Azzam Isa. Paul didn't hesitate to push Isa hard, and the ugly Arab stumbled into his living room. Hayk followed and pulled the door closed behind him; while training his rifle on Isa.

"What's the meaning of this?" Azzam Isa asked with genuine surprise.

"We're liberating your Armenian concubines," Paul said in Arabic, before he went through the archway. That was a carpeted room with a large bed, scene of much unwanted abuse, and a curtain covering another arch. Paul brushed that aside to be in a room with three black suffahs, which were their beds. Three women in black were embroidering, and momentarily Paul wished he knew their names.

"Do you remember me from last time?" he asked in Armenian.

Two nodded with their eyes lit up in hope, bordering on disbelief.

"Come with me now," he said. They went to a chest, obviously to get their belongings, but that wouldn't work on the back of a horse. "We can't take your belongings," Paul said. "You must come with me now."

He led the two women to the living room where Hayk had Isa pinned into the corner.

"You go and I follow," Hayk said.

Paul led the women past Aren to their horses, where Aren mounted his. Moments later Hayk appeared, and he cupped his hands for one of the women to climb behind Aren. Paul sensed something, and spun around to see Azzam Isa aiming a rifle from his front door. Without hesitating and just as he practiced with Mama, Paul aimed and squeezed his trigger. Azzam Isa stumbled backwards into his living room, and Paul ran after him. Isa had a wound on his shoulder but was still breathing. Paul ejected the cartridge, loaded a fresh bullet into the breech of his rifle, and grabbed Isa's rifle just as he heard commotion in the street. Outside, Hayk was on his horse. Paul tossed Isa's rifle away, slung his own rifle over his shoulder, and cupped his hands to allow the other woman to mount that horse. All around Arabs, some with rifles, were murmuring and asking who they were and what was going on. More rifles appeared as Paul mounted Ira, and that was a dangerous situation.

"Ride away and I will protect you," Paul shouted.

They rode at a canter while Paul trained his rifle on the gathering crowd. *Now what?* He kicked Ira and his gentle, Arab gelding knew what to do.

Still training his gun, Paul was balanced in the saddle just as he noticed one of the women fall into the dirt. *Scheissen!* Paul quickly dismounted, cupped his hands once more, and helped her climb on.

"Hold very tight!" he shouted, before turning to face the approaching crowd. He fired his rifle above their heads which stopped them, before reloading and mounting once more. Again he kicked Ira, and again the gelding followed the two mares along the main road. Paul turned in his saddle to see one man in the crowd with his rifle lowered and aimed. Paul fired in the general direction of over their heads, as best he could from a saddle, to be met with that man firing back, but fortunately his bullet missed them. At a canter they left the village behind, and after a time they slowed to a walk while Paul kept checking the road was clear. For once having horses was more than a symbolic expression of power, because the more typical Arab donkey had no chance. In the heat of the midday sun, they settled to a steady walk north to Sousian.

Hayk stopped their convoy at a small waterway, where Paul dismounted to help the women from their horses. They led the three horses to drink while Paul shared his canteen with one of the women, but the water was unpleasantly tepid.

"I remember you and that woman," she said in Armenian.

"My name's Paul Lang and that woman is my wife," Paul said.

"My name's Lusig Balkan and my friend's Ina Tertian."

"Parev Lusig Balkan," Paul said. "We're going to Sousian which we should reach mid-afternoon, and where we will stay overnight. There we have another rescue before returning to Aleppo. We will help you both to recover and to be ready for the world, and then arrange a new home in France. There are six other women in our refuge, and I'm sure you will find support from them, and from my wife and her mother."

She handed the canteen back and Paul screwed the cap tight.

"When you left that time, I thought that was the end of my life," Lusig Balian said. "I barely believed it when I saw you once more."

Paul saw that in her eyes. "I'm sorry about what you've been through, and perhaps your new life starts today."

Lusig Balian nodded. "It's time for a new life for me," she said quietly. She looked into Paul's eyes. "If this hadn't happened; I would have died in that camp."

"I know."

Hayk mounted his horse, Aren likewise, and Paul helped the two women before he mounted Ira to follow. It was well into the afternoon, and Paul was looking forward to a meal at the cafe in Sousian, with a well-deserved rest to follow.

* * *

They stood outside the miserable-looking house of Mahir Awad, surrounded by sand reflecting the morning sunshine.

"Same as last time," Hayk said. "I detain this man; you search for the woman, and Aren keeps watch outside while looking after Lusig and Ina."

Paul knocked on the door and when Mahir Awad opened it, Hayk burst into the room to pin the pudgy, middle-aged Arab to the corner of his living room. Paul went through the curtained arch to a bedroom, and through a second curtained arch to the harem. There was Fatima, alone.

"Do you remember me?" Paul asked in Armenian.

She nodded. "I do."

"Do you want me to rescue you?"

"Yes I do."

"Come with me now."

Paul led Fatima to the living room where Mahir Awad warily pondered Hayk's Lee-Enfield semi-automatic. Paul wanted to tell Awad that he could have had 50 gold coins for the same result, but that was childish. Awad knew that already. Paul took Fatima outside where Aren was alert despite nothing stirring.

"What's your real name?" Paul asked Fatima.

"Magi Dorian," she replied.

"Parev Magi Dorian. We're taking you to Aleppo where we have a refuge. We rescued Lusig and Ina yesterday, and we have six more women at the refuge."

"Thank you so much."

"How do we do this?" Paul asked Hayk.

Nothing stirred in the bleak wasteland of Sousian.

"We're not under threat, thank God, so we walk. How far?"

"About four hours. Are you ladies alright to walk with us?" Paul asked.

"As long as we get away from here," Magi Dorian said.

The men mounted their horses, and surrounded by women in dark, Arabic robes, they headed out of town on the trail towards Aleppo. It was hot by the time they arrived at Tal Shar; where they watered their horses before eating lunch at a cafe. They eventually reached the stables by mid-afternoon. Paul suggested that Hayk and Aren go home and gave them his key, while he led the three women to the refuge. There, Karine and Mama helped them settle in while Paul washed. All was peaceful and calm at the refuge, once more at capacity, when they handed over to Kohar Petrosyan from the Union of Armenian Women of Aleppo. Paul sensed something about Karine, but didn't quite know what it was. She should have been pleased they rescued those women, but she seemed unsettled. They walked home in silence with Karine absorbed in her own world.

"We went to seven villages and rescued six women, and left three women behind," Karine eventually said. "If we had more money we could have rescued Lusig and Ina, and offered more money for Magi, although we got them in the end. It's been more than one woman for each village, and there are about one-hundred villages in the near vicinity, and maybe two hundred further out. So that's more than three-hundred women, but we have less than half that money. Even then we can't afford some of these women, and we have to put our lives in danger to rescue them."

"We're making progress," Paul said automatically.

"This should never have happened! These are my people, and this should never have happened!"

Paul put his arm around Karine's shoulder and felt her boiling anger. That didn't show very often, but she was right. The massacres, the barbarity and the suffering should never have happened. It was almost inconceivable that one race would set out to exterminate another race. But it was less than that. Three people, and a few others, were the architects of this atrocity. One in particular, Talaat Pasha; without him, the atrocity would never have happened. In total, seven or eight men were responsible for the worst atrocity in the history of humanity. It was almost impossible to believe that those men did what they did.

When he got home, Paul bathed. Later, when he dressed in a clean shirt and a pair of shorts, he thought he heard crying. He climbed the stairs to their bedroom where Karine was slumped against the wall; crying her heart out. He sat beside her where she rested her head on his shoulder, and he held her.

"It's hopeless," she sobbed. "We won't be able to rescue half of them, leaving too many women in the most wretched of conditions. Some will wish they'd never been born. What sort of life is that?"

Paul held her tighter. He could say that every rescue was a victory, but Karine was right. Too many women would never be rescued.

"And poor Mama," she cried. "Almost everything's been taken from her. Her husband, one of her daughters, most of her family, love. How can she to find love in a city of widows and married couples? And me! I can't have children because I was sold to that brothel! What did we do to deserve this? How did the men who killed one and a half million people, and ruined the lives of hundreds of thousands more, walk away without punishment?"

Paul held Karine tighter still while she cried so hard. He remembered the look of relief from Lusig and Ina; who until then must have wished they'd never been born. He remembered the starvation at the camp, the women on the crosses, and the night he found Karine. What happened defied reason and defied understanding. "I'm a doctor," he said quietly. "I took an oath to do no harm. But if I came across the men responsible for this atrocity, I would kill them."

She looked into his eyes, and Paul knew she believed him. If he found them, he would kill them.

Chapter Twenty Eight
Berlin, Germany – Late January, 1921

Soghomon Tehlirian strode beside Shahan Natalie along busy Berlin streets on the way to Berlin Hauptbahnhof. There, Shahan was to catch a train to Rome, hopefully to intercept Talaat Pasha at a meeting of Turks. They passed through the tall, imposing entry and into the busy train hall, smelling of smoke and echoing of the noise of trains, and of thousands of conversations. They pushed their way through the crowd to Shahan's train, waiting. Shahan climbed into his carriage while Soghomon watched from the low platform. There he noticed a big man approaching. He turned to study this man carrying a cane, and wondered if he was the man they'd been searching for. As this man approached, two young men and young woman arranged themselves as a type of honour guard, along with a fourth, older man. The young woman kissed the big man's hand and said, in Turkish, 'they're inside, Pasha'. The big man used his cane to rap a window of the train, before nodding his head in acknowledgement to the person inside, and then rejoined the men and the woman who'd called him Pasha. They stepped back as the train whistle blew, the carriage lurched, and the train pulled out of the station.

Soghomon followed the group and noticed the younger people trailed the big man and the older, darker man by a few steps. Their route passed Tiergarten until they reached number four Hardenbergstrasse, where the young men and the young woman bowed deeply and moved off. The big man and the dark man went inside the apartment building, leaving Soghomon to ponder if that big man really was Talaat Pasha. He must be! He was the man they'd been searching for. The brass plate beside the door had a name in Turkish script: Ali Salih Bey.

Next day, Vaza discovered Ali Salih Bey was a merchant, and his rental was arranged by the Turkish embassy. When told, Soghomon knew no businessman would have his accommodation arranged by the embassy, but he had to be sure this man was really Talaat Pasha. But if he was Talaat they had to act quickly, or else the worst murderer in history, the man who obliterated his family, wouldn't be punished for his horrendous crime. That night Soghomon slept badly; dreaming of fields of bodies.

Every day Soghomon kept vigil near four Hardenbergstrasse; tracking this big man's moves. One night Soghomon took the photo given to him by Armen and scratched away the moustache. Then it was clear! That man was Talaat Pasha!

But nothing came of it. His many colleagues remained to be convinced. They couldn't afford to kill the wrong man. Soghomon was convinced, but he had to follow orders.

After stalking this man for weeks, Soghomon was told by Shahan that he received a letter confirming the man at number four Hardenbergstrasse was Talaat Pasha, and Shahan rented an apartment across the road at 37 Hardenbergstrasse. Soghomon could move on Sunday.

Hazor helped Soghomon with his move into an immaculate and clean apartment, with a bed, a dresser, an armchair, and a desk and chair beneath a large window overlooking the street and number four. Hardenbergstrasse was busy with traffic, pedestrians swarmed by, while Soghomon kept a vigil through a gap in his curtains. He studied Talaat Pasha's apartment where lights burned late into the night.

That night Soghomon walked along the street with Shahan. "You know how this must be done," Shahan said. "You must wait by the body and allow yourself to be arrested, and through that we can tell our story to the world."

"I understand," Soghomon said.

"In your trial, we will reveal the worst crime in human history."

They reached 37, and there Shahan handed a pistol to Soghomon. "It's been tested and it's ready for your finger."

The next morning Soghomon studied number four through the gap in his curtains when he saw his prey emerge from the building. It was early and not Talaat's usual routine. Soghomon grabbed the pistol, jammed it into his belt covered by his jacket, and raced downstairs, only to find the gate to the street was frozen! He struggled with that lock but it wouldn't budge. He ran inside and grabbed Fraulein Weber, and she helped dismantle the latch. But by the time Soghomon reached Hardenbergstrasse, Talaat Pasha was long gone. He went to his colleagues at the tobacco store but they'd seen nothing. Soghomon returned home, past a tradesman repairing that useless lock.

All night Soghomon was convinced that Talaat had discovered their plot and left Berlin. Soghomon was so close but he'd let Talaat Pasha slip away. He could barely wait until morning. Early, he rang Shahan who promised to come by straight away.

Knocking on the door, and Soghomon let Shahan into his small room.

"I couldn't get out because the lock was frozen, and now Talaat Pasha is gone," Soghomon blurted out. "He's left Berlin."

Shahan grabbed Soghomon by the shoulders and looked him in the eyes. "He hasn't gone," he said. "There's no reason for him to suspect us. In fact, this is an opportunity. You have papers linking you to us, and now we can clear your room. This way, the plan will survive."

They drank glasses of cognac each, and Shahan left with letters, the notebooks and the binoculars.

The next morning Soghomon studied number four when he heard knocking on his door. It was Frau Dittman with Fraulein Weber, and he wondered what Frau Dittman was saying. Had he been discovered spying? No, something about the lock. She gave Soghomon a new key and he replied with 'danke'. Silence for a moment, before Frau Dittman and Fraulein Weber left. Soghomon returned to the desk beneath the window and stared through the gap in his curtains once more. No movement; nothing at all. Had Talaat Pasha slipped away after all?

Soghomon kept his vigil late into night, but apart from a brief flash of a light, saw nothing from Talaat's apartment. That night he slept badly. He dreamed of his mother sharing a breakfast of bread and honey, and then lying dead at his feet. His pillow was wet with sweat, despite the cold. In the morning he washed from the basin on his dresser before pulling on his clothes and sitting at the desk once more. A black car pulled up and the dark man from the railway station, accompanied by a beautiful woman, entered the apartment building. That woman must be the wife of Talaat Pasha, who was reportedly beautiful. Soghomon wondered how a monster like Talaat could have such a beautiful wife. Although it was said she was involved with her husband's affairs.

The next morning the beautiful woman left the building, and Soghomon went downstairs to follow her from a distance. She went to a fountain, while Soghomon pondered that with her knowledge and on the command of her husband, many thousands of beautiful women were condemned to die from starvation, or to be imprisoned in brothels and harems for the rest of their miserable lives.

The next morning Soghomon saw Talaat on the balcony of his apartment. If he followed his usual routine, Talaat Pasha would soon go for his walk. Soon, the big man left the building, dressed in an overcoat but no hat as always. Soghomon jammed the pistol behind his belt, and pulled on his jacket before he went downstairs. He had to be sure. He had to get a good look at Talaat's face but not alert him in any way. He tracked the big man from the opposite side of Hardenbergstrasse, and then he went ahead and crossed the street. Soghomon turned and approached Talaat Pasha; his heart beating fast with excitement while he sought to calm his breathing. Soghomon glanced at the man's face and he was Talaat Pasha, their eyes meeting for a moment as they passed.

Soghomon stopped just past Talaat, drew his pistol, pressed it to the side of Talaat's thick neck, and squeezed the trigger. The big man fell on his face with a sound like a branch sawed from a tree.

So effortless.

Soghomon stood above the body, his pistol in his hand, while blood flowed profusely. That was for the blood this man had spilled. Slowly Soghomon became aware of the chaos around him; men shouting and women screaming in their language he couldn't understand. His soldier's reflexes took over and he ran from the scene. Nobody tried to stop Soghomon as he turned into Fasanenstrasse. There, men caught him. They pulled at him; they slapped and even punched him, and something sharp tore at his face. An anonymous man pushed his way into the violent crowd and hauled Soghomon away.

"What do you want?" Soghomon shouted to the crowd. "I'm Armenian, he's Turkish; what is it to you?"

Soghomon was dragged to the policemen at their small outpost by Tiergarten Gate. The two policemen grabbed Soghomon, one on each arm, and led him past the body of Talaat Pasha still lying where he fell. The crowd surrounded them, shouting and angry, but the policemen kept them at bay. A police truck rolled up and Soghomon was pushed into the rear. Shortly after, he was in a cell in Charlottenburg Police Station.

Chapter Twenty Nine
Berlin, Germany – June 2, 1921

Soghomon felt calm despite the chaos in the courtroom. He rehearsed his story with Shahan many times over the past weeks, and he could make it seem like he was a part of the atrocity despite being far away and fighting the enemy of the Armenian people, like his brother Misak. Then Soghomon came home and his family was dead, his friends were dead, most Armenians in his town were dead, Armenians in his province was mostly dead; his people were mostly dead. He heard many stories of what the Turks did and he'd been there since, so he was sure they would believe his story. As long as the world heard what happened, then his mission would have purpose. Beyond that, he, Soghomon Tehlirian, had brought justice to the man responsible for all of that death and misery. If Soghomon had to spend his remaining years in jail, then that was a worthy price to pay.

At the table were his lawyers: Dr Adolf von Gordon, Dr Johannes Wurthaner and Dr Kurt Niemeyer; and Soghomon's interpreters Kevork Kaloustian and Vaza, who was really Vahan Zakarian. Ahead were Judge Erich Lehmberg and his lawyers, at an adjacent table were the prosecuting lawyers, and to the side was the jury of 12 people. There were many in the gallery above; including reporters.

Through those reporters the story of the Armenian atrocity would become known world-wide.

Soghomon was sworn to tell the truth, and then he was asked many questions by Judge Lehmberg with Vaza translating. Soghomon told the story he rehearsed with Shahan of the rape and murder of his sisters, the murder of his brothers, and the murder of his mother and father. He told how he escaped the deportation caravan and fled through the lands of the Kurds. He was lucky, he said. He was hit on the head and fell with his brother's body on top of him. When that happened the Turks would have thought he was dead. When he woke, he was able to get away from the massacre. The hushed silence of the court showed his story had an effect. So many horrific murders, and Talaat Pasha was responsible for all that.

But then Judge Lehmberg asked questions about his time since then, and of course Soghomon couldn't tell them the truth about that either. He was a language student in Berlin, although he didn't speak the language. Sometimes the questions were hard, but he managed to answer well enough, thanks to his practice with Shahan.

Soghomon then told of his return home, and how there were only a few survivors of the deportation. Then he told the story suggested by Shahan that he dug up gold coins buried in the yard, which explained how he supported himself these past years.

Dr Niemeyer asked if Soghomon knew that Talaat Pasha had been sentenced to death and Soghomon said he knew. Dr Niemeyer then asked if Soghomon planned to kill Talaat and he told them that he saw Talaat was living nearby, and his mother told him to kill Talaat Pasha in a dream. Then he woke up and decided to do it.

The judge questioned Soghomon about his sicknesses and then asked about the murder and what happened after, and Soghomon stuck to his story. Dr von Gordon also asked about the murder, and Soghomon still stuck to his story.

Other witnesses were called while Vaza translated in Soghomon's ear. After each witness, the judge asked more questions but Soghomon was pleased with the answers he gave. He stuck to his story as closely as he could.

Christine Terzibashian told of her experience of the massacre and deportation of good Armenian people. Her story was horrific, and at times her story was so bad that the trial was interrupted by onlookers in the gallery overcome by hearing about such atrocities. Germans testified and then Krikoris Balakian, who knew and said that Talaat Pasha was personally responsible for what happened. Finally, Soghomon's doctors spoke to the court, and said that Soghomon's sickness was due to the shock of what he'd endured. That was the end of the day and Soghomon was taken to jail once more.

The next day the lawyers and Judge Lehmberg spoke in German for a time, before they took turns to address the jury with Vaza translating to Soghomon. This took a long time and was very detailed. The jury went away and everyone else was allowed out of the courtroom, but not for long because the jury reached their decision quite quickly. The leader of the jury said something which Vaza translated, but Soghomon didn't believe that. That didn't seem real or even possible. Vaza repeated that Soghomon was free. Soghomon never imagined he would be released for killing a man in front of many witnesses on a busy street in Berlin.

Soghomon stood on the street of Berlin a free man. He killed Talaat Pasha, the man most responsible for the horror committed against his people. He and other Armenians told of these horrors, and this was now known throughout the world. And after all that he was able to live his life in freedom. Nothing could bring back his family, but Soghomon felt at peace knowing that he did the right thing.

Chapter Thirty
Rome, Italy – July 2, 1921

Arshavir Shirakian arrived at busy Roma Termini station mid-afternoon, after a train journey from the port of Napoli. He wandered the streets looking for accommodation, but not at a hotel because he didn't want to show his documents or sign a register. He saw a sign in a nearby window: Stanza in Affitto. He went inside where a middle-aged man rented Arshavir a room. He unpacked, carefully hid his Browning pistol and his photographs, stripped off and went to bed early to recover from his journey. Safely hidden in his wardrobe were photographs of the ten men on the list of criminals to be executed, and many of those men were based in Rome.

The next day, Arshavir strapped his gun to his thigh, before staking a seat in a cafe across the road from the Turkish embassy, to watch for the men from his photographs. He'd studied those photographs so many times that he knew his targets without needing to refer to their pictures. A few men came and went from the embassy, but none from his photographs, before activity died down in the evening and Arshavir returned to his room. The next days and evenings were similar, where he saw nobody of interest. The following morning Arshavir bought the newspaper to pass time, and noticed an advertisement asking for a woman to rent a comfortable room in the apartment of a widow.

Which twenty-two year old man wouldn't want to rent a room with a widow? Not only that, as a private rental he wouldn't have to show his documents or sign a register. Arshavir checked his map and it was maybe ten minutes away. With map and newspaper in hand, he headed off.

Via Cola di Rienzo, 28; was a multi-storey apartment block in stucco, guarded by a dark brown door along the side lane with bell pushes to one side. Arshavir pressed the bell for apartment two, and the door clicked. He went inside and climbed the steps to the first floor, and there he knocked on door number two. Moments later the door opened to reveal a middle-aged woman, who laughed when she saw Arshavir holding the newspaper; obviously amused that a man had answered their advertisement. Moments later a beautiful young woman dressed in black; slim with dark eyes, long lashes, and jet black hair, like an Armenian woman, appeared.

"Buongiorno," Arshavir said. "Mi chiamo Arshavir Shirakian."

"Buongiorno Arshavir Shirakian," she said. "Mi chiamo Signora Maria Rossi." She contemplated Arshavir quite seriously. "Why have you have come?" she asked in Italian.

"I'm a war orphan from Greece, and I've enrolled in the School of Agriculture here in Roma. I'm looking for comfortable accommodation."

She nodded approvingly. "Would twenty lira be reasonable?" she asked, while counting twenty with her fingers.

Arshavir barely believed that, for such a nice apartment. "That would be very good," he said.

Signora Rossi took Arshavir's hand and guided him through a beautifully furnished living room, with many pictures of a solider in uniform. That explained why Maria Rossi wore black, and why black curtains all but blocked the sun. She took Arshavir to a room further on; very nicely furnished. It was a lovely room in fact: light, bright and spacious, with a bed, a wardrobe, a dresser, a desk and a chair. It had a lovely view over the street.

"This is your room," Signora Rossi said.

"This is very nice, thank you," Arshavir replied, wishing that he knew more Italian so he could express his gratitude better. "Can I move in tonight?"

"You can move in anytime you wish."

Arshavir terminated his rent on the room near the station, and returned to the home of Signora Rossi. He hung his shirts in the wardrobe, placed his underwear over his gun and photos in the dresser, and slid his case under his bed. Now what? Fit in so as not to be suspicious, and return to the embassy the next day.

They ate dinner together, conversed even though Arshavir's Italian was still quite basic, and then he went to bed.

The next day Arshavir was at the cafe across the road from the Turkish Embassy; watching men come and go. Each midday he ate with Maria, she wanted him to call her Maria, and then he returned to the embassy until evening. When he returned home later, Maria always waited for him. Then they would stroll along the streets of her suburb. Over those weeks Arshavir noticed a change in Maria: she discarded black and often dressed in blue and sometimes even lighter colours, and the black curtains gradually disappeared too. Even some of the photographs of her late husband disappeared. They talked as friends, and Maria shared much of her past life with Arshavir. Their walks became more intimate: holding hands while they walked together. Eyes meeting in glances, glances held for longer.

One evening Arshavir spotted one of the men from his photographs: Dr Nazim who then went to a nearby restaurant. Sadly Arshavir lost track of Dr Nazim, and he returned home disappointed. Arshavir returned to the embassy the next day, but there was nobody.

"You're busy every day and evening," Maria said while they strolled together on their usual route. "It's not my business to pry, but I'm glad you can find time for me too."

"I like you a lot," Arshavir said, and he meant that too. "You remind me of the beautiful women of my homeland."

Their eyes met and she squeezed his hand tighter. "Grazie," Maria said.

"You've changed these past weeks," Arshavir said.

"A handsome young man changed me."

"Perhaps a beautiful woman is changing me."

"I think we're changing each other."

They returned to the apartment building where Maria unlocked the outside door, and the inside door too. She led him through the living room to the corridor and stopped. She opened the door to her room.

"This is my room," she said.

Arshavir knew. He watched her go inside her room, and he followed her. She closed the door behind them, before embracing Arshavir. He rested his hands on her hips while they kissed.

* * *

For weeks leading into months, Arshavir went from place to place near the Turkish embassy, without finding any leads. Then he saw Tafvik Azmi; not on his list but a bodyguard of former Grand Vizier, Saïd Halim Pasha. Saïd Halim was the head of government of the Ottoman Empire and signed all deportation orders. When Armenian patriarchs asked him to stop these terrible deportations, Saïd Halim was dismissive; stating that reports of atrocities were significantly overstated.

For his role in the deportation process, and for his refusal to represent Armenian interests to the Three Pashas, Saïd Halim Pasha was put on the list of criminals to be executed.

Tafvik Azmi caught a tram with Arshavir following. Azmi got off at a tourist lookout to meet with two other Turks. Arshavir hid out of sight but was close enough to hear that Enver Pasha and Dr Shakir were expected in Rome soon, and Saïd Halim was raising funds for the war conducted against Armenians and Greeks by Mustafa Kemal. It was late by then so Arshavir ate a meal in a restaurant and then walked home, having missed the last tram.

Arshavir continued to keep watch in the area around the Turkish embassy until he saw Azmi meet an unknown man, and bow and behave respectfully to this short and plump figure. Arshavir had no idea who this man was, until he realised that Azmi was bodyguard to Saïd Halim Pasha! Then that respectful behaviour made sense. Arshavir followed the pair at a distance until they went to the Palace Hotel. Arshavir decided to stake-out the Palace Hotel over the next few days. One day Saïd Halim Pasha arrived by carriage, which meant he lived in Rome. When they left in that carriage, Arshavir followed on foot by pretending he was jogging, all the way to a grand villa on Via Eustacchio.

The next day while keeping watch on the villa on Via Eustacchio, Arshavir noticed an attractive young woman smiling at him from her window. He smiled back, and realised that a friendship with that woman would be a good cover. He went inside her apartment building and knocked on her door to meet Helena who spoke Italian, but when Arshavir gave his cover story of being a student from Greece, he discovered Helena was Greek herself, which was a language Arshavir spoke much better than Italian. He invited Helena outside for a walk.

"This is a beautiful city," Arshavir said. "Beautiful weather, beautiful streets," he looked deeply into his companion's eyes. "Beautiful women."

Helena put her head down.

"No, I mean it," Arshavir said. "You have beautiful blue eyes." She did have beautiful, blue eyes too.

"Thank you," Helena said quietly. "You're a handsome man."

"Thank you."

They walked hand-in-hand while Arshavir kept watch over the villa, and later departed with a promise to meet again. That evening, Maria begged Arshavir to accompany her to the opera to see a performance of Faust. Of course he couldn't disappoint his lover, as any other behaviour would have been suspicious. What Arshavir didn't realise was Saïd Halim Pasha also had an interest in the opera. There, in a box so close, Saïd Halim watched Faust with his bodyguard. Arshavir could easily have gone to that box and killed Saïd Halim Pasha, but only at the cost of several casualties and mass panic. The assassination of Saïd Halim Pasha would have to wait for another day.

The next day Saïd Halim Pasha took his carriage to Roma Termini station where a train was leaving for Genoa. Arshavir felt Saïd Halim slipping through his fingers for a second time, until he realised the Turk was merely seeing Dr Nazim off. Arshavir vowed that he would make his next chance count.

Back at Via Eustacchio, Arshavir whistled at the window of Helena and they went for a walk. While they talked Helena got more personal; stating that her father was away for a while. That was a subtle hint, but Arshavir didn't want to take that sort of advantage of a young woman. Maria was quite different of course; she was a widow and they genuinely liked each other. Helena must have wondered why Arshavir was so shy and unwilling.

That evening, December four, Arshavir resolved to carry out his mission the next day. He cleaned his gun and loaded a full magazine, before returning to Maria's room. The next morning he woke at his usual time, ran a bath, dressed in a new suit and shirt, and left home with a newly-bought, wide-brimmed had that better hid his face. He walked to the villa of Saïd Hallam Pasha while wearing his overcoat on a cool morning, but didn't whistle at Helena's window. He kept watch over the villa as the sun got hotter, so he unbuttoned his overcoat. For hours nothing stirred until Helena approached, which was the last thing Arshavir needed! He tried to ignore her but still she came to him.

"What's the matter?" she asked in Greek. "Are you sick?"

"No I'm not sick," Arshavir replied. "My father will be arriving any minute, and I don't want him to see us together."

"But you said your father was dead," Helena said.

"Yes I did say that, but now he's here. He's angry that I've been doing badly in my studies, so that's why I don't want him to find us together."

"Why would he meet you in this street?"

It was nearly four in the afternoon. Soon the builders at the end of the street would stop work for the day; the street was filling with the afternoon rush of pedestrians, and Arshavir had this stubborn girl pestering him! Then he heard the clopping of horses' hooves and the rumble of a carriage.

"Goodbye; go!" Arshavir said firmly. "My father's here."

Saïd Halim Pasha was in the carriage with Tafvik Azmi. The carriage stopped at the villa and Saïd Halim Pasha got out to pay the driver. Arshavir strode to Saïd Halim while drawing his gun from his pocket, and shot Saïd Halim Pasha once in the back of his neck. Tafvik Azmi reached for his gun.

"Throw your gun away or I will kill you!" Arshavir ordered in Turkish, and he did.

Then Arshavir ran; the coachman immediately gave chase, and others chased too. Arshavir ran through the crowds, losing his overcoat trailing behind him, and losing his hat as well. Arshavir crossed the street just in front of a tram which then blocked his pursuers. Arshavir continued to run while he heard people searching for him in nearby streets. Arshavir jumped a wall, ran through a front yard to a stream at the back of the house. He crossed that stream on a plank of wood, pulled it up and threw it away, and buried his gun in a nearby mound of dirt. Arshavir walked home, and feeling unsettled he went straight to his old room.

The next morning, Arshavir bought a new hat and coat, and returned home before midday. He hung his hat and coat on the stand, as usual.

"I'm sorry about my behaviour yesterday," Arshavir said to Maria. "I wasn't feeling well. This morning I went to see a doctor."

On the table was the newspaper Corriere Della Sera, with a headline article about the killing of Saïd Halim Pasha. There were many pictures including a picture of his hat and coat, with the caption 'find the owner of this hat and coat and you will find the murderer'. Arshavir looked up to see Maria studying his new hat and coat on the stand.

Arshavir wanted to get far away from that newspaper. "Let's eat at a restaurant," he suggested to Maria.

"No, no, no!" she said firmly. "Cook has prepared lunch and we will eat in."

"We will eat in on one condition," Arshavir said. "That we eat out tomorrow instead."

"I accept," Maria said. "Did you see the newspaper?" she asked innocently. "There's a picture of a hat and coat."

For sure Maria knew. "What has Cook prepared for lunch," Arshavir asked to change the subject.

"There's no lunch for bad boys," she said with a bright smile, and Arshavir knew that he was safe with his lover.

They went to the dining room, where Cook had prepared macaroni.

"Did you read the newspapers?" Maria asked.

"I did," Arshavir said. "A murderous, Turkish Pasha was killed."

"The newspaper said the same thing. I will go to my villa for a few days rest." Maria looked at Arshavir. "You should come too."

A few hours later they were in the countryside south of Rome, surrounded by forest with a peaceful lake nearby. Arshavir and Maria relaxed in chairs on the veranda overlooking the lake.

"As you know I have property beyond my apartment and this villa," Maria said.

Arshavir knew that, and he said nothing.

"My property generates good income, and I'm available," Maria continued. "Life could be good."

Arshavir studied his beautiful companion, who he liked very much. He knew he could spend his life with her; free of the stresses and anxieties of life, and free to indulge in the pleasures they shared. But there were many who were yet to be brought to justice, and he wondered if it was possible to have a good and peaceful life while knowing those monsters were still free. That evening they shared their pleasure, and the next morning they went fishing in a boat: Arshavir rowing and Maria with the rods. Over the next days they cooked together, talked together; made love together. After a wonderful time spent relaxing and recovering from his mission, Arshavir knew it was time to bring that to an end.

"I have wealth, property and income," Maria said as a temptation to stay.

"I must return to Rome," Arshavir said quietly.

"Return to Rome?" she snapped. "Why?"

"I have an important job."

"What job?" she snapped again.

He lightly touched her hand. "You know what my job is."

Maria slipped into silence; the rest of the evening passed in silence, and there was silence in their bed too. The next morning Arshavir rose, washed, dressed and packed, and Maria joined him shortly after.

"Now it's time for me to go," he said. He held her firm chin and looked into those lovely, dark eyes framed by long lashes. "I will remember you for always."

"I will remember you too."

"Our farewell should be here in peace, and not in the chaos of a railway station."

She nodded.

Arshavir kissed her lips, grabbed his suitcase, and headed out the door towards the station. He knew if he looked over his shoulder at Maria watching him, he would turn around to stay.

Chapter Thirty One
Berlin, Germany – February 1, 1922

Although he would have preferred to be in Baku to stalk Enver Pasha, Arshavir was sent to Berlin to meet with Shahan Natalie, Aram Yereganian, Arshag Yezdanian and Hayk. They had a number of targets, with the key criminals being Cemal Azmi and Dr Behaeddin Shakir. Azmi, the Butcher of Trabzon, went beyond following orders to the most debauched behaviour imaginable. He separated pretty girls aged 10 to 13, put them in a hospital as a huge harem, and 'gave' some of these girls to his son as well. Other women and children he drowned at sea by throwing them off boats. He emptied orphanages to put children into Muslim households, and he stole huge amounts of Armenian property, especially gold and silver. Shakir was the detailed architect of the extermination of Armenians, so he was next most important after the Three Pashas. He was also heavily involved with the disastrous Armenian – Azerbaijani war.

The room Arshavir rented from Herr and Frau Sack was convenient and comfortable; it didn't require him to show his documents, but it didn't have the other benefits of renting from a beautiful and lonely widow! After the assassination of Saïd Halim Pasha, it was probable that police in many countries realised there was a conspiracy against Turkish war criminals. All Armenian agents had to be vigilant, and renting a room from a policeman like Herr Sack was one way to avoid being noticed. As long as he didn't give away what he was doing, Arshavir was safer there. He even offered to walk their German Shepherd named Robert, each day.

Hayk posed as Mehmed Ali and made friends of Kemal, the son of Cemal Azmi, and he also made friends with Hayriye Talaat Bafralı; the attractive widow of Talaat Pasha. Every time Arshavir met with Hayk, he complained about pretending to enjoy their stories of 'the old country', which invariably were stories about the massacre of their people. That was hard for Hayk to stomach. Arshavir wondered how far Hayk had to go to be a 'friend' of Hayriye, but he never said any more than he was her friend.

Eventually they discovered that Shakir and Azmi generally went for an evening walk along Uhlandstrasse with members of their families, and that was the best opportunity to get at them, although not ideal. Unlike Rome, Arshavir couldn't act unilaterally and had to wait for Shahan to give the order. That was planned for Monday April 17, for Arshavir and Aram.

It was a pleasant spring evening when Aram and Arshavir went for dinner at the Schildkroete Restaurant on Uhlandstrasse. They ordered their meals and ordered wine as well.

"There will be too many people around," Aram grumbled. "Family, friends, and it's busy there."

Arshavir made the sign of a cross. "This is like the last supper," he said.

"This isn't a time to make jokes."

"Who said I was joking?"

"I've the rest of my life to look forward to."

Arshavir briefly thought about Maria, and the reasons why he left her. "This is justice for a million and a half killed, and the hundreds of thousands who still suffer."

Aram drew a deep breath. "Then the last supper this will be."

Their veal schnitzels arrived, which was one of the best German dishes. That, and a glass of Italian red wine. Again Arshavir thought of Maria and her massive wine cellar under her villa. He ate his meal in silence, and glanced at the clock.

"It's time to go," Arshavir said.

They headed into the busy, Berlin street, and hid in shadows along a lane. Arshavir rolled his right trouser leg and slipped his Browning from behind the straps wrapped around his thigh, before stuffing it behind his belt. A clock struck ten, and shortly after Arshavir caught sight of Dr. Rusuhi Bey, followed by Azmi's wife, daughter, and mother, and Shakir's son's fiancee. Then Djemal Azmi and Dr Shakir arm-in-arm, trailed by Hayriye Talaat Bafrali and Shakir's wife. At a distance behind was a man with blond hair, who was most definitely German and probably a bodyguard for the family group. All about, the street bustled.

Arshavir moved but Aram grabbed his arm.

"It's too busy," he whispered.

Once again that night, Arshavir crossed himself. "It's time to do this," he said. "I'm taking them from behind, and you can come with me or not."

Arshavir ran across the street and knew Aram was following. He reached behind his flowing jacket and pulled out his gun. Bafrali screamed and tried to pull at him. Arshavir easily broke free from her grasp just as Azmi turned around, and Arshavir shot Azmi in the face. Shakir said something and Arshavir replied 'yes', before squeezing his trigger a second time. Aram also shot Dr Shakir, and then they ran into the crowd.

Berliners chased them; desperate to stop these murderous criminals, just like in Rome.

"What do these people want?" Aram shouted while they ran. "What are they saying?"

In their homeland, seeing someone get shot was a sign to flee or take cover; but not in European countries!

Their pursuers didn't chase for so long, and Arshavir and Aram were able to dodge into Pariserstrasse unmolested. There they hid in a doorway while they got their breaths back.

"I killed Shakir," Aram said.

Arshavir knew that. "I think I only wounded him." He wondered if they both were dead. "We ought to go back."

"They're dead."

"You can come or not."

Arshavir tucked his gun behind his belt, and strolled into bustling crowds on Uhlandstrasse once more. Further north, a large crowd gathered at the scene of the execution, with two widows crying hysterically. Those widows knew what their husbands did, but did they shed a tear for millions killed? Not likely. It was rough justice, but justice came in the end.

Police poured from the back of a police truck and it was time to go.

"Murder on the street like that is terrible," Arshavir said in German to a man standing nearby.

"It is," the man agreed.

There was a man in his thirties, a woman about the same age, and a young girl.

"This isn't a scene for your daughter," Arshavir suggested.

The man nodded and moved on with his wife. Arshavir slipped his arm through the girl's arm, and moved on with them, straight past a line of policeman blocking the street.

Chapter Thirty Two
Tbilisi, Georgia – July 22, 1922

Stepan slipped open the envelope and read the telegram. Send the package to Tbilisi. He sighed. The 'package', Djemal Pasha, was in Tbilisi, and he had to travel from Batumi to Tbilisi. He sighed again. He'd been doing this for too long. It was important to deal with Djemal, a monster who left a trail of corpses no matter where he went; be they Armenians in Anatolia or Jews in Palestine or Arabs in Syria; but he'd been doing this for far too long. When this was over, he would give it up. At age 36, it was time to hand over to younger men.

One thing at least: the country was a mess. The chaos that the Soviets brought upon Georgia may work in his favour. He packed his big bag, went downstairs and handed over his key, before walking two blocks to the station. The train was due to leave at ten or just over an hour's time, so Stepan went onto the platform to smoke a cigarette and wait. As passengers boarded the brown carriages, he butted his cigarette and went inside. He stared out the window while more boarded, the train whistle blew, and they jerked away. Stepan put his head back to sleep, if he could.

* * *

The train arrived late afternoon, around five, and Stepan wearily followed passengers through the station building, and headed to the rented apartment of Bedros Der Bohemian, who was hosting Stephan's nephew Artashes Kevorkian. It wasn't far, about ten minutes or maybe a bit more, and Stepan was knocking on a dark brown door while neighbours scurried in and out. The Sovietisation of Georgia created a certain degree of paranoia as well. The sooner he could head home; the better.

The door swung open to reveal a smoky apartment with three men. Stepan greeted Artashes and Bedros.

"Stepan Dzaghigian," Bedros said. "This is Zareh Melik-Shahnazarian."

"Parev Zareh," Stepan said while they shook hands.

"Parev Stepan," Zareh Melik-Shahnazarian responded.

"How was your journey?" Bedros asked.

Stepan grimaced.

"This will be over soon," Bedros said. "We have to deal with Djemal and Enver, and then it's finished. These two are most guilty, so we have to convict, sentence and execute."

Stepan sat on a threadbare brown sofa and lit a cigarette. "Do you have any plans?" he asked.

"We've followed them for more than a week. The best opportunity is each afternoon around four, when Djemal goes for a walk protected by two bodyguards."

Stepan nodded in acknowledgement. "Tomorrow at four show me, and we do it the day after."

318

"Do you want something to eat? Something to drink?"

"A glass of cognac."

Bedros left the room, while Stepan absent-mindedly smoked his cigarette.

* * *

Stepan and Bedros walked along David Guramishvili Street, hands in pockets while they smoked cigarettes. On the opposite side of the road was Djemal Pasha, trailed by two younger men wearing jackets despite the warm weather. It was quiet with very few people around. They passed a large building where beyond was a side-street which might make for a good escape route. Not many civilians and an escape route made that place ideal. When the threesome got out of sight, Stepan crossed the street and checked the side-street, Gvazauri Street, which took them towards quarries and wasteland. He doubled back to David Guramishvili Street.

"What's this building?" Stepan asked.

"Headquarters of the Chekov." Bedros replied.

The Soviet Secret Police. "We'll do it here and escape down that street there."

"What about the bodyguards?"

"We'll surprise them, and with all of us we'll outnumber them."

"That's true."

Stepan clapped Bedros on the back. "We'll tell the others."

* * *

Once more just after four in the afternoon, Stepan walked south on David Guramishvili Street, trailed by Bedros, Artashes and Zareh. Ahead were the Turk and the two bodyguards, with a few pedestrians some distance away. Stepan casually crossed the street while slipping his hand behind his jacked. He closed on them, aimed and fired six times, and heard a barrage of bullets from his colleagues. Stepan checked that Djemal Pasha was done for, before continuing into Gvazauri Street and away from the scene.

Early the next morning there was loud knocking on the door before it was kicked in. Police in green uniforms, red stars prominent on hats, filled the apartment with much shouting and noise. Stepan, Bedros, Artashes and Zareh were shoved downstairs, and bundled into a truck with fellow Armenians. With the door of the truck locked shut they were on their way, and when the door opened they were at the scene of the assassination. At the Cheka Headquarters, several trucks disgorged many Armenians. They were taken to the basement and thrown into cold, dank cells smelling of sewerage. More and more until there was barely room to move. Cell doors clanged shut and the police left. Stepan went to the bars and looked towards the locked door leading to the stairwell. It wasn't supposed to end that way.

Chapter Thirty Two
Aleppo, Syria – August 9, 1922

Paul came home and smelled food, so he went to the kitchen where Karine cooked at the fireplace. She left that to hug and kiss him, and he put the newspaper on the table to hug her too. She felt good in his arms.

"I have good news for you," he murmured in ear.

"That newspaper?" she asked.

"Read it."

She sat and turned the pages, until something pricked her interest. Paul sat beside to read the article once more:

> *Since November 1921, convicted war criminal Enver*
> *Pasha has been leading the army of Muslim people*
> *seeking independence from the Soviet Union, which is*
> *known as the Basmachi Revolt. Red Army*
> *Commander, Armenian Yakov Melkumov, has been*
> *involved with suppressing this revolt for some years*
> *now. On Friday August 4, the day of the Kurban*
> *Bayrami holiday, Melkumov took advantage of many*
> *Basmachi soldiers being on leave to stage a surprise*
> *attack on the headquarters of Enver Pasha, near the*
> *village of Ab-i-Derya. The skeleton force retained by*
> *Enver Pasha stood no chance, but Enver Pasha*
> *managed to escape by horse. Yakov Melkumov*
> *disguised some of his men in order to locate Enver*

Pasha, who some four days later was found hiding near the village of Chaghan. Melkumov not only led the attack on Enver Pasha but personally killed him, thereby ending the life of the last man associated with the massacre of the Armenian people.

"Well, that is good news," Karine said with a big smile. "Yet again, justice has been done, and again it was an Armenian who did it."

"That's the end of it, except for Dr Nazim Bey safe in Constantinople." Paul wondered. "The killing of Enver Pasha was a military operation, and he was a vain man who loved uniforms and titles, so he was the one most likely to be involved in a war such as that one. But the other killings seem more than coincidental to me."

Karine put her hand on his. "Are you saying that my people assassinated those most responsible for the near-extermination of my race?"

He looked her in the eyes. "Yes I am. But the world didn't seem to care, or perhaps welcomed those assassinations, so that's how they happened."

"It's called justice, and its liberation for those of us who survived, and it's in remembrance of those who perished. At the time we stood no chance, Mama's battle at Ourfa shows that, but in the end we fought back." Karine went to the mantel above the fireplace and grabbed a letter. "Speaking of Mama, we received this today."

Paul read it.

'To my darling son and daughter. It's had to believe that two years have passed since our wedding in Aleppo. A great Armenian wedding with music and dance, and a wedding which I will remember for always. So much has happened since then. As you know I am happy here in France, especially with Henri who I always knew would be good for me. Taniel is doing well at school now that he's grasped the language, and he still wants to be a doctor! Paul was a good influence for him and I hope Taniel achieves his dream. Last month we went to Marseilles again to visit more of the women we rescued. Some of our women have married, and even more are engaged to be married. Some of our women are expecting children, which is wonderful news. We gave their lives back, and I'm proud to have been a part of our rescue mission. Astrid and her daughter Zora are living with Tapni and her husband, one of the first we rescued, and they are caring for Zora as if she were there own. Astrid is still too young for engagement and marriage of course, but life is good for her and I'm sure she will have a bright future. Mina and her son Ara are living with a couple in town, and I'm sure she

*will have a bright future too. Henri wrote an article
about our women, and maybe the Red Cross will
receive more donations to rescue more women. It's sad
that Armenians have been forced to leave their homes
in Cilicia. Henri wants to publicise their plight so we
will be visiting Aleppo shortly. When I have the
details I will send you a telegram. You can't believe
how much I'm looking forward to visiting my family
and returning to my home. France is lovely and the
people here have made me feel like I belong, but I miss
the broad horizons, the spaciousness, the colour and
excitement and all that goes with our homeland. I will
be seeing my family in Aleppo soon, but until then you
know that you all have a space in my heart.'*

"Mama was always like that," Karine said. "She had a
space in her heart for everyone. She must have the biggest
heart in the world."

"I'm very happy for Mama," Paul said. "I can't imagine
what it was like to lose so much, and I think that hurt her
more than she ever admitted. But now Henri is good for her,
as she says."

"Mama," Ari said from the door. "Lilit is awake."

Karine turned around. "I will be there in a moment.
Motherhood never ceases," she said to Paul.

"I don't think it's an emergency," Paul said. "It's just he's attached to his sister."

"Who can blame him?" She kissed Paul on his cheek. "Perhaps all mothers have spaces in their hearts." Karine left the room while Paul thought about the refugee camp, from where they adopted Ari and Lilit. The defeat of the Ottoman Empire resulted in a Western Armenian homeland in Cilicia, and an Eastern Armenian homeland in the eastern part of Anatolia. Under Mustafa Kemal, the Turks set to reclaiming those homelands; challenging the war-weary French, British and Americans to intervene. That resulted in 20,000 refugees from Cilicia escaping to a collection of huts in a dusty field outside Aleppo, where they couldn't stay forever. They would be resettled; mostly to America and France. On the positive side a small Armenian homeland was carved out of the Caucuses, which in turn was taken over by the Soviet Union, but that was for displaced Eastern Armenians.

The future for Western Armenians was bleaker. They were to be spread all over the world; in time to lose their culture, and even to lose their language. The removal of Armenians from their homeland of Anatolia, started by the Three Pashas and continued by Mustafa Kemel, had been devastatingly effective. Except for a lucky few settled permanently in northern Syria and in Lebanon, Western Armenians would become American citizens or French citizens; or citizens of other countries, and no longer be themselves. The assassinations of the men most responsible for the biggest crime in history meant something, but could never begin to compensate for that which was lost.

One million, five hundred thousand were killed, while hundreds of thousands of survivors suffered in horrific ways, and still suffer. Paul hoped the atrocity against the Armenian people would be the first and the last. Unfortunately the rest of the world had moved on; millions of Turks in Anatolia were richer and more powerful than a few hundred-thousand dispossessed Armenian survivors, making it possible for someone to commit an atrocity against another race and culture. Paul hoped that wouldn't happen, but those who cannot remember the past are condemned to repeat it.

Epilogue

Following the defeat of the Ottoman Empire, representatives of the empire signed the Treaty of Sèvres in 1920, which partitioned the empire to a number of occupying powers, including partitioning Anatolia to occupying powers and the creation of a large Armenian homeland to the east. Mustafa Kemel objected to this treaty, and formed an army to win back Anatolia for the Turkish people. This Turkish War of Independence was concluded with the Treaty of Lausane in 1923, which formed the Republic of Turkey as the successor to the Ottoman Empire. This republic occupied what was previously Anatolia plus a large part of Eastern Armenia, while to the east there was a small Armenian Soviet Socialist Republic (later the Republic of Armenia).

Over the next years there was a rise in Turkish Nationalism, including the notion that Anatolia was the source of Turkish culture, and that after their invasion in 1071, Turkish people had built a new civilisation in Anatolia. Pre-existing Greek, Kurdish and Armenian civilisations were wiped from official Turkish history. Maps with references to Armenia or Kurdistan were banned, and a large number of places in Turkey had their formerly non-Turkish names changed to Turkish names, including the village of Gamursh which was renamed Dağeteği, but which still has the

Armenian Apostolic Church. This process of changing non-Turkish place names continued until relatively recently.

In 1944, Raphael Lemkin coined the term 'genocide' to describe the intentional action to destroy a people, in whole or in part. That covered the Holocaust genocide happening at that time, but Lemkin originally became interested in genocide because of the action taken by Turks to destroy the Armenian race beginning in 1915, and later by Germans against Jews and a number of other races. Turkey has always denied the historical factuality of the Armenian Genocide, as has Azerbaijan. In 1943, the remains of Talaat Pasha were removed from Berlin and re-interred in the Monument to Liberty at Istanbul (formerly Constantinople). In 1996, the remains of Enver Pasha were removed from Ab-i-Derya and re-interred in the Monument to Liberty in Istanbul. Djemal Pasha had been buried at Ezurum, Anatolia, after his assassination. The grandson of Djemal Pasha, Hasan Jemal, recently said that to deny the Genocide would mean to be an accomplice in this crime against humanity.

The United Nations, the International Association of Genocide Scholars, the Roman Catholic Church, the European Parliament, and the parliaments of 29 nations have formally recognised the Armenian Genocide of 1915. In fact, a number of nations have laws which make denial of the Armenian Genocide a crime. My country of Australia has not recognised the Armenian Genocide, although two states of

Australia have. The United States of America has not recognised the Armenian Genocide, but 46 states of the USA have recognised the genocide.

The year 2015 saw a large number of nations formerly recognise the atrocity called the Armenian Genocide.

One million, five-hundred thousand died, and in many cases entire families were eliminated, leaving nothing more than witness statements, survivor testimonies, and a few hundred grainy photographs. The least we can do is to keep the victims of this genocide in our memories.

While we do that we should pause and consider that it's well about time for religious-based hatred and violence to come to an end. In their memories we should do this.

www.ingramcontent.com/pod-product-compliance
Lightning Source LLC
Chambersburg PA
CBHW060517180626
46817CB00002B/387